COMMAND PERFORMANCE

Magrane checked his rifle one final time and settled down to wait.

He was not nervous, but supremely confident. His superiors would be proud of him. He had set up this operation by the book, without a single mistake.

Now, in just two hours, his target would come into view, and into his rifle-sights. Then Magrane would complete his assignment, following his orders right down to the letter.

Magrane was mad, of course.

But that was nothing compared to the madness that would engulf the world when he pulled the trigger. . . .

BACKFIRE

CLIVE EGLETON

BERKLEY BOOKS, NEW YORK

BACKFIRE

A Berkley Book / published by arrangement with
Atheneum Publishers

PRINTING HISTORY
Atheneum edition published 1979
Berkley edition / December 1983

ISBN: 0-425-05438-1

A BERKLEY BOOK ® TM 757,375
Berkley Books are published by The Berkley Publishing Group,
200 Madison Avenue, New York, New York 10016.
The name ''BERKLEY'' and the stylized ''B'' with design are
trademarks belonging to Berkley Publishing Corporation.
PRINTED IN THE UNITED STATES OF AMERICA

1 . . .

MAGRANE got out of bed and walked across the room in his bare feet. In another ten minutes or so, Stanislaus Klepacz, the ward orderly, would collect his breakfast tray, and he'd learned from experience that it was advisable to be washed and shaved before the Pole arrived. The hospital staff had a thing about personal cleanliness, next to godliness, you might say, which was a little odd because, officially, God didn't exist in the Soviet Union. Hospital staff? Magrane scowled at his reflection in the mirror above the wash basin. What the hell kind of double-talk was that? He was being held in an interrogation center deep inside Siberia and when they were satisfied that they'd pumped him dry, he would end up in one of those lunatic asylums that Solzhenitsyn was always writing about.

Magrane eyed the battery shaver on the wooden shelf and reached for it, a slow smile replacing the scowl. The battery shaver represented a small but important victory, because it was a sign that they were beginning to trust him again. Of course, in the early days of his captivity, the guards had allowed him to use a safety razor, but that was before Trooper Cashmore had committed suicide, secreting a blade which he'd used later to cut his throat from ear to ear.

Cashmore had been a good soldier, steady and reliable, but in all the years he'd known him, he'd never suspected that the Norfolk man was such a fanatic that he was ready to take his own life rather than crack under interrogation. Perhaps he'd known the Russians would break him sooner or later; maybe they had even threatened him with a lobotomy and, fearful of becoming a vegetable, he'd chosen what he believed was the easy way out? Whatever his reasons, Cashmore had certainly given the staff a nasty shock, with the result that the commandant had tightened up on security, making life even more difficult for the inmates. On the colonel's instructions, the staff had removed everything a man could conceivably use as a weapon for self-destruction, and for several months he'd had to suffer the indignity of having his beard shaved by one of the Polish trusties.

Magrane switched off the shaver and placed it carefully on the shelf, rubbing a hand over his jaw to satisfy himself that his skin was smooth enough to pass muster. The face in the mirror still looked gaunt, the cheeks sunken, the flesh pallid and stretched tight across the prominent cheekbones, but at least his eyes were no longer dull and listless. Persuading the KGB doctors that he had changed his attitude in the last five weeks and was now prepared to be cooperative had been a master stroke. It hadn't been easy to hoodwink them, but he'd persisted with the ruse until finally they had been convinced that they could take him off the depressants. That had been a major breakthrough, because it meant that there were no more Nembutal, Amytal, Mandrax or Seconal pills; no more barbs, bleepers, downers or mandies, whatever it was they called those little pink, blue, green, yellow and red capsules that the orderlies had been pushing at him for the past nine months. Beyond any doubt, he had taken the first tentative step on the long road to freedom.

Freedom? Well, naturally the Russians had a word for it, but they had never known what it really meant, no more so now than when the Romanovs had occupied the Winter Palace. Curious people, the Russians: kind and gentle one minute, cruel and barbarous the next. Their surgeons had done a good job on his chest and the bullet wound had healed nicely, but their psychiatrists were intent on scrambling his mind, to brainwash him so that at some future date he could be produced at an international press conference as the latest defector from the United Kingdom, the former SAS officer who, without any prompting, would denounce Her Majesty's Government for their imperialistic designs on the Third World or some other load of shit that happened to appeal to the Kremlin at the time. In all probability, the KGB were already busy preparing a suitable script for him which he would be expected to learn by heart. But he had bad news for them: there wasn't going to be any bloody press conference.

A bolt slid back, a key turned in the lock and the door opened inwards. Looking up, Magrane caught a glimpse in the mirror of the all-too-familiar wizened features of Stanislaus Klepacz as he entered the room. Stanislaus Klepacz, a frail old man at fifty-seven, hollow chested and damn near crippled with arthritis. Stanislaus Klepacz, the Pole with the tubercular cough and the morose expression.

"Hullo, Stan," he said cheerfully. "And how are you today?"

"I think I've got a cold coming on." The Pole produced a grubby handkerchief and wiped his nose, as if to underline the point. "And you, sir?" he asked politely.

"On top of the world. What's the weather like outside?"

"Cold, bitterly cold. We had another fall of snow during the night."

Magrane glanced at the barred window and felt a shiver run down his spine even though the room was centrally heated. The hillside was virgin white, the belt of fir trees in the middle distance encrusted with a thick layer of sugar icing. The sky was leaden, holding a promise of more snow to come.

"Well now, that's what I call a real Siberian landscape, Stan."

"Yes, I suppose it is."

The Pole was slipping. There had been a momentary hesitation and the doubtful note in his voice had given him away. The camp was situated in Siberia all right, somewhere to the east of the Urals. He had always thought this was the case but it was good to have the supposition confirmed. Half-filling the basin, Magrane washed his hands and face.

"I've never known a winter like it."

"Oh?" Lids half closed in case the remains of the soap ran into his eyes, Magrane groped for the paper towel on the handrail. "How long have you been in this part of the world, Stan?"

"Almost thirty-three years, sir."

Thirty-three years was about right. Klepacz had been one of General Bor-Komorowski's men and had taken part in the Warsaw uprising on the first of August, 1944, when the Polish Home Army had attempted to seize the capital. Sixty-three days later, with the Red Army still holding back on the outskirts of the city unwilling to intervene, he had been marched off to a prisoner-of-war camp along with the other survivors. Klepacz was in Siberia now because after the war he'd made the mistake of returning to Poland where he was regarded as a dangerous subversive.

"I'm afraid the newspapers haven't arrived this morning." Klepacz cleared his throat. "The roads are impassable."

It was a valid enough excuse but Magrane knew there was more to it than that. In all probability, the Aeroflot TU 144 which brought the newspapers from London had been delayed at Heathrow by the bad weather. The KGB were extremely thorough and it was no secret that they had built an exact replica of a small English town complete with a branch of Lloyds Bank at Kazanakov, but even they couldn't control the weather.

"Do you think the railwaymen really will come out on strike, sir?"

"No chance, Stan. The government will give in to the unions."

He thought Klepacz looked relieved, which was understandable. A few minutes ago, the Pole had made a bad mistake and the question had been his way of wallpapering over the crack, a crude attempt to maintain the illusion that the hospital was situated in the Highlands of Scotland as opposed to Siberia. This elaborate charade was just one of the mind-bending techniques employed by the KGB to disorientate a prisoner, to undermine his confidence and powers of resistance to the point where he was receptive to brainwashing. Not for the first time, Magrane thought it was fortunate the SAS had briefed him what to expect should he ever fall into Soviet hands.

"The senior medical officer will be making his rounds in another hour, sir."

"Yes, I know. He always does on a Monday, Stan."

The Pole nodded gravely, collected the breakfast tray and walked out of the room, looking and bolting the door behind him.

The senior medical officer duly put in an appearance towards midmorning. A short, rather tubby man with a balding head, his bearing and manner reminded Magrane of an amiable schoolmaster on the verge of retirement. According to the Dymo name tag on his white housecoat, he was Colonel G. L. Carr, M.D. Like most English-speaking Russians, his accent carried a transatlantic drawl. As usual, Carr was accompanied by the matron, a formidable woman with the makings of a moustache on her upper lip and a physique that a good many shotputters would have envied.

Carr spent some minutes examining the temperature and weight charts clipped to the foot of the bed and then looked up, beaming a smile at him. "Eleven and a half stone; you've gained another three pounds. That's the style."

"Is it?"

"You bet. We can't have Captain Magrane here looking like a scarecrow, can we, matron?"

"I should think not," the Amazon said emphatically.

"You get the picture?" Carr closed one eye in a knowing wink. "If matron has anything to do with it, you're going to become a second Charles Atlas."

"It's not just my body that needs feeding, Colonel."

"Come again?"

"The mind." Magrane tapped his forehead. "It has to be nourished too. I get bored lying here all day with nothing to do."

"Make a note, matron." Carr snapped his fingers. "We'll have the occupational therapist look in on Captain Magrane."

"I'm not interested in basket weaving. I'd like something to read."

"Sure, why not. When does the librarian visit this ward, matron?"

"This afternoon, sir, between two and three o'clock." A fleeting smile lit up her severe features and her voice almost purred. "Unfortunately, that's when Major Daniel will be interviewing the patient."

Magrane clenched his hands under the bedclothes, digging the nails into his palms. Daniel was bad news, the headshrinker to beat all headshrinkers, the four-letter man who was out to prove that he was the best interrogator in the business. Daniel was about his build and roughly the same age—thirty-one going on thirty-two—but there the similarity ended. The KGB psychiatrist had a lot in common with Reinhard Heydrich; like Hitler's SD man, he too was part Jewish, completely ruthless and highly intelligent, a combination that made him dangerous.

"Oh, that's too bad." Carr tugged at the lobe of his right ear and looked thoughtful. "Tell you what, I'll get the librarian to leave you a few books. Who are your favorite authors?"

"Well, there's Solzhenitsyn for one. I've always wanted to read *The Gulag Archipelago*."

"I don't think we have a copy."

"No, I thought that might be the case," Magrane said dryly. "And I bet you don't have anything by Pasternak, Orwell or Huxley either."

The smile slowly faded from Carr's face. "We'll see what we can do," he said curtly. "Sadly, we only carry a modest stock of books in our library."

"Anything by Marx or Engels then—they're bound to be on the shelves."

The amiable façade crumbled and Carr's lips met in a thin, straight line. For a moment it looked as if he was going to lose his composure, but he managed to keep his temper in check and turning away, stalked out into the corridor. The matron didn't say anything either, and Magrane doubted if her vocabulary could have done justice to the venomous expression on her face. Clutching a clipboard to her ample bosom, she flounced out of the room, slamming the door behind her. The way she turned the key and threw the bolt home suggested that locking him up gave her a great deal of pleasure.

As near as Magrane could figure it, lunch was still an hour away. Kicking the sheets and blankets aside, he got out of bed and proceeded to do twenty push-ups, part of the gruelling program of physical exercises he had devised to get himself fit again. While he was busy working up a sweat, the first hesitant snowflakes began to fall from the leaden sky.

Joseph, the male nurse who collected Magrane at two o'clock to escort him down the corridor to Daniel's office, could have been the matron's twin brother except that his hair was much fairer. He was a taciturn sort of man, and no one in his right mind would have actually let him near a patient, but put Joseph in the ring with a wrestler and he'd have his opponent on the canvas begging for mercy seconds after the bell had gone for the first round.

Reinhard Heydrich had been an outstanding fencer, but it seemed that winter sports were more in Daniel's line. Seated behind a functional steel desk, the KGB man was wearing a turtleneck sweater, stretch pants and thick woollen stockings which reached as far as his knees. A bright red anorak was draped over the back of his chair, a knitted woolly hat and a pair of ski gloves were drying off on the radiator. Magrane noticed that the snow had melted from his lace-up boots to form a small puddle of water on the brown linoleum.

"You must be a fanatic."

Daniel looked up from the file he was reading and stared at him, a hostile expression on his face. "A fanatic?" he asked coldly.

"About skiing."

"Oh, I see. Well, I do a bit of langlaufing now and then." He pointed to the chair in front of the desk. "You can sit there, Andrew."

"We're giving the couch a miss this time, are we?"

"That rather depends on you."

There was no need for Daniel to elaborate. To be thought uncooperative was to invite the electric shock treatment or a shot of pentothal. Magrane sat down, conscious that Joseph was standing behind his chair, ready and only too willing to restrain him should the necessity arise. The atmosphere was distinctly tense and he tried to think of a way to lower the temperature.

"I haven't seen Sergeant Franklin lately," he said idly. "How's he coming along?"

"I thought you knew." Daniel allowed himself a bleak smile. "Franklin made a complete recovery. He was sent on convalescent leave weeks ago."

They had turned Franklin then, bending his mind so that now he would respond exactly as they wanted him to. Convalescent leave? Balls. They were keeping Franklin on ice somewhere in Moscow until they had finished brainwashing him. Two defectors were always better than one.

"Let's talk about Operation Damocles, Andrew."

"Why? We've been over that ground before. Anyway, it was a training exercise, not an operation."

"Really?"

"Of course it was. Look, the whole thing was cleared with the Libyans in advance. The Navy put us ashore near Tripoli and we had to infiltrate through the beach defenses to reach a small oasis some thirty miles inland from the coast."

"So why was the exercise called off before it was completed?"

"We weren't acclimatized; five members of the patrol got heatstroke."

It was a parody of the truth, but it was the story Daniel wanted to hear. There had been no prior clearance from the Libyans for one very good reason: somebody in Whitehall had decided that Qaddafi had to go, and the SAS had been landed with the job of ambushing him. Unfortunately, the operation had been a disaster from start to finish. The unexpected presence of two Soviet frigates in the area had compelled the commander of their Oberon-class submarine to shut down the diesel engines and adopt a silent routine to avoid detection. That chance encounter had made a nonsense of their timetable, delaying the final approach by some two and a half hours. By the time they had concealed their inflatable assault boats, it had been evident that they would be lucky to reach Tripoli before daybreak.

"It was an abortive exercise then, Andrew?"

"Yes."

Abortive was an understatement. As things had turned out, they were still roughly three miles from the outskirts of Tripoli when first light had appeared over the horizon. And since the Navy had planned to pick them up the following night, they had been forced to go to ground in an area where there was precious little cover. Almost inevitably, they had been spotted and towards midday the patrol had found themselves surrounded by a company of infantry. Even now, he found it hard to understand how the fire fight had started, but within a matter of minutes, five members of the patrol had been killed and he'd finished up with a gunshot wound in the chest.

"And after the exercise was over, your troop returned to the U.K. from Muscat in an RAF Hercules?"

The big lie, one that Goebbels would have been proud of. Instead of a troop, there had been an eight-man patrol of whom three survivors and five dead men had been transported to the Soviet Union in an Antonov 22 from Libya.

"Isn't that right?" Daniel insisted.

"You should know."

"I see. What does Case Black mean to you?"

"Nothing, absolutely nothing."

"Allow me to refresh your memory, Andrew." Daniel tapped the file cover in front of him. "Case Black projected the circumstances in which it might be necessary to detain certain people under Section 18(b) of The Defence of the Realm Act. You were to be in charge of one of the arresting parties."

The Libyans had never brought Operation Damocles to the attention of the UN and, during the long months of his captivity, he had often wondered why the Kremlin had persuaded Qaddafi to remain silent about the affair. Now he thought he knew the answer. Before the general election of February, 1974, when it had seemed the country was becoming ungovernable, there had been talk of a possible military coup d'etat. There had never been any substance to the rumors but four years after the event, it seemed the KGB intended to prove that such a contingency plan had existed.

"You know what your trouble is, Daniel? You've got an all too vivid imagination."

"Yes? Well, perhaps that's one thing we do have in common, Andrew."

"I doubt it."

"Maybe you're right." Daniel rested both elbows on the desk and leaned forward, his mouth creasing in a furtive, knowing smile. "Why do you hate Virginia?"

"Virginia?"

"Your wife." A slim hand opened the file and extracted a photograph. The long-legged blonde was standing by a swimming pool in a one-piece bathing suit. The pose looked professional.

"Remember, Andrew?"

Magrane avoided his gaze and stared at the window beyond him. The snow was falling heavily now and a gale force wind had sprung up. There was no perimeter fence outside and no prowler guards either, and he could understand why this should be so. The constant blizzards of a Siberian winter and the vast emptiness of the wastelands were sufficiently intimidating to discourage any would-be escaper.

"I asked you a question, Andrew."

He could remember Virginia all right, could remember returning home early one fine morning to find her in bed with a stranger. Any other man would have thrown her out on her ear, but she had always been able to twist him round her little finger. Virginia was his Achilles' heel and the KGB knew it. Somehow they would find a way to use her to break him.

"I don't hate Virginia."

"I think you do."

"I don't give a shit what you think, Daniel." His voice rose in anger. "Once and for all, get this straight—I don't give a fuck."

Daniel stood up and moved towards the small table under the poison cabinet in the corner of the room. Using a pair of tongs, he lifted the lid from the sterilizing tray and fished out a hypodermic needle.

"Please take off your dressing gown," he said coldly.

"Why should I?"

"Do you want Joseph to do it for you?"

"No."

"Then be a good fellow and do as I say. Take it off, roll up the sleeves of your pyjama jacket and then lie down on the couch behind the screen."

Pentothal: Daniel intended sending him to the land of dreams so that he could look inside his head and expose the dark thoughts. How long did Stan the Pole say he had been in this god-awful place? Thirty-three years? Jesus Christ, was that what the future held in store for him? His eyes began to prick and a tear ran down his cheek. His mind formed one word: no.

"I'm waiting, Andrew."

Magrane stood up and slipped his arms out of the dressing gown. Turning round, he handed the robe to Joseph and then hit him in the throat, smashing the larynx so that the male nurse was dead before he hit the floor. Hearing a strangled gasp behind him, he whirled about to face Daniel.

"Don't, Andrew."

"What?"

"Please don't make things any worse than they are. Killing me won't solve anything."

The KGB man swallowed nervously, and he liked that. It showed the bastard was afraid of him.

"Maybe not," Magrane said in a low voice, "but it would give me a great deal of satisfaction."

"Look, I want to help you."

"Yes?"

"You must believe that."

"All right, if you really want to help me, you can make a start by putting the syringe down on the desk."

"Yes, of course."

"And strip off."

"What did you say?"

"I need your clothes—it's cold outside."

"You'll never get away with it."

"What's the matter? Are you tired of living?"

Daniel pulled the sweater off over his head and dropped it on to the desk. "May I sit down to take off my boots?" he asked quietly.

"If you come out here and sit in the middle of the floor

where I can keep an eye on you." Magrane backed towards the door and, reaching behind him, turned the key in the lock. "Two's company," he said, "and I aim to keep it that way."

"You won't last five minutes if you go outside in that blizzard, Andrew."

"You're wrong; I'm a born survivor. I can speak Russian too. I bet you didn't know that."

"No, I didn't." Daniel got to his feet and stripped off his ski pants. "But I doubt if it will help you very much out there."

"Did anyone ever tell you that you look very cute in your vest and underpants, Doc?"

"I'm not in the mood for jokes, Andrew."

"Neither am I. Get down on the floor again and lie flat on your stomach."

"Now, look here—"

Daniel suddenly doubled up as Magrane moved in close and kneed him in the groin. His legs gave way and he sank down on to his knees, mewling softly like a kitten. Gradually, he stretched out and lay flat, his head over to one side, a dribble of bile escaping from the corner of his open mouth.

"What happens now?" he groaned.

"Nothing spectacular; you just go to sleep."

Magrane picked up the syringe and pressed the plunger to send a jet of pentothal spurting into the air. Bending over the KGB man, he jabbed the needle into the main artery of his left arm and slowly emptied the hypodermic. On his instructions, Daniel started counting and got up to five before he passed out cold. Some moments later, his loud snores disturbed the silence in the room.

"To sleep; perchance to dream; ay, there's the rub; For in that sleep of death what dreams may come . . ." Why did he remember that quotation now? Had he been dreaming? Magrane shook his head. This was no nightmare. There were two men lying on the floor, one dead, the other breathing heavily. What was it Daniel had said? You won't last five minutes if you go outside in that blizzard, Andrew. Well, so what? It was Hobson's choice; in killing Joseph, he'd as good as signed his own death warrant anyway. Better to die out there in the cold than be put up against a wall and shot. Reaching for the pile of clothing, he began to dress hurriedly, pulling the ski pants on over his pyjamas.

Ten minutes later, he walked out of the room and on down the corridor towards the swing doors in the entrance. A medical orderly was on duty in reception, but he didn't even bother to look up from the book he was reading as Magrane strolled past the window. Once outside, he found the langlauf skis wedged in a snowbank and, putting them on, he set off in the direction of the pine forest he'd seen from his bedroom.

Such light as there was faded rapidly and the night closed in around him. Darkness was his friend and so too was the blizzard that covered his tracks. By the time he stumbled upon the log cabin, Magrane had covered approximately fifteen miles.

2 . . .

MAGRANE stirred and, slowly opening both eyes, became aware of a chink of grey light showing in the gap between the drawn curtains in the window. Suddenly wide awake, he sat bolt upright in the armchair, his pulse racing as he looked round the unfamiliar living room. The bright red anorak on the clotheshorse and the ski boots which had been left to dry in the hearth set his mind at rest and the momentary feeling of panic rapidly evaporated. The peat fire in the grate had gone out during the night but fortunately, the quilt eiderdown had kept him warm and insulated him against the bitter cold. Draping the quilt round his shoulders like a cape, he padded across the floor in his stockinged feet, drew back the curtains and rubbed a peephole in the skin of ice which had formed on the inside of the window pane.

Although it had stopped snowing, the view depressed him immeasurably. The log cabin lay in a wide but shallow valley, a great white wilderness devoid of any noticeable features, which stretched as far as the eye could see in the prevailing light. There wasn't another dwelling place in sight, which explained why there were no roads, no telegraph wires or power cables. For all Khrushchev's proud boasts, Siberia was still the frozen arsehole of the world.

He still hadn't the faintest idea where he was, and the old man who had taken him in last night hadn't been able to enlighten him. Despite the fact that his Russian was fairly fluent, they had been unable to communicate with one another because the peasant spoke a different dialect, one that he couldn't recognize. In an attempt to make himself understood, the old man had scribbled a few sentences down on a scrap of paper, but the ill-formed letters were not from the Cyrillic alphabet and the words hadn't struck a chord with him.

Magrane glanced at the wristwatch he'd stolen from Daniel and was surprised to see that it was past eight o'clock. Either the old man was a late riser or else he was still sleeping off the effects of the night before when they had drunk the best part of a liter of vodka between them. At least, he assumed it had been vodka. The spirit had been colorless, slightly oily and far from smooth, the first mouthful burning his throat on the way down so that the tears had come to his eyes and he'd coughed and spluttered. After that experience, he'd learned to take it slowly, enjoying the warm glow in his stomach that had subsequently spread through the rest of his body. Tiptoeing across to the adjoining room, he put his ear to the hardboard partition and, hearing a faint snore, decided it was safe to raise the latch and open the door.

The old man was lying flat on his back buried under a mountain of blankets and a sheepskin coat. Too tall for the narrow single bed, the man had hung his feet over the edge, the bedclothes reaching only as far as his shins. Both matted socks were holed at the toes and smelled as if they hadn't been changed in weeks. Considering that he had downed three tots to his every one, Magrane thought it remarkable that the old man hadn't been sick during the night. Backing out of the room, he closed the door quietly behind him.

The time to leave was now while the old man was still dead to the world and, dumping the quilt in the armchair, he put on the anorak and zipped it up. Food? He wasn't particularly hungry, but there was no telling when he would eat again and in this inhospitable climate, it paid to stock up.

The greasy remains of last night's stew in the pot on the cooking range looked singularly unappetizing and, hastily replacing the lid, he went into the larder, an airless cubbyhole darker than the Black Hole of Calcutta. Groping around, he found a flashlight on one of the shelves and switched it on. The batteries were down to their last dregs, but the weak beam was sufficient for him to see that the old man had stored enough potatoes, carrots, onions and swedes to last him through the winter and well into the summer. A hare hung from a hook in the ceiling and, looking inside a barrel, Magrane saw that the carcass of a deer had also been salted away. There were unlabelled cans of what looked to be flour, dried yeast, sugar, herbs, raisins, black-eyed peas and haricot beans as well as several earthenware jars of salt. However, apart from a loaf of homemade bread and some goat's cheese, there was precious little in the way of perishable food. Bread, cheese and onions were not the usual things he would have chosen for breakfast, but they would provide plenty of nourishment. Tucking the flashlight under his left arm, he helped himself to a couple of onions, picked up the loaf and the dish of cheese and turned to leave. It was then that he noticed the rifle wrapped in a canvas covering and propped against the wall in the corner nearest the door.

A hunter? That had to be the answer. The old man lived off the land during winter, hunting deer to supplement the root crops he scratched from the poor soil in late spring and summer. Perhaps he even trapped for furs on the side and was amongst the last rugged individualists left in the Soviet Union who managed to survive outside the regimented system. Leaving the bread, cheese and onions on the kitchen table in the living room, Magrane returned to the larder and collected the rifle.

The canvas protecting the breech mechanism had been tied together with two pieces of string, and he had to cut the knots to remove it. The rifle was a museum piece dating back to World War I, but it was nevertheless in very good condition; among other things, the sights had been recently blackened and the bolt action lightly oiled with a special low-temperature lubricant. At first, the general configuration led him to believe it was a Mosin-Nagent, but on examining the die stamp on the breech more closely, he saw that the weapon was a model

P14 Lee Enfield, manufactured in the U.S.A. under license
by Remington Arms.

As a subject of interest, history had always fascinated him
and he knew that there were only two possible ways the rifle
could have entered the Soviet Union. Either it was originally
part of the consignment of small arms that had been sent to
Admiral Kolchak's forces at Omsk via the Trans-Siberian
Railway from Vladivostok, or else it had been left behind in
the Ordnance Depot at Archangel when the British Army had
pulled out of northern Russia. Two possible explanations,
both equally valid, both equally useless because neither one
helped him to pinpoint his position. Archangel and Omsk
were twelve hundred miles apart and he was somewhere in
between.

Magrane spread some of the goat's cheese on a slice of
bread and munched it slowly. The rifle might be a museum
piece, but it would keep him in food if he could find the
ammunition. ''If'' was the major stumbling block; the old
man was just about the untidiest person in creation and there
was no telling where he might have put the cartridges. More
in hope than expectation, he opened the left-hand drawer in
the kitchen table and immediately struck gold.

The twelve .303 rounds in the cardboard box were discol-
ored with age, the brass cartridge cases dull yellow instead of
bright chrome. Had it not been for the game in the larder, he
would have said they were probably dud. Charging the magazine with five rounds, he depressed the W spring so that it
was possible to close the bolt without chambering a bullet.
That done, he squeezed the trigger, applied the safety catch
and pocketed the rest of the ammunition.

As a matter of course, he went through the other drawer,
but none of the assorted junk inside was of any use to him
and, leaving the table, he sat down in the armchair and
slipped his feet into the ski boots. Without a compass, he
would have to navigate by the sun and the stars, and in this
latitude there were precious few hours of daylight and the
stars were often hidden by a dark overcast. However, if worst
came to worst, he supposed he could always find north by the
growth of moss on the tree trunks. Murmansk: if he could just

reach Murmansk, there was a chance he could stow away on an ore ship bound for Narvik in Norway. It wasn't much of a plan, but at least he now had a definite aim in mind.

Magrane eyed the loaf on the kitchen table, decided his host could spare half and sliced it in two. Cramming the hunk of bread into the other pocket of the anorak, he picked up the Lee Enfield and was about to leave when the door opened and the old man shuffled into the room, scratching his stomach. He seemed amiable enough, if a little hung over, until he noticed the rifle and then the inane grin faded rapidly and he became extremely agitated. For somebody under the weather, he was surprisingly quick off the mark and before Magrane could ward him off, they were locked together in a violent tug of war over the Lee Enfield rifle.

The contest should have been a one-sided affair, but the old man was a lot stronger than he'd bargained for and a sudden twisting movement almost broke his hold on the weapon. Although he didn't want to hurt him, Magrane's reaction was instinctive, one that had been drilled into him, and he lashed out, kicking his right leg to break the bone above the shin. Then, backing off a pace, he clouted the old man with the butt, wielding the P14 like a scythe to open a deep gash in his skull. The blow would have felled an ox and looking at the still figure lying at his feet, Magrane realized with a sinking feeling that he was dead.

Was this the price freedom entailed? To kill an old man who'd shown him only kindness? Slowly, he turned away and stumbled out of the cabin, a bitter taste in his mouth. As if in a dream, he walked into the lean-to shed where the peat was stored and collected the langlauf skis.

For a few moments, Donaldson received a panoramic view of the camp below as the Wessex helicopter banked through a hundred-and-eighty-degree turn to approach the landing pad marked out in the snow. Once a Commando battle school, Strathconan had been allowed to run down despite the fact that after the war it had been retained by the Ministry of Defence on a ''care and maintenance'' basis. ''Care and maintenance'' was an expression open to any number of interpretations and with the Treasury keeping a tight rein on the purse strings, he supposed it was inevitable that most of the Nissen huts at the top end of the camp should now be derelict. Only a sudden volte-face had saved the camp from extinction; five years ago, under mounting public pressure to withdraw from Dartmoor and Lulworth Cove, the Army had managed to persuade the civil servants to give Strathconan a new lease on life.

The Wessex went into the hover and then set down on the landing pad, the downwash from the rotor blades whipping up a flurry of snow. Suddenly aware that the winchman was giving him a thumbs-up sign, Donaldson unclipped the seat belt, grabbed his overnight bag and jumped down from the helicopter. Although there was no need to do so, he found it psychologically impossible not to duck his head as he trudged away; the rotor blades were a good fifteen feet above him but the subconscious mind always seemed to reject this fact out of hand. He was still bent double, still only halfway to the long, wooden barrack hut where the two-man reception committee was waiting for him, when the Wessex lifted off again and roared over his head.

As he drew near, the taller man stepped forward to greet him, one arm outstretched to shake hands, a ready smile on his lean face.

"My name's Hugh Tamblin," said the stranger. "And you must be Major Donaldson."

"That's right."

"Splendid." Tamblin beamed and pumped his hand enthusiastically. "I'm with Public Relations at the Ministry of Defence. And this gentleman is Mr. Lloyd; he's from the Home Office, Police Department."

Lloyd was in his mid-forties but, unlike most men of that age in a sedentary occupation, he looked extremely fit. There wasn't a spare ounce of flesh on his body and Donaldson got the impression that he was something of an athlete. He had none of Tamblin's bonhomie and his cold, appraising glance suggested that he did not suffer fools gladly. It soon became apparent that he could be very direct.

"I assume you know why you're here," he said.

"Not really. I was just told that there had been a spot of bother at Strathconan and since everyone else was tied up I was to get up here as fast as I could to liaise with the civil authorities."

Lloyd raised both eyebrows and then with a trace of impatience turned to face Tamblin. "You led me to understand that this officer had been briefed by Special Forces, Hugh."

"That's what I was told."

"It would seem you were misinformed then."

Donaldson thought Tamblin wasn't the only man who'd been misinformed. If Lloyd believed that he had been handpicked for the job, he didn't know the Army. There had been no selection process; the assignment had come his way because it just so happened that he was available. It was as simple as that.

"Yes, I'm afraid you're right." Tamblin stamped his feet in the snow and clapped his gloved hands together. There was a resigned expression on his face. "I should have known there'd be a cock-up. Too many people had their fingers in this particular pie."

"Is that really so unusual for the Ministry of Defence?"

"I wouldn't say that. I daresay the same sort of thing goes on in the Home Office." The smile was still there on Tamblin's face, but it was becoming tighter by the minute. "We all have our faults."

"Indeed we do. Will you give Major Donaldson the background story, or shall I?"

"Well, since the police are involved, I think it might be better if you brought him up to date."

"As you wish," said Lloyd. "Let's go inside the hospital, it's damn cold out here."

Poetic license was all very well, but Donaldson thought it a gross distortion to call the barrack hut a hospital. A medical center or a reception station would be a more accurate description. As he followed behind the other two, he gave the signboard by the entrance a thump, dislodging the snow to reveal the letters MRS stencilled in black below the Red Cross symbol.

"Ever met an officer called Andrew Magrane?" asked Lloyd, holding the door open for him.

"The name doesn't ring a bell."

"That's funny; he's a captain in the SAS."

"We're a different breed," said Donaldson. "I'm a para-trooper; we don't have much to do with the SAS."

"But you're familiar with their methods?"

Lloyd halted in the corridor, opened a door on his left and waved him inside. The room was standard size and furnished in accordance with minimum barrack scales. The poison cabinet on the wall and the couch behind the folding screen indicated that it was used by one of the doctors attached to the Medical Reception Station.

"I mean, you know how they operate in the field?"

"It's no great secret," said Donaldson.

"Good. This office we're using belongs to Major Daniel. Magrane was one of his psychiatric patients."

"One?"

Lloyd not only ignored the question, but sniffed in a way that suggested he thought it totally irrelevant. "Normally, Magrane was docile enough," he continued, "but yesterday afternoon for some inexplicable reason, he became very violent. To put it in a nutshell, he killed one of the male nurses, overpowered Major Daniel and escaped."

Donaldson recalled the vague briefing he'd had from Vaughan and tried to hide his anger. To refer to murder as a spot of bother had to be the understatement of the year, even by Vaughan's standards. An ex-cavalryman, Vaughan prided himself on being cool, calm and collected when, in fact, he was merely lethargic. His experience with Special Forces and clandestine operations was somewhat limited, but the selection board had seen fit to promote him to full colonel in charge of the cell at Headquarters U.K. Land Forces, perhaps in the belief that he would add a little tone to the branch.

"Daniel is a keen winter sports enthusiast." Lloyd shoved both hands into the pockets of his wool-lined suede coat and leaned back against the wall. "Keeps himself in trim by skiing to and fro between the hospital and the Married Quarters patch. Magrane simply stole his langlauf skis and vanished into the snowstorm."

"I assume the local police are already looking for him?"

"Not actively," said Lloyd.

"What does that mean?"

"They've got a lot on their plate and it's a question of priorities. The blizzard piled up a mass of snowdrifts, some of them over thirty feet deep. Just about every village in Ross and Cromarty is cut off and things aren't much better in the adjoining county. I understand the railway line is blocked north of Inverness."

"So Magrane is hardly their number one concern?"

"Not at the moment. Fortunately, we can call on the troop of Royal Marine Commandos who are up here training for winter warfare. That's where you come in."

"In what capacity?"

"As a coordinator. The troop commander is comparatively inexperienced and we'd like you to vet his provisional patrol program."

Donaldson frowned. Inexperienced or not, the Marine officer would be resentful to say the least. That the Ministry of Defence had thought it necessary to send an officer from another service to hold his hand only added insult to injury. He also couldn't help wondering whether his journey had really been essential. Between the two of them, Lloyd and the Marine officer should have been capable of organizing a search operation.

"Ross and Cromarty is one hell of a big area," he said thoughtfully. "Can we get any helicopter support?"

"Not a chance," said Lloyd. "The Secretary of State has ruled that the Highlands are to be treated as a disaster area. Every available helicopter has been put at the disposal of the local authority for rescue work."

"That figures."

"Do you have any other questions?"

"Only one," said Donaldson. "If Magrane was a psychiatric case, why was he being treated up here instead of at Netley?"

Lloyd turned towards Tamblin. "I think you should answer that question, Hugh."

"It was a matter of security."

"Come again?"

"Security." Tamblin cleared his throat. "Magrane had been working undercover in Belfast. The IRA got on to him, there was a shoot-out and he was badly wounded. There was a feeling in some quarters that the IRA might try to finish him off. Since it is no military secret that Netley is a psychiatric hospital, it was considered that he would be much safer up here at Strathconan."

The explanation made sense; yet, all the same, Donaldson couldn't shake off a feeling that it wasn't the whole story, that Tamblin was deliberately holding something back. It could be just his imagination, but he thought the PR man seemed a mite anxious.

The Whirlwind belonged to the helicopter rescue flight based on Lossiemouth, but since early that morning it had been operating out of Inverness in support of the local authority. By midday the crew had completed four missions, delivering essential heating oil to outlying farms and airlifting one very pregnant young woman to a hospital. Now, toward fifteen thirty, with the light fading rapidly, they were flying their fifth and last mission of the day, making for an isolated croft on the fringe of Strathconan forest in Ross and Cromarty.

Surveying the white wilderness below, the pilot wondered how the lonely old man could bring himself to live in such an isolated and inhospitable place. The police at Marybank had said that he was a recluse, and he needed to be; nobody in his right mind was going to beat a path to his door.

Presently, the log cabin came in sight and the pilot thought that one swift circuit above it ought to suffice. Providing there was no SOS marked out in the snow and smoke was coming out of the chimney, they could then push off back home for tea and crumpets at Inverness, if the temporary Officers' Mess could run to such a delicacy. His mouth watered at the prospect, but not for long. Although there wasn't an SOS, the chimney was dead and that spelled trouble.

The snow looked treacherous and the pilot was damned if he was going to risk it. Putting the Whirlwind into the hover, he spoke to the crewman over the intercom and instructed him to take a quick look round. The quick look lasted all of fifteen minutes, the time it took the crewman to discover that the old man was dead and to have the corpse winched up on a litter. Low on fuel, the Whirlwind finally made it back to Inverness in the pitch dark.

Some two hours were to elapse before the police at Marybank decided to inform Lloyd.

3 . . .

THE yellow flagpin which Lloyd had pressed into the map was about the size of an average thumbnail. Since it marked the approximate location of the log cabin where Davie Tulloch had been found dead, Donaldson thought it would have been more appropriate if he had chosen a black one. The flagpin affected them all, but in different ways, and it was clear that he, Lloyd and the Royal Marine would have to get together and come up with another plan because obviously they had started off on the wrong foot. For Carr, the senior medical officer, and Daniel, the dark-haired psychiatrist, it was another reminder that they had failed their patient, while, in Tamblin's case, it would mean fending off a host of awkward questions from the press once they put two and two together and guessed that Magrane had been involved. The news of his escape had already sparked off a number of inquiries and if the past few minutes were anything to go by, it now looked as if Tamblin was going to spend most of his time on the telephone in the office next door answering a whole spate of questions.

"I suppose it couldn't have been an accident?" The hopeful expression on Carr's face was a sign that he was grasping at straws, looking for any excuse that would get him off the hook. "After all, Tulloch was getting on in life and when a man reaches the age of sixty-seven, he's apt to be none too steady on his feet. He could have slipped and struck his head against the table or something like that."

"I'm afraid not." Lloyd glanced at the notes he'd taken down when the telephone call had come through from Marybank. "The police are satisfied that the wound was caused by a blunt instrument."

"And the tracks leading northeast from Tulloch's place were definitely made by langlauf skis?"

"That's what the crewman reported, Colonel, and the helicopter pilot backs his opinion."

"Well, that's it then." Carr sighed. "It has to be Magrane."

"Yes. Unfortunately, it would appear the Marine Commandos have been searching the wrong area. You'll have to do something about that, Robert."

Donaldson launched himself from the chair and walked over to the map. The sudden use of his first name didn't fool him. Almost in the same breath, Lloyd had put up the umbrella, making it clear to the others that he hadn't been responsible for the abortive patrol program. Tulloch's death was proof that the attack on Joseph and Daniel had not been an isolated act of violence. Magrane had shown that he was prepared to kill anyone who stood in his way, and he had to be stopped before there was another victim.

"It's a pity the Chief Range Warden didn't tell you about Tulloch's place."

"I don't suppose it occurred to him," said Donaldson. "It's a good fifteen miles from here and way outside the training area."

The Commando troop had been split into four patrols and in the absence of any positive information, they had simply described a circle on the map with a radius of ten inches centered on Strathconan camp. Ten inches represented ten miles on the ground, the maximum range of the A41 manpack radio set. After quartering the circle, each patrol had then been given a segment to search. Those who hadn't already returned to base would have to be recalled and the whole troop moved forward to Tulloch's place, ready to continue the hunt at first light tomorrow. As briefly as he knew how, Donaldson told Lloyd what he had in mind.

"I don't like it." Lloyd tapped the wall map with a finger-nail, making a noise like a woodpecker. "Magrane already has a big enough head start on us. By calling off the search now, you'll be giving him another twelve hours."

"We could miss his tracks in the dark."

"There's a strong possibility they won't be there tomorrow. According to the latest weather forecast, this area can expect light to moderate snow showers during the night."

"Then the local authority will have to release a couple of helicopters."

"We may think finding Magrane should take priority over everything else, Robert, but they might have other ideas. Right now it would be a help if we knew what had prompted him to take off in a northeasterly direction."

"He's making for the coast," said Daniel.

"Really?" Lloyd turned about to face the psychiatrist. "You seem very sure, doctor," he said. "Is that an educated guess or an informed opinion?"

"A bit of both." Daniel managed a faint smile. He was still feeling the effects of the pentothal and his face looked pale and haggard. "Magrane is under the illusion that this place is somewhere deep inside Siberia. He was also convinced that he was being held for questioning by the KGB."

"He's pretty far gone then?" said Donaldson.

"It certainly wasn't easy to reach him. Of course, looking back, I can understand how the illusion was fostered. I mean, the landscape is not all that dissimilar and we've had a bad winter up here."

"Not to mention the various nationalities around this place." Carr leaned forward, resting both elbows on the desk. "People like me, for instance. I joined the British Army thirty years ago, but I still haven't lost my Canadian accent, and that was enough to convince Magrane that English wasn't my native tongue. That's why he used to needle me about Pasternak and other writers banned in the Soviet Union. I confess it annoyed me because it showed he was slipping back just when I thought he was beginning to improve." Carr frowned. "And then there's Stanislaus Klepacz."

"Who's he?"

"A Pole, like the rest of the civilian staff. Most of them got to know this part of the world when they were stationed up here during the war with the First Polish Parachute Brigade. Klepacz married a local girl in 1944, so it's not surprising he decided to settle here after he was demobilized. Actually, he's one of the range wardens, but we were temporarily misemploying him as a hospital porter."

There was nothing freakish about the fact that the camp staff were Polish. Klepacz was a casualty of the last war, one of many that Donaldson had encountered elsewhere, men who had found it impossible to return home for one reason or another. Half the mess waiters at the School of Infantry had served with General Anders's Corps in Italy.

"Would the illusion persist outside the confines of this medical center?"

"You mean when he met up with Tulloch?" Daniel hooked a leg over the arm of his easy chair. "One can never be a hundred percent sure about these things, but it's more than likely. In Magrane's present state of mind, he'll bend the facts to suit his preconceived ideas. For example, if he was confronted with a sign in English, he would reason that it was written in the Cyrillic alphabet. You may find that hard to swallow, but as far as Magrane is concerned, this is Russia, not Scotland, and he has an uncanny ability to explain everything to his own satisfaction. Take the newspapers we gave him. According to Andrew, they were always a day late because this place is four thousand miles from London. It was the same with the radio. The BBC programs he heard were all recordings made by the KGB in Moscow. To put it in a nutshell, *Magrane believes what he wants to believe*. And who knows what he may choose to believe next?"

"But he must have spoken to Tulloch. Wouldn't that have broken the spell?"

"Perhaps I can answer that question," Lloyd cut in swiftly with an apologetic smile for Daniel. "In my view, Tulloch probably confused him even more. There are a large number of Gaelic speakers in Ross and Cromarty, the vast majority of whom are completely bilingual, but the police told me that Tulloch was one of the very few Highlanders who either couldn't or wouldn't speak English. I don't suppose they knew what to make of one another, especially if Magrane addressed him in Russian.''

"Can he?"

"What?"

"Speak Russian," said Donaldson.

"I wouldn't know." Lloyd glanced away, a faint smile appearing on his mouth as the door opened and Tamblin walked into the room. "You'll have to ask Hugh."

"Ask me what?" said Tamblin.

"Robert wants to know if Magrane can speak Russian."

Tamblin hesitated, his eyebrows meeting in a quizzical frown. For a fleeting moment, his demeanor was akin to that of an actor who'd forgotten his lines and was waiting for a cue.

"Is it important?"

"Robert appears to think so."

"Well, as a matter of fact, he qualified as a second-class interpreter back in 1972. That was after a two-year language course."

Lloyd and Tamblin; coupled together, their names sounded like a double act. For two complete strangers who'd only met one another on the way up to Strathconan, Donaldson thought it remarkable that they should have established such a close rapport in so short a time.

"I'm afraid I've got to land you with a fast ball, Robert," Tamblin said apologetically.

"What sort of fast ball?"

"A press briefing. You see, Magrane is headline news now whether we like it or not. I've been talking to PR at the Ministry of Defence and they agree it's the best way to handle the situation."

"Why pick on me?"

"Well, you helped to organize the search operation and we do need a military spokesman."

"Terrific."

"Don't worry, I'll be there to hold your hand." Tamblin moved into top gear, developing a line of sales talk that rolled off his tongue with practiced ease. "Anyway, if I know reporters, most of them will give it a miss. The village hall at

Carnforth is handy for us, but it's a fair old drive from Inverness even though the road has been reopened. On a night like this, I fancy they'll prefer to prop up the bar in the Station Hotel.''

''We're just going through the motions—is that the idea?''

Tamblin pressed a finger against his nose. ''Mum's the word,'' he said. ''Whatever you do, don't let on to the press.''

''No, we don't want any gaffes, Robert. In the circumstances, I think it would be a good idea if you and Hugh put your heads together and thrashed out a statement.''

Lloyd placed a hand on his elbow and gently but firmly steered him towards the door. He was the perfect civil servant, smooth, efficient and very persuasive, a man who was used to talking his way out of a tricky situation.

''Don't worry about the redeployment.'' He stretched his face in a smile that was meant to be reassuring. ''The troop commander and I can handle that small problem.''

There was a bad smell about the Magrane affair and now that the Ministry of Defence had decided to smother it, everybody up at Strathconan would be skating on very thin ice. If they weren't careful, someone was going to get his feet wet, and the way things were shaping up, Donaldson had a hunch that he was the most likely candidate.

Magrane halted on the crest, kicked off the langlauf skis and immediately dropped flat. The village was directly below him, almost within hailing distance, and strung out in a thin straight line. From the number of lights showing, he figured there were about twenty houses in all. Although only a dot on the map, the hamlet was obviously important enough to be connected to the national electricity grid, and that could be ominous.

Perhaps there was a Soviet Air Force base in the vicinity? If so, it would explain why their Hound helicopters had been able to keep him pinned down for most of the day. The Hound bore a close resemblance to the Westland Whirlwind and had much the same range and endurance, which meant that it was good for three hours' flying time. To his certain knowledge, one of the Hounds had spent two and a half hours conducting a box search of the area where he'd been hiding, leaving the pilot just thirty minutes to return to base.

A quick piece of mental arithmetic convinced him that his assumption about the Air Force base must be wrong. In thirty minutes, assuming the pilot maintained an average speed of seventy knots, the Hound would cover forty miles, almost twice the distance he had logged in the whole day.

Magrane studied the village with renewed interest. Cold, tired and hungry, he didn't fancy his chances in the open now that it had started snowing again. If you were reasonably fresh and equipped with the right tools, building a shelter was a simple enough job, but it was an impossible task when you were practically dead on your feet and had to scrape out a hole in the hard-packed snow with your bare hands. Not surprisingly, the more he looked at the isolated house on the outskirts of the village, the more attractive it became.

After some deliberation, Magrane climbed to his feet and unlooped the rifle from his back. Working the bolt to chamber a round, he applied the safety catch and passed the leather sling over his head so he could carry the weapon across his chest. The occupants of the isolated house were unlikely to welcome him with open arms, but the Lee Enfield would persuade them to stifle their objections. Clipping his toecaps into the skis, he set off downhill, the langlaufs cutting neat parallel lines in the virgin snow as he gathered momentum.

Seen from a distance, the house resembled a shot box and appeared to be constructed of prefabricated slabs of concrete. Drawing nearer, he was surprised to find that it also possessed a small back garden enclosed by a hedge. It was definitely an oddity; one which contradicted the mental picture he had formed of Siberia from geography textbooks he'd read at school. Maybe he had been wrong about Khrushchev, maybe the former premier had succeeded in changing the wastelands out of all recognition.

He peered over the hedge, wondered if he should try the kitchen and then decided that it would excite less suspicion if he knocked at the front door. Moving down the side of the house, he opened the front gate, left his skis beneath the hedge and walked up the path, the rifle butt cradled under his right armpit.

The young woman who answered the door dressed in a pair of tan-colored denims and a turtleneck sweater was about five feet two and slim, the very opposite of the butch matron back at the detention center. She had fair hair and a narrow, almost childlike face. The half-formed, tentative smile on her lips disappeared when she saw the rifle levelled at her stomach.

"Who are you?" Her voice was hoarse with alarm. "What do you want?"

Magrane stared at her, his pulse racing. English. The young woman had spoken to him in English, and there was a peaked cap on the hatstand, a dark blue one like the kind worn by the Soviet civil police. She and her husband obviously belonged to the elite. They had been sent to a language school to learn English, and she knew enough to guess that he was the escaped prisoner the police were looking for.

"There's no need to be frightened," he said quietly. "I won't hurt you."

Suddenly the penny dropped and her eyes grew wider. "You're the one they're looking for," she whispered.

"That's right, I'm the man who escaped from the prison camp." Magrane gave her a gentle prod with the rifle, stepped inside the hall and closed the door behind him. "Did they also tell your husband that I killed one of the guards?"

"My husband?"

"He's a policeman, isn't he?"

"Yes."

"Call him."

"He's not at home." A small pink tongue explored the bottom lip. "He left early this morning to join the rescue team."

"What rescue team is that?"

"The main line is blocked with snow and a train has been derailed."

"Whereabouts is that?" he asked sharply.

"Just east of here on the coast."

Magrane advanced down the hall, checking out the rooms on either side as the woman retreated before him towards the kitchen. A railway on the coast in Siberia? Either something was terribly wrong with the geography or else the bitch had told him a pack of lies. If the woman had lied, it could only be that she was playing for time because her husband was still somewhere in the house. Perhaps he was lying in wait above? No, that couldn't be right; he didn't remember seeing any lights in the upstairs rooms as he approached and then circled the house.

"What happens now?"

A pertinent question delivered in a relatively calm voice. Magrane had to admire the way she had recovered her composure. In a similar situation, his wife Virginia would have been reduced to a quivering jelly by now.

"You make yourself comfortable over there." He dipped the Lee Enfield, using the rifle like a pointer staff to indicate the kitchen table. "We're going to have a quiet chat."

"A chat?"

"About the geography of this place."

She looked incredulous as if he had taken leave of his senses. A muscle twitched at the corner of her mouth, but she didn't say anything and, drawing out a chair, she sat down at the table. For a while, she seemed at a loss to know what to do with her hands, but finally she clasped them together in her lap.

"What's your first name?" he asked.

"Alexandra," she said, "but everyone calls me Sandra."

Alexandra—a good old Czarist name, none too popular with the Soviets after the Romanovs had been shot in the cellar at Ekaterinburg, but obviously the wheel had turned full cycle and it was now back in fashion again. Magrane moved a few paces to the left and stood with his back to the wall. In that position, while watching his prisoner, he could cover both the hall and the back door and have the drop on any intruder.

"Tell me, Sandra, what's the winter been like up here?"

"One of the worst on record. We haven't had storms like it in twenty years." Her voice died away. "Or so they say."

"Who's they?"

"The weathermen."

It was very cold, but not intolerably so. Magrane figured he must have notched up close to twenty-five miles and that was good going in a day. As a matter of fact, it was better than good now that he came to think about it. In Siberia, when the temperature reached minus thirty, it was not unknown for a man to drop in his tracks, totally exhausted after a few miles. This wasn't Siberia then. The climate and the topography had more in common with the Baltic States.

"Where are we? Latvia, Lithuania or Estonia?"

Sandra stared at him, a wary expression in her eyes. "Where? . . . er . . . Estonia," she stammered.

"You don't seem very sure." Magrane pushed the safety catch forward and curled his finger round the trigger. "I think you're making it up."

"No." Sandra shook her head. "No, I wouldn't lie to you. This is Estonia."

"How far are we from Tallinn?"

"Oh, four or five miles."

Five miles. With warm food in his belly he could reach the coast tonight, steal a boat and make the home run to freedom across the Gulf of Finland. Of course, he would have to do something about Sandra, otherwise she would raise the alarm. There was bound to be a length of clothesline or rope in one of the drawers with which he could tie her up.

"I'd like something to eat, Sandra. What have you got?"

"There are some eggs in the larder."

"And sausage?"

"Yes."

"Good." Magrane applied the safety catch again and smiled at her. "Sausage and eggs will suit me fine," he said in a dreamy voice.

4 . . .

THE village hall at Carnforth was nothing to write home about. A large wooden structure with a corrugated iron roof, it had been erected in the immediate postwar period, an era when building materials had been in short supply and austerity the watchword of the day. Although the hall had obviously been redecorated on a number of occasions since then, it seemed that no one had given any thought to changing the original color scheme and the walls remained a muddy chocolate brown and cream. Over the years, the floor had been polished so often that most of the pine strips had now turned black and were deeply ingrained with a mixture of surplus wax and dirt. The central heating was a fairly recent innovation, but there weren't enough heaters to do more than take the chill off the air. One look at the drab surroundings was enough to convince Donaldson that Tamblin would have been hard pressed to find a more depressing venue for the press conference.

Despite Tamblin's confident prediction that most of the press corps would be propping up the bar in the Station Hotel back at Inverness, some thirty reporters had showed up for the briefing. As yet, no one had complained that his journey had been a waste of time and effort, but it was evident from their jaundiced expressions that quite a number of those present were thoroughly disenchanted. Donaldson could understand how they felt. To have braved the weather for a load of crap that could easily have been put across in a press handout was beyond a joke.

Nor had the police spokesman made things any better. In the absence of a press information officer, they were represented by a Chief Inspector, a dour, humorless man of few words who had simply stuck to his brief and refused to answer any questions of a speculative nature. Sensing the atmosphere turning sour, Tamblin had pulled out all the stops, using his considerable charm to create a favorable impression. For a while, he almost had them eating out of his hand, but now that he was being pressed for details of Magrane's Army career, his evasive answers were beginning to arouse a certain amount of hostility.

Donaldson lit a cigarette and reached for the glass ashtray in front of Tamblin. The questions were still coming thick and fast and he wondered how much longer the war of attrition between the platform and the assembled correspondents would last. A chair scraped at the back of the hall and out of the corner of his eye he saw the earnest young stringer from the *Daily Express* on his feet again, determined to push Tamblin into a corner. His question seemed to go on forever and while Donaldson thought it had something to do with the sequence of events that had preceded Magrane's nervous breakdown, there was an element of doubt in his mind. He found it difficult to concentrate on what the reporter was saying because the girl in the far left-hand corner of the room was staring at him intently.

He had noticed her earlier when he'd tried to explain why the Marine Commandos had failed to run Magrane to ground. She hadn't bothered to take any notes but had merely sat there watching him, an attractive-looking woman in her late twenties with straight black hair reaching to her shoulders. At one point he'd thought she was about to ask him a question, but the small inquisitive frown hadn't amounted to anything. Unable to resist the temptation any longer, he slowly turned in her direction to sneak another look.

The girl was leaning forward, one elbow resting on her

knee, her chin cupped in the palm of the right hand. The press briefing was a damp firecracker, but unlike the other reporters who were at least going through the motions, her notebook still lay unopened on the adjacent seat. But for the fact that no one had been allowed in without a press card, he would have said she was a gate-crasher.

"Are there any other questions?" Tamblin glanced round the hall with an encouraging smile that was wholly false. "We don't guarantee satisfaction, but we'll certainly give you a straight answer."

For a few moments it looked as if there were no takers, but then the dark-haired girl suddenly rose to her feet.

"My name's Linda Warwick," she said, "and I have a question for Major Donaldson."

Tamblin nodded and waved a hand inviting her to proceed.

"I'm interested in the selection procedures used by the SAS. To be specific, I'd like to know if they are quite as thorough as we've been led to believe?"

Her tone was provocative, like the question, and Donaldson had the feeling that Linda Warwick was hiding an ace up her sleeve. It stood to reason that she wouldn't have stuck her chin out, implying there was something wrong with the system, unless she had a few facts and figures at her fingertips.

"I'm in the Parachute Regiment," he said disarmingly, "so I'm not really an expert on the SAS. However, for what it's worth, their requirements are much the same as ours. They only take the best, men of above average intelligence who are extremely fit and very determined, those who will keep going long after others have given up. It isn't enough to pass the selection tests. Every volunteer for the SAS knows that he will have to take a step down in rank just to get into the regiment. The competition is that fierce."

"Then how did Captain Magrane slip through the net?"

"No system is foolproof." Donaldson stubbed out his cigarette in the ashtray. "You could say he was the exception that proves the rule, but I don't think it's that simple."

There was a sharp intake of breath from Tamblin as if a tooth somewhere at the back of his mouth had given a twinge. In a none too subtle way, the PR man was warning him to watch his step. But it was too late in the day for that; he'd already gone over the top and there was no turning back now.

"For months on end, Magrane had been working undercover in Belfast and he must have known that he'd been blown long before the IRA got to him."

"So he was the odd man out? Is that what you're implying?"

"Yes."

"Supposing he wasn't the only man who'd cracked up?"

"Is that a hypothetical question, Miss Warwick?"

"Oh, absolutely," she said sweetly.

"Well, in that case I imagine the SAS would take another look at their selection procedures."

"Thank you, Major Donaldson."

Her mouth curved in an impish smile and then she sat down, crossing one elegant leg over the other. To Tamblin's evident relief, there were no more questions from the floor and the meeting broke up, the reporters streaming towards the exit like homeward-bound commuters eager to get the hell out. Significantly, Linda Warwick was the last to leave.

"There's one young woman who doesn't have to meet a deadline," Tamblin observed with a sniff.

"You know her?"

"I've met her before in London. She used to be with *Time* magazine, but now she's gone free-lance. A very sharp young lady. I wish to God she would go back home to America. We've got quite enough investigative journalists as it is without importing some of the *Washington Post* variety."

Tamblin broke off to say good-bye to the Chief Inspector who'd tapped him on the shoulder to let him know that he was leaving. There was a lot of handshaking, but the Whitehall bonhomie didn't go down at all well. As a Highlander, he wasn't used to the instant friendship routine.

"Do you think she's onto something, Hugh?"

"Who? Linda Warwick?" Tamblin gathered his papers together and stuffed them into the government-issue briefcase. "No, she's just fishing for information."

"In other words, she knows there's more to the Magrane affair than we're prepared to admit."

"Nonsense, we haven't got anything to hide."

"You must think I was born yesterday," Donaldson said irritably. "Look, there's a public relations officer to every

Military District in the U.K. Now, suppose you tell me why the Ministry of Defence chose to send you all the way up here when they had a perfectly good man in Edinburgh?''

''The Ministry of Defence tends to overreact.'' Tamblin smiled. ''You must know that, Robert.''

''And the same goes for the Home Office, does it? They weren't happy to leave things to the Chief Constable of Ross and Cromarty.''

''Well, that's the way it is in Whitehall.''

''Balls,'' Donaldson said angrily. ''Linda Warwick didn't pose a hypothetical question. Magrane wasn't the only man who cracked up. Lloyd virtually let the cat out of the bag when he said that he was one of Daniel's patients.''

''You must be mistaken. I'm sure he said no such thing.''

''There's nothing wrong with my hearing. According to you, Magrane was wounded in August, 1974. He underwent an emergency operation at the Royal Victoria and was then transferred to the Millbank in London as soon as he was off the danger list. By June, 1975, he'd made a complete recovery and was discharged from the hospital. That should have been the end of the story, but then the poor bastard had a nervous breakdown in May, 1977. Now, I don't want to rock the boat, but something must have happened in the intervening two years to send him off his rocker, and I think I'm entitled to know what.''

Tamblin looked up at the ceiling, his eyes half-closed as if seeking guidance from the Almighty. Presently his right hand began to play a slow five-finger exercise on the briefcase.

''I'm supposed to be the official military spokesman, Hugh. Unless you're prepared to risk a cock-up with the press, I have to know what's going on behind the scenes.''

Tamblin sighed deeply, suggesting that the weight on his shoulders had become an intolerable burden.

''Do you know anything about psychochemicals, Robert?'' he asked wearily.

''Not a lot, apart from the fact that the Americans have been experimenting with LSD, trying to assess its military potential as an incapacitating agent.''

''So have we. Just over three years ago, the Chemical Warfare Establishment at Porton managed to produce a derivative of LSD, a volatile liquid agent that was tasteless, odorless and invisible to the naked eye. In due course, an evaluation report was sent to the Ministry of Defence where it was considered by a steering committee. On their recommendation, it was eventually decided to go ahead with a field trial in May, 1977."

"And that's where Magrane came in?"

"The SAS was asked to find thirty-five volunteers and a troop was formed under his command. The field trial, which was known as Exercise Damocles, was held in Oman for reasons of security. Magrane's troop was required to mount a conventional infantry attack against a strongpoint. Shortly after crossing the line of departure, they were exposed to a dose of the incapacitating agent and the attack gradually broke down. I'm told their antics were quite hilarious; when the soldiers weren't dancing with one another, they were rolling about on the ground shrieking with laughter. The section commanders tried to get them into some sort of order, but within a matter of minutes, they too were affected by the drug. The troop sergeant, whose name was Franklin, managed to keep going for some time but, in the end, only Magrane reached the objective and when the umpires found him, he was crying his eyes out. Oddly enough, the rank and file suffered no aftereffects, but unfortunately that wasn't the case with Franklin and Magrane. Both of them had nervous breakdowns, the only difference being that Franklin responded to treatment. He's now on convalescent leave."

"Now I know why they were being treated at Strathconan. You wanted them kept out of the way in case the press got to hear about Exercise Damocles."

"You're forgetting the rest of the troop."

"Oh, you didn't have to worry about them, Hugh. They were bound by the Official Secrets Act, and besides, they hadn't suffered any aftereffects. The only newsworthy thing about Exercise Damocles was the fact that two men had gone round the bend and you made damn sure the press were kept in the dark about that."

"What would you have wanted us to do? Make a clean breast of it and hand the results of our research work to the Russians on a plate?"

"That's a convenient excuse and you know it. No matter how you try to dress it up, the fact remains that the experiment backfired and Magrane was driven insane. Somebody high up authorized the scientists to gas those thirty-five soldiers and I'm damned if I can see why he and the rest of the bloody government should hide behind the Official Secrets Act."

"A word of advice, Robert." Tamblin picked up his briefcase and moved towards the steps leading down from the stage. "You're a professional; unless you want to change your occupation, you'll have to take a leaf out of my book and learn when it's politic to keep your mouth shut."

The *Sunday Times,* the *Observer* or the *Sunday Telegraph?* Linda Warwick frowned. The *Sunday Times* had already commissioned her to do a feature on North Sea oil, so it would only be ethical to let them have first refusal. It would be no use phoning Lionel Harkness at the office, though; the editorial staff would have finished their meeting long ago. Better to call Lionel's home number.

Lifting the phone off the hook, she flashed the hotel switchboard to connect her with 0483-66342. Even though she had spent the last five years in London, the vagaries of the GPO telephone service never ceased to amaze her; she could dial a number with no problem, but whenever she had to place a call with an operator, the delay was usually such that it seemed to her the engineers were still laying the line to the number she wanted. On this occasion, however, there were no gremlins on the line.

A tired voice said, "Guildford 66342."

"Lionel?"

"Yes. Don't tell me—it's Linda Warwick—right?"

"How did you guess?"

"I recognized your voice. How's the piece on North Sea oil coming along?"

"It's almost finished. But I think I may have a better story for you, Lionel."

"If it's the weather or the Magrane business, I'm afraid you're out of luck. Both those news items are already being covered by our regular correspondents."

"Perhaps story is the wrong word—I should have said feature."

"What sort of feature?"

"Suppose I can prove there's a cover-up, that Magrane isn't the only SAS man who went bananas. Could you find a home for it in—say, the Insight column?"

There was a long pause while Harkness thought it over. Holding the receiver in place with her right shoulder, Linda opened her handbag, took out a packet of cigarettes and lit up.

"Do you have a source?" Harkness asked eventually.

Linda smiled. The commitment was scarcely unequivocal, but Harkness was nibbling at the bait and she knew she could land him. "It's my story, right?"

"Agreed."

"Okay, the source is a man called Stanislaus Klepacz. He's one of the range wardens up at Strathconan, but for the past eight months it seems the Army has been misemploying him. According to friend Klepacz, they turned him into a hospital porter. So far I've only seen the tip of the iceberg and I need to do a lot more digging before we can go to print. There's a sort of troika running the show up here. We have a public relations officer from the M.O.D. called Tamblin who's as slippery as an eel, a civil servant by the name of Lloyd from the Police Department at the Home Office who is keeping a very low profile and a Major Donaldson. Donaldson is the odd man out. I could be wrong, but I have a hunch he isn't too happy with the situation. If I went to work on him, I think he could be persuaded to open up. And that's where you come in."

"I thought there might be a snag," said Harkness.

"Donaldson is supposed to be with Special Forces at Wilton. Can we check that out?"

"Wilton is the home of Headquarters U.K. Land Forces. If he's on the staff there, his name will be in the Army List."

"Fine. And I'd like anything else you can dig up on him, Lionel. You know the sort of thing—career, home background—personal stuff like that. I want all the ammunition you can give me."

"It won't be easy."

"I know that, but do the best you can. One other thing; I want an extract from the hospital admission book and I may have to grease Klepacz's palm to get it. How high can I go?"

"Up to a hundred," Harkness said quickly.

Linda pulled a face. "Boy, you're generous. But if that's the way it is, well, okay."

"We have to watch our expenses, Linda."

"I guess you do. Look, you can reach me at the Station Hotel, Inverness, room 303. If I'm not in, leave a message with the desk clerk and I'll call back. Okay?"

"Yes. Well, keep in touch and good luck."

"Thanks. I may need it."

Linda hung up in a thoughtful frame of mind. Harkness had never said a truer word, she was going to need all the luck in the world. Taking on Whitehall was like tilting at a windmill. Just when you thought your aim was dead center, the target moved away and you were left thrashing the air.

The cigarette burned down between her fingers, scorching the flesh. In her haste to get rid of the thing, she dropped the stub onto the bed where the ember burned a neat round hole in the counterpane before she could sweep it into the ashtray.

Raising the afflicted finger to her mouth, Linda gingerly licked the burn. Donaldson: now there was a man with an interesting face who most definitely wasn't a creep. His features weren't exactly handsome, but they certainly caught the eye. Strong, that was the adjective she was looking for, *le bon mot*. She also suspected that he was a very likeable man once you got to know him. But, hopefully, she would be proved wrong, because if Donaldson really was a nice man, it wouldn't be easy doing a hatchet job on him.

Magrane rubbed his jaw, feeling the stubble under his gloved hand. It might not be Tallinn, but the tiny fishing port tucked away in the sheltered bay protected by the headland was the answer to all his prayers. Luck, absolute pure luck, there was no other way to describe it. It was a good job he hadn't stuck to the directions Sandra had given him because there was no telling where he would have ended up. Go east, she'd said, go east and you'll hit the railway. Well, he had news for Sandra. There wasn't a bloody railway within miles of her village and if instinct hadn't prodded him into turning north, he would never have found this fishing port. The stupid little bitch hadn't known what she was talking about. Or had she? Perhaps she was cleverer than he'd allowed for, perhaps she had deliberately set out to mislead him? What the hell, it didn't matter a damn now. He moved on again, pushing one ski in front of the other, making his way past the dark, silent houses towards the harbor.

There were eighteen boats in all, twenty-five-foot fishing smacks with small diesel engines forward of the well deck. Eighteen boats moored in pairs along the mole, there for the taking. Moving to the far end of the mole, Magrane kicked off the langlauf skis and slid down the stern mooring line. Although he tried to land silently, his boots struck the deck with a hefty thump; to his sensitive ears the noise sounded loud enough to wake the dead. Scrambling over the gunwale into the adjoining fishing smack, he cast off fore and aft, grabbed a boat hook and pushed off. Slowly, all too slowly, a gap opened between the two vessels.

Nobody was going to stop him now, neither the KGB nor the Soviet Baltic Fleet. There was a strong wind blowing and as he raised the sail and the canvas filled, Magrane knew beyond any shadow of a doubt that he was going to make it. Full of confidence, he went into the tiny wheelhouse and put the wheel hard over, pointing the bows towards the mouth of the inlet. It was tempting to start the diesel engine to cram on more speed, but he forced himself to wait until he was satisfied that no one ashore would hear the noise.

Magrane had been underway for roughly an hour before it occurred to him to try the radio. There was a lot of static about and the reception was poor but he caught the words— "Cromarty—Firth—Tyne—northeasterly severe gale force 9, increasing storm force 10—imminent." A skip transmission? Yes, that was it; the overcast was bouncing the transmission over an incredible distance, enabling him to pick up the shipping forecast on the BBC. As a small boy, he could remember one freakish occasion when the Chicago police net had practically blasted Geraldo and his orchestra off the air.

A force 10 gale in the North Sea? Well, the weather wasn't any too good in the Gulf of Finland either.

Making a steady eight knots, Magrane sailed on down the Dornoch Firth.

5 . . .

TAIN lay to starboard and as they swept over the Dornoch Firth, the sergeant pilot raised a gloved hand and pointed to the cluster of houses in the distance.

"That's Keebleloch ahead," he grunted, his voice crackling over the intercom. "Edderton is just behind us on the left."

Donaldson pushed the boom mike closer to his mouth. "How much longer?" he asked.

"Five minutes. We'll be there by ten thirty, give or take a bit."

The Scout helicopter had been making heavy weather of it against the strong headwind and they were about a quarter of an hour behind their estimated time of arrival. Before setting off from Strathconan, there had been an even chance that the press would beat them to it, but now it was a stone-cold certainty. The professionals were bringing up the rear, and that was bad for the image PR and the Ministry of Defence were so keen to impress upon the public. The snort of disgust which reverberated through his earphones told Donaldson what Tamblin thought of it.

"I assume somebody will have had enough sense to mark the LZ?"

Lloyd's voice sounded acid over the intercom. Although the Home Office didn't advertise their own efficiency, it appeared he was equally disgruntled.

"There'll be trouble if they haven't," the sergeant said laconically.

Keebleloch lay in a narrow, sheltered inlet. A tiny fishing village with a population of one hundred and eighty-seven, according to the last census, it was sustained by one kirk, three pubs and eighteen fishing smacks. Or at least there had been eighteen before Magrane took one down the Dornoch Firth.

Donaldson stared at the angry whitecaps below. The weather was bad enough in the comparatively sheltered waters of the Dornoch Firth, but Magrane was somewhere out in the North Sea braving a force 10 gale in a twenty-five-foot boat that was normally used inshore. Unless he had already decided to turn back, it was quite possible that the owner would never see his fishing smack again.

The pilot approached the village from the sea, spotted the H pad on the quayside and went straight in, losing height so rapidly that Donaldson was sure his stomach had been left behind. As the helicopter closed on him, the ground handler suddenly raised both arms and began flapping them like a harassed parking lot attendant trying to guide a learner driver into a vacant slot. Seconds after the Scout touched down, the sergeant cut the switches to complete a landing in record time even by the standards of the Army Air Corps.

Aside from the local population, most of whom had apparently turned out to watch their antics, the press and television reporters were also there in force at the far end of the quay. Tamblin grimaced and muttered something about keeping everybody sweet and then hurried to join them, displaying his usual instant smile.

"You'd think Keebleloch was celebrating the Silver Jubilee all over again," Lloyd observed sourly.

Donaldson followed his gaze. "It beats me how the press got hold of the story."

"Some people aren't averse to taking a backhander, you know. I daresay one of the local stringers in Inverness has a contact at the central police station." Lloyd jammed both hands into the pockets of his suede coat and hunched his shoulders against the wind. "You'd better stay here, Robert, while I have a word with the Inspector."

Donaldson nodded. He'd suspected that Tamblin had some ulterior motive in mind when the PR man had idly suggested he might like to come along for the ride, but now it was beginning to look as if he'd misjudged him. Perhaps both men had thought it might appear a little odd if two civilians were seen to arrive in an Army Air Corps helicopter and he was merely there to allay suspicion? If that was the case, he was just a glorified tailor's dummy in a combat suit and red beret. Turning his back on the crowd, Donaldson walked to the opposite end of the quay and stood there gazing out to sea.

"Not much of a view, is it?" A hand tapped him lightly on the shoulder and he turned to find Linda Warwick at his side. "At least not on a day like this. Is it true what they say about the weather up here? If you think it's bad now, stick around, it can only get worse?"

"Oh, I don't know, Miss Warwick, I understand they had a pretty good summer up here last year—nobody died of exposure."

"Is that a fact?"

"It was meant to be a joke, Miss Warwick."

"My name is Linda," she said firmly. "Miss Warwick sounds kind of stuffy."

"Yes, I suppose it does." Donaldson suspected she was angling for his first name, but didn't enlighten her. He preferred to wait and see how much she already knew about him.

"Okay."

"If you don't mind me asking, why aren't you with the others?"

"I got tired of listening to friend Tamblin. He hasn't got anything to say, he's just trying to be one of the boys."

"And you're not?"

"Do I look it?"

The beige-colored trench coat and dark slacks were more

practical than stylish, but there was no disguising the fact that she had a very attractive figure.

"Hardly," he said.

"Well, Robert, now that we're agreed on that, how do you rate Magrane's chances out there in the North Sea?" He was right then. The sudden use of his Christian name was proof that she had put in some spadework on him.

"We don't know for sure that he did steal the boat."

"Oh, come on, a pair of langlauf skis were found on the quayside."

"So I hear."

"And he also broke into a house at Cullicastle not ten miles from here. He's a funny guy, isn't he?—a mass of contradictions." Linda shook her head, a small frown adding to her air of bewilderment. "I mean, he killed two men in cold blood and yet he went out of his way to reassure Mrs. Johnstone that he meant her no harm."

"Mrs. Johnstone?"

Linda smiled. "Now who's pumping who? Mrs. Sandra Johnstone—he broke into her house while her husband was away. After she'd fed him, Magrane tied her up with a length of clothesline. Mrs. Johnstone said he was very apologetic about it. Now, don't tell me you didn't know?"

It confirmed what Lloyd had said to him a few minutes ago. Somewhere, some bloody policeman had taken a backhander and shot his mouth off to the press. "Will you be able to sell the story?" Donaldson said, changing the subject.

"Maybe. Depends on how well I do my homework." Linda brushed a strand of hair from her eyes and turned her back to the prevailing wind. "How did you know I was a free-lance journalist? Did Hugh tell you?"

"Yes, he mentioned it."

"And warned you off at the same time, no doubt."

"You don't like him much, do you?"

"Not a lot. Most of the PR men I've met are honest enough to admit that their one aim in life is to project a favorable image and to that end they're prepared to gild the lily a bit. That's something Hugh Tamblin would never concede; he's very smooth and far too slippery. I'd watch him if

I were you. Hugh's the sort who'd pull the rug from under your feet before you had time to blink.''

"You make him sound a real four-letter man, Linda, and I don't think that's true."

"You'd better believe it. Can you guess what he said just now when one of the reporters asked him why Magrane thought he was in Russia? He said he didn't know who was the bigger nut—Magrane or the psychiatrist. It got a cheap laugh." Linda stamped her feet and drew the coat across her throat. "God, it's cold out here," she said. "Why don't I buy you a drink? The pubs are open."

"It ought to be the other way round."

"I can put it down to expenses and you can't. That gives me the edge. What do you say?"

"I'd like to very much, but it'll have to be some other time." He pointed to Lloyd who had returned to the helicopter and was now looking expectantly in his direction. "It seems I'm wanted."

"I guess you are." Linda smiled wryly and shook his proffered hand. "Still, never mind, you've got a rain check. If we don't run into each other again up here, maybe you'll give me a ring next time you're in London?"

She smiled again and then walked away. Donaldson stared at the visiting card she had pressed into his palm and wondered what the hell she was up to. Slipping the card into his pocket, he strolled towards Lloyd, a puzzled expression on his face.

"Who's the young woman?" asked Lloyd.

"Linda Warwick." Donaldson turned his head and watched her enter The Fisherman's Arms. "I think she was trying to pump me about Magrane."

"Does she know anything?"

"I'm not sure, but she's certainly looking for a different angle."

"I see." Lloyd fingered his jaw. "Did she mention anything about a rifle?"

"What rifle?"

"According to Mrs. Johnstone, Magrane held her at gunpoint. The police think he must have stolen the rifle from Davie Tulloch. It appears the old man joined the Home Guard in 1941 and was issued with a P14 Lee Enfield. Obviously he held on to the bloody thing after the war, probably kept it to do a bit of poaching.''

Everything fitted together like a jigsaw puzzle, but it didn't get them very far. Magrane was out there in the North Sea beyond their reach. With a rifle. If he put about and landed somewhere down the coast, they could have victim number three.

"Well, I suppose that's it then," said Donaldson. "I might as well go back to Wilton. You don't need me any longer."

"What?"

"Finding Magrane is a job for the RAF. I assume you'll be asking them for a Nimrod?"

"Who do I get in touch with?"

"You could try Strike Command."

"Well, if you don't know, who does?" Lloyd shook his head. "No, Robert, I'm afraid I can't afford to let you go just yet. The Armed Services have a language all their own and I must have someone who understands the jargon. Of course I'll clear it with the M.O.D. first, but I'm sure they'll agree to you staying on up here until we find the boat or what's left of it."

Donaldson stared at Lloyd. Lloyd's face was quite expressionless, but there had been a certain nuance in his voice which suggested he wouldn't be sorry to learn that Magrane had drowned.

Although Magrane had gone about to run before the wind, the change of course hadn't made a whit of difference as far as he could see. The waves were still just as high, the troughs equally deep and the boat was still shipping water over the bows. The diesel engine had packed up on him shortly after daybreak and now that the sail was almost ripped in two, it looked as if he was going to lose it at any moment. Once that happened, it was doubtful if the smack would answer to the helm and sooner or later she would broach to and capsize.

Magrane peered at the horizon, his eyelids partly closed. A huge wave had smashed the glass in the wheelhouse and with the spray lashing his face, his vision was somewhat impaired. Even so, he was sure the coastline should have been in sight long ago. He went over his calculations again, looking for an error which might indicate where he had gone wrong. From zero zero three five hours he had steered northeast for exactly five hours and twenty-five minutes at roughly eight knots before turning due south, a course he'd held ever since zero six hundred that morning. Five and a half hours at a steady eight knots added up to fifty nautical miles for the outward leg. According to Daniel's wristwatch, it was now two forty in the afternoon and that meant he must have covered at least the same distance on the shorter, reciprocal course, even allowing for the fact that his speed had fallen off. If there was nothing wrong with his original calculation, he could only assume that the compass had gone haywire.

The chart he'd found in the drawer was next to useless. The coastline was shown in white in the bottom right-hand corner and most of the named landmarks were smeared with greasy thumbprints which made them illegible. It also purported to show an area bounded by longitude two degrees west and latitude fifty-eight degrees north, and he knew that couldn't be right because Estonia lay farther to the east. A sudden pistol crack startled him and, glancing over his shoulder, he saw that the mast had snapped in half above the boom and was hanging over the starboard side.

He needed rope to lash the wheel and an axe to cut the spar free. Since neither was readily at hand, Magrane reasoned he couldn't very well leave the wheelhouse to go and look for them because it was vital to keep on course. What seemed only common sense one moment became lunacy the next, however, as the smack ploughed into a deep trough and heeled over, listing dangerously to starboard. There was no time to weigh the risks and reach a pragmatic solution. Survival depended on doing the obvious, regardless of the hazards involved and, leaving the wheelhouse, he ran aft.

There were three lockers in the well deck. One contained a large coil of rope, the second revealed a set of rusty tools for the diesel engine and the third, assorted fishing tackle and a collection of murderous-looking knives. Choosing one with a six-inch blade, he slashed the canvas from the boom and then went for the halyard, using the knife like a saw to cut through the line and release the shattered spar. As he heaved the wreckage overboard, the smack began to turn broadside on.

Magrane turned and ran back to the wheelhouse, his feet skidding wildly on the treacherous surface of the deck. Kicking the door open, he stumbled inside and made a frantic grab for the wheel, turning it hard to starboard to bring the bows round. Slowly, grindingly slowly, the boat began to answer the helm, but she was still wallowing like a pig when the next wave struck her. The torrent which swept through the wheelhouse knocked Magrane off his feet and slammed him against the binnacle. As he lay there dazed, he could see the wheel spinning like a top.

The boat crabbed into the trough listing heavily and, closing his eyes, he waited for her to keel over. The long road to freedom was coming to an end and somehow it didn't seem to matter. He had tried and failed, but at least he would go quickly and that was infinitely preferable to spending the rest of his life in a prison camp. He thought about his wife Virginia and wondered what she would do with the money that was coming to her. Ten thousand pounds with profits, according to the man from Sunlife. Well, there wouldn't be much in the way of profits because the policy was only six years old, but ten thousand was still a tidy old sum. He imagined Virginia would have the time of her life while it lasted: a shopping spree in Paris and a flight to the nearest fashionable resort. A spark of anger flared within him and he scrambled to his feet again, determined that while the fishing smack was still afloat, the bitch would damn well have to wait for her money. The wheel fought him as if it had a mind of its own, but, exerting all his strength, he managed to bring the vessel round.

At first Magrane thought the cliffs were simply a hallucination. Not half an hour ago the horizon had been empty, but now, less than a quarter of a mile off, there were dark granite crags rising almost vertically from the sea. As the boat drew closer to the shore, he could see waves breaking over a reef that extended some distance out to sea.

The boat would founder on the rocks, and if he left it too late, there was a chance that he would go down with her. He was a good swimmer and the tide seemed to be running in his favor, although he suspected there was probably a strong undertow. The current would still be there whether he took the plunge now or waited until later. Hesitating no longer, Magrane stripped off his anorak, left the wheelhouse and, taking a deep breath, dived overboard.

The ski boots weighed him down and he came up slowly. By the time he surfaced, his lungs felt as if they were on the point of bursting. Treading water, he caught his breath and then struck out for the shore. As he struggled towards the cliff face, it slowly dawned on Magrane that he was pitted against an ebb tide that threatened to take him back out to sea. Summoning up his reserves of strength, he powered his way forward until at last his feet touched bottom on the reef and he was able to wade ashore.

The cliff rose above him like a devil's causeway. For some minutes he studied the face carefully, looking for foot- and handholds. It was a difficult climb, but he had seen worse, much worse. Compared with Rakaposhi, which he'd conquered back in 1969, the granite cliff was an insignificant molehill. He climbed slowly, taking his time because there was no need to hurry. Reaching a narrow shelf some thirty feet up the face, Magrane decided to rest a while before tackling the chimney which stretched all the way to the top.

Incredibly, the fishing smack was still afloat and had actually drifted farther out to sea. She seemed to be lying very low in the water, but it was hard to tell from a distance. As he watched, she finally broached to and slowly heeled over. He expected her to go straight down but the hull remained buoyant, kept afloat by a pocket of air. Turning his back on the scene below, Magrane wedged himself into the chimney and started climbing again.

Some twenty-five minutes later he reached the top. A gusting northeast wind cut through his body and the lowering sky looked ominous. Before very long there would be another shower of snow or sleet, and the white, featureless plain which stretched before him looked very inhospitable. No matter what the risk, Magrane knew that he had to find somewhere to shelter, otherwise it would only be a matter of time before he died of exposure. Deciding to move inland, he set off at a brisk jog trot. Surprised to find that there was only a thin carpet of snow on the ground, he gradually increased his stride, eventually finding an economical rhythm which he was able to keep up for mile after mile.

One hour later, he encountered a narrow, sunken lane running roughly north to south. It was the last thing he expected to find and there seemed to be no logical reason why it should be there at all. There were only bare fields as far as the eye could see, but obviously it had to lead somewhere and after some deliberation, he decided to push on south. Presently, the lane merged with a wider road that had been gritted. And there was a signpost. Brushing the snow from one of the arms, he stared at the directions in total disbelief.

Balmedie two miles, Aberdeen nine. Had the whole world gone mad, or was it only him? If Carr and Daniel were not KGB officers, why had they tried to brainwash him? Had it been some kind of test to measure his powers of resistance under prolonged interrogation, the kind of specialist training that everybody in the SAS was subjected to at one time or another?

His stomach took a nose dive. It had been an exercise all right, but the directing staff had allowed the damn thing to get out of hand, and as a result, two men had died. The Army would claim that he was insane because it was the only way they could explain the whole lousy rotten business without getting egg on their faces. Broadmoor: he could spend the rest of his life in Broadmoor unless he did something about it. He would have to start again with a new identity in a different country. The simple answer to the problem, but easier said than done.

He would just have to take one step at a time beginning with Balmedie. Yes, that was it. He would choose the right house and then wait until it was dark.

With dusk closing in, the Air Sea Rescue Center at Lossiemouth decided to suspend the search operation until first light the following day and the Nimrod was therefore ordered to return to base. While still some distance from Arbroath, one of the radar operators on board noticed a tiny blip on his screen, and descending below the cloud base, the pilot and crew eventually spotted the upturned hull of a small inshore fishing boat lying off Cruden Bay.

Once the Peterhead lifeboat had confirmed that the partly submerged wreck was the *Margaret Rose* from Keebleloch, Donaldson supposed it was almost inevitable that Tamblin should want him to attend another press conference.

6 . . .

FROM the hillside above Balmedie, Magrane watched the young couple leave their semidetached house in the cul-de-sac and drive off towards Aberdeen. The light in the hall had been left on, but all the other rooms in the front of the house were in darkness. It was difficult to see what sort of car they had, but it appeared to be a two-door job, and as there wasn't a baby-sitter, he assumed they were childless. There were ten semidetached dwellings on each side of the road and theirs was the second one down on the right from where he was standing. It was also the only one empty at the present moment.

Leaving the hillside, Magrane worked his way round to the right and crossed an open field to approach the house from the rear. The small back garden was enclosed on three sides by a woven fence about four feet high which looked strong enough to bear his weight. Levering himself up and over, Magrane dropped into the garden and crept towards the kitchen, staying close to the dividing fence to avoid being seen. The curtains were drawn in the living room next door and the light appeared to be coming from one corner, suggesting to him that the neighbors were watching television.

The back door was locked and although it was mostly

glass, he didn't want to smash a pane unless it was absolutely
necessary. Noise carried at night and even if the people on
either side didn't notice, it might start a dog barking. The
kitchen, which faced the garden, had one large picture and
two side windows, both with quarter windows, one of which
had been left slightly ajar in the absence of an exhaust fan.
Climbing up onto the sill, Magrane opened the quarter window to its fullest extent and, leaning inside, reached down and
unlatched the side window. There were a number of potted
plants on the shelf under the window and these he moved
carefully out of the way before standing on the drainboard.
Once inside the kitchen, he sat down and slowly placed one
foot at a time on the floor. Finally, he closed the side window
and left the quarter window slightly ajar.

His wristwatch was no longer working, but according to
the electric clock on the facing wall above the serving hatch,
it was now eleven minutes past seven, which meant the
owners must have left the house around six thirty. A faint
smell of fried bacon and the two plates drying off in the rack
indicated they had probably snatched a quick meal before
going out. Six thirty was an early start to the evening and
they had been in a hurry as if anxious not to be late. It was
unlikely to have been an emergency, though, because the
kitchen had been left neat and tidy, and while he had been
unable to hear what they were saying to each other, their
demeanor had seemed happy enough. A night in town then:
either at a pub, a cinema or the football ground. Wherever
they'd gone, Magrane thought he could rely on them being
away for at least another two hours.

Two hours in which to find money, a change of clothes, a
stiff drink and some food. He needed a stiff drink all right;
his teeth wouldn't stop chattering and he was chilled to the
bone. As quickly as his numb fingers would allow, he unlaced
and removed the ski boots and then went out into the hall,
hastily closing the door behind him in case the light streamed
into the kitchen. His eyes had become accustomed to the
dark, but the glare from the hundred-watt bulb undid all that.
Luckily, there was a flashlight on the hall table and he was
able to mask the beam with the fingers of his left hand after
he'd switched it on.

The lounge and dining room were combined in one and it didn't take him long to find the sideboard. The drinks were in the right-hand cupboard and his light swept over a decanter of dark, sweet sherry, four bottles of beer and an assortment of mineral waters before coming to rest on a bottle of whisky that was still three parts full. He drank the whisky neat, enjoying the warm glow it brought to his stomach and, gradually, to the rest of his body. After the equivalent of three doubles, Magrane felt on top of the world.

There were three bedrooms upstairs: two doubles and a single that was little bigger than a cupboard. The drawn curtains showed that only the large double at the front of the house was in use. Her clothes took up most of the space in the wardrobe, but crammed into one corner behind a sports jacket and flannels was a dark two-piece suit which he pulled out and placed on the double bed. From the collection of ties draped over a hanger behind the door, he chose one in a neutral color that would fit in with the suit and match the pair of black loafers he found on the floor of the wardrobe. The shirts in the chest of drawers were size sixteen and a half and would be loose around his neck, but Magrane doubted if anyone was going to take much notice of that. Going through the remaining drawers, he took out a pair of dark grey socks, a vest and a pair of underpants. Satisfied that he now had everything he needed, Magrane picked up the clothes and went into the bathroom to strip.

Removing his sodden clothes, he dumped them in the bath for the time being and then towelled himself dry from head to foot before changing into the clean vest and underpants. His beard felt decidedly rough and he had a quick shave, using the electric shaver he discovered in a plastic case on top of the medicine cabinet. That done, he finished dressing and returned to the bedroom to check his appearance in the full-length mirror behind the wardrobe door. The trousers and jacket sleeves were a bit on the short side, but he thought they would pass muster.

Magrane looked round the room, saw there was a handbag on the chair beside the dressing table and sorted through the contents. The handbag was no treasure trove. Leaving it on the dressing table, Magrane went downstairs.

There were three jars on the top shelf tucked away behind the bottled fruit and labelled Electricity, Milk and Summer Holiday. The holiday money contained an I.O.U. for eight pounds which showed that she wasn't quite as efficient as he'd supposed. Nevertheless, the jars yielded twenty-nine pounds fifty between them and that was more than enough for the train fare to London. As long as he didn't touch the money in her purse and put everything back as it was, there was a chance they wouldn't realize that they'd been burgled for quite some time. He made a start with the jam jars and then carefully rearranged the potted plants he'd disturbed before going upstairs again.

The suitcases were stored in a cupboard in the single bedroom and, choosing a zipper bag, Magrane returned to the bathroom and packed the ski clothes which he'd worn over his hospital pyjamas. He then cleaned the bath, hand basin and floor, using an old dishcloth he found on top of a can of cleanser on the bathroom shelf. Carefully refolding the towel he'd used earlier, he draped it over the rack and withdrew to the bedroom, carrying the zipper bag.

The woman had left her handbag on the chair facing outwards with the clasp undone. Before placing it in exactly the same position, he checked the contents again and discovered a key ring. Of the two Yales, one obviously belonged to the front door while the other probably opened the garage. The garage? Why would she need a key to the garage unless there was a second car? Magrane stared at the bunch of keys in his hand. Four suitcases in the cupboard, four small keys on the ring and two spare; one was for the ignition and the other for the trunk. Christ, she had a Mini. Her husband parked his car on the drive and she kept hers in the single garage. It was as simple as that.

The lucky breaks were certainly coming his way. Money in his pocket, a change of clothing and now a car. What more did he need? Food; yes, he might as well have something to eat before he moved on. Returning to the kitchen, he packed the ski boots and then made himself a plate of cheese and onion sandwiches.

Magrane ate quickly, one eye watching the luminous minute hand on the kitchen clock creeping towards nine o'clock.

The two hours he'd allowed himself were almost up, but there was still some tidying up to be done. Swiftly he brushed the crumbs into the wastecan, washed and dried the plate he'd used and put the bread knife back in the drawer. Using a dry mop, he cleaned the floor, removing the footmarks made by his ski boots, and then wiped a dishcloth over the drainboard.

Eight minutes past nine—time to go. But the news would be on television and it would be nice to know if the police were looking for him. Magrane went into the lounge, switched on the set and, punching the button for BBC 1, turned the volume down low.

He caught the tail end of a report from Salisbury concerning Ian Smith before the camera cut away and he heard his own name mentioned. A map appeared on the screen, with a white cross superimposed on the sea off Cruden Bay, and then a film clip started. An airfield on the coast somewhere, the camera panning from the runway to the Operations Room where a reporter was interviewing the RAF Station Commander and an army Major, somebody by the name of Donaldson with Special Forces. Special Forces: a staff branch at Headquarters U.K. Land Forces down at Wilton. 22 SAS had had some dealings with them as he recalled, something to do with the allocation of training areas and maneuver rights over private land.

The Group Captain was doing most of the talking, explaining how the Nimrod had found the capsized fishing boat off Cruden Bay, but it was Donaldson who interested him. He had a strong face and looked as if he was the sort of man you could trust. He watched the reporter turn to Donaldson and heard him confirm that everything pointed to the inescapable conclusion that Magrane had been swept overboard and drowned.

Slowly, as if in a trance, Magrane switched off the set. It was not given to many people to hear on television that officially they were dead, but Magrane knew there was more to it than that. Donaldson had been speaking directly to him, to let him know that his death was a cover-up. Naturally the authorities in Whitehall would ensure the story was repeated in the national newspapers tomorrow because they couldn't afford to rely on one television interview to get their message across. In a very clever, very subtle way he had been given the green light. The operation was on. Case Black or Damocles? It didn't matter now. Donaldson would brief him when they established contact with one another tomorrow. For the present, it was enough to know that he would be controlling the mission.

Magrane went out into the hall, left the flashlight on the table and helped himself to a shabby raincoat hanging on the rack inside the door. Checking to make sure he hadn't left anything behind, he let himself out of the house.

The nearest street light was about thirty yards away and the neighborhood seemed as quiet as a graveyard. Opening both garage doors, he dumped the zipper bag in the car and pushed the Mini out into the drive. His pulse racing, he closed and locked the garage and then got into the car, taking care not to slam the door. The Mini was an old one, but it started the first time and, reversing out of the drive, he drove off down the road towards Aberdeen.

There was no ignoring the shrill summons of the telephone, even had Linda Warwick been of a mind to do so. Scrambling out of the bath, she wrapped a towel around her and ran into the bedroom, leaving wet footprints on the fitted carpet. Snatching the receiver off the hook, she heard the hotel switchboard telling the caller that the extension wasn't answering, and there followed the usual three-sided crosstalk before the operator eventually got off the line.

"Linda?" The voice at the other end was still full of doubt.

"Yes, who's that?"

"Lionel, Lionel Harkness. I haven't called at a bad moment, have I?"

He had, but she let it pass. "No, I'm quite alone, if that's what you mean. Did you catch Donaldson on the nine o'clock news?"

"Yes, that's why I called. Do you have your notebook handy?"

The notebook was in her handbag and the handbag was where she'd left it, on the dressing table, just out of reach. Still holding on to the phone with one hand and practically bent double, Linda took a pace forward and managed to grab it before the bath towel ended up round her ankles.

"Okay, Lionel," she said. "I have my pencil poised and ready to go."

"Right. For openers, I looked Donaldson up in the Army List and he is a GSO 2 Special Forces."

"A what?"

"A General Staff Officer, second grade. I had a few words with a friend of mine who's a spare-time soldier and he remembers Donaldson when he was doing a two-year stint with the Territorial Army as Adjutant of his T.A. Parachute Battalion. Donaldson was married in those days and very happy by all accounts, until it was discovered his wife had leukemia. She died four years ago."

Harkness paused and Linda realized she was expected to make some kind of comment, but every phrase that sprang to mind sounded either trite or unsympathetic.

"That's tough," she murmured, and felt embarrassed because it was difficult to express genuine sympathy for someone you hardly knew.

"Yes." Harkness cleared his throat. "There wasn't much else he could tell me about Donaldson except that he's done a couple of tours in Northern Ireland and is a lot more intelligent than you might suppose on first acquaintance. Anyway, how's the story shaping up?"

"I think I've run up against a brick wall."

"Oh, in what way?"

"With Stanislaus Klepacz. I tried to call him twice this evening and on both occasions his wife answered the phone. First she told me she was expecting him home at any moment and then when I called back an hour later, she said he was feeling poorly and had gone to bed. I have a feeling that Klepacz has been told to keep his mouth shut."

"That could be a story in itself, Linda."

"Maybe. However, we don't want to go off at half cock, do we?"

"No, we certainly don't want a libel suit. When are you coming back to London?"

"I'm not sure." Linda frowned at her reflection in the mirror. "I thought I might stick around for another day or so in case anything breaks. Why do you ask?"

"Well, I don't know how significant it is, but I couldn't find Lloyd in the 1977 edition of *Whitaker's Almanack*. His name doesn't appear among the Assistant Secretaries, the Principal or Senior Executive Officers of the Police Department at the Home Office. Of course, it's possible he only joined the department a few weeks ago. You know how it is with Whitehall, they never stop playing musical chairs."

"I think there's more to it than that, Lionel," she said, choosing her words carefully.

"So do I, but watch your step. Okay?"

"Don't worry, I won't put my foot in it. Anyway, thanks for the tip."

"Don't mention it," said Harkness. "Bye, Linda."

She hung up and drew the bath towel over her shoulders, holding it across her chest like a shawl. Her skin was covered with goose pimples, but the change in temperature wasn't the only reason. The more she learned about the Magrane affair, the more sinister Lloyd became. Their paths hadn't crossed yet, but she had a nasty feeling that he already regarded her as a possible adversary.

Maybe she ought to forget the whole business and do the story she'd originally had in mind about North Sea oil and the effect it was having on Inverness? Like hell she would. Nobody, least of all Lloyd, was going to frighten her off the Magrane affair. She would type a draft article and send it to Donaldson, care of Special Forces at Headquarters U.K. Land Forces. That would really put the cat among the pigeons.

Magrane drove into Aberdeen on the A 92 and made straight for the city center. Turning into Union Street at the bottom of King Street, he went past the Town Hall and, ignoring the sign pointing the way to the main line station, continued on over the railway bridge. Although he had never been to Aberdeen before, he was quite certain he would find a parking lot within reasonable walking distance of the station.

Presently, a metal sign attached to a lamp post caught his eye and, slowing down, he saw a white capital P on a blue background. The directional arrow took him into College Street and a multistory garage. Leaving the Mini on the third floor, he walked back to the station and caught the last train to London.

On the overnight sleeper from Inverness, Donaldson was also travelling south.

7 . . .

MAGRANE stepped off the train and walked towards the barrier. Surrendering his ticket to the collector, he passed through the gate into the main concourse of King's Cross. He glanced towards the baggage check department, wondered if he should deposit the zipper bag when it opened for business and then decided against the idea. These days, they were apt to become suspicious and call the police if hand luggage wasn't collected again within a few hours. When the IRA bombing campaign had been in full swing, passengers had been obliged to show the contents before the staff had even been prepared to accept their luggage.

Twenty past seven by the station clock. The train had arrived ten minutes behind schedule, but it was too early to go home yet. The school where Virginia taught was only just round the corner from their house and she rarely left home much before eight thirty. Better to make it a quarter to nine to be on the safe side; that would give the latest boyfriend time to get himself off to work, always assuming the bastard wasn't unemployed.

Breakfast. He was hungry enough to eat a horse and it would help to pass the time, but first of all, he wanted a newspaper. Veering away from the subway, Magrane walked

over to the newsagent and bought a copy of the *Daily Mail*.
Retracing his steps, he followed the subway down to the
Underground station where he obtained a ticket to Piccadilly
Circus from one of the vending machines in the hall.

The northbound platform was practically deserted and he
sat down on one of the vacant bench seats, the zipper bag
between his feet while he scanned the headlines. In a perverse
sort of way, Magrane was disappointed to find that he rated
only half a column. Nor was there a photograph. Still, that
was understandable; the SAS made damn sure their people
remained faceless. That nobody had interviewed Virginia was
also readily explained; the next of kin enjoyed the same kind
of anonymity and while the press might scream blue murder,
the Ministry of Defence would not disclose his wife's name
and address. An officer from the Adjutant General's branch
would have told her that he was dead before the news was
announced on television, but even if there had been a slip-up,
he doubted that Virginia would have been too upset. Like as
not, as soon as she'd heard the news, the bitch had gone
straight to the writing desk to look for the Sunlife insurance
policy. A faint breeze stirred the newspaper and, folding it in
half, he picked up the bag and moved forward to meet the
incoming train.

Four stops: Russell Square, Holborn, Leicester Square and
then Piccadilly Circus. Four stops in about fifteen minutes,
time enough to reflect and get things straightened out in his
mind. Those bloody quacks at the mock interrogation center
had certainly overstepped the mark. They hadn't just bent the
rules, they'd thrown the bloody book out of the window. You
went into one of those kinds of exercises knowing they were
authorized to break one of your little fingers and dislocate a
second to make it realistic, but as far as he knew, nobody in
authority had sanctioned the indiscriminate use of pentothal
and scopolamine.

And what about Daniel? Hell, that shrink had fairly made
him jump through the hoop, he had really dug into his past,
making him remember the Cashmore incident. How long ago
was it now since Private Cashmore had been killed? Eleven
years? That would be 1967. He'd been a second lieutenant in
the Royal Anglian Regiment in those days, serving in that

arsehole of the world, the Aden Protectorate. Cashmore—
Private, Arthur Harold; a fun-loving, cock-happy soldier who'd
gone out of bounds to visit one of the local brothels. He
hoped good old Arthur Harold had enjoyed his last night out
on the town because when the police found him three days
later, Cashmore was lying on a dung heap in the Arab quarter
of Aden with his throat cut from ear to ear and his mutilated
penis stuffed in his mouth. Qaddafi, far away in Tripoli, had
hailed it as a great victory, another nail in the imperialist
coffin. Well, he had news for the colonel; as soon as Donaldson
gave the word, he would have the chance to even things up a
little. One fine day, God willing, he would persuade the
colonel to open his loud mouth just one more time so that he
could slip the two-and-a-half-inch barrel of a Wesson .357
magnum between his milky-white teeth and blow his fucking
head apart. Magrane looked up, suddenly aware that the train
had arrived at Piccadilly Circus, and hastily left the compartment.

There was no snow in London, only a dark early morning
sky, a persistent drizzle and a chill wind that drove the fine
rain into his face. Turning left into Coventry Street, he strolled
towards Leicester Square, eventually finding a coffee bar
open on the corner of Oxenden Street. Perching on a stool at
the counter, he asked the Pakistani waiter to bring him an
order of two fried eggs and four rashers of bacon.

Seven forty-five by the clock on the wall. Another three
quarters of an hour to kill before he caught a train out to
Harrow-on-the-Hill. Magrane opened the *Daily Mail* again,
turning to the gossip page to learn who was having it off with
who.

Magrane left the station at Harrow-on-the-Hill and turned
into Clarendon Road, thankful that at least it had stopped
drizzling. It would take him only a few minutes to reach their
house in Angel Crescent, and now he began to think about all
the things that could go wrong. He could easily bump into
one of their neighbors in the street or some nosey-parker
might see him enter the house. No, that was unlikely, the
street was virtually deserted between the hours of nine and
five. Virginia then. What if she was feeling upset or poorly

and had decided to take the day off from school? No, Virginia wouldn't be upset by the news of his death. Their marriage had broken down; Daniel had known that even though he'd tried to deny it. If she hadn't been a Catholic, they would have been divorced long ago. She could be poorly, though; February was a bad month for colds.

He reached the corner of St. Anne's Road and waited for a break in the traffic. The school was just up the way, a hundred yards to his right, and her classroom was in the front of the building. It might be possible to catch a glimpse of Virginia from the opposite side of the road, but it wasn't worth the risk of being spotted. He nipped across the road, strolled past The White Swan and turned into Angel Crescent.

Their place was halfway down the left-hand side of the street. The estate agent who'd sold them the small detached house had said it was in a desirable neighborhood and that, while it was a fairly old property, it had been completely modernized by the previous owner. Although the description was not entirely inaccurate, he had neglected to tell them that the previous owner had been a do-it-yourself fiend whose expertise was questionable. The central heating system which he'd installed had only functioned in fits and starts and eventually it had cost them a small fortune to have an expert put it right. The neighborhood was desirable all right, but strictly from a burglar's point of view. With so many husbands and wives away at work all day, a thief could take his pick. He'd tried to point out all the disadvantages before they'd signed the contract, but Virginia had refused to listen to him. She'd wanted a place of her own, somewhere to put down roots while he was serving abroad, and the house in Angel Crescent was the only one they could afford on their joint incomes.

Magrane opened the front gate and followed the path round to the side of the house. The wooden shed erected by the previous owner opposite the kitchen was always left unlocked and, stepping inside, he pulled out a drawer in the workbench and took out a can of nails. For all that she prided herself on being efficient, Virginia was inclined to be a bit scatterbrained, and the number of times she'd locked herself out of the house had to be some kind of record. This annoying habit had always been a bone of contention between them, but this was one time when he had reason to be grateful for her forgetfulness. Hidden beneath the nails was the spare key to the back door.

So far so good. He slipped the key into his pocket, found a pair of pliers in the toolbox and moved to the far end of the shed. Wheeling an old wheelbarrow out of the way, he knelt down and extracted four rusty nails whose heads protruded slightly above the surface. The floorboard hadn't been lifted in months and he had to insert one of the nails into the join to pry it loose. Once removed, he was able to reach inside the cavity and bring out a small canvas wallet.

The wallet contained a Bernardelli .25 automatic and a Wesson .357 magnum revolver with a two-and-a-half-inch barrel. Both pistols were souvenirs from his first tour of duty in Northern Ireland. Things had been somewhat disorganized back in those days and a lot of officers and men had preferred to acquire their own handguns rather than use the Army issue 9mm Browning. There was nothing wrong with the accuracy and reliability of the Browning, but if you were obliged to wear civilian clothes, it was an impossible weapon to conceal. Also, it wasn't a pistol you could draw quickly, another reason why it had been unpopular.

There were twelve rounds for the Wesson, eight for the Bernardelli, and two handmade, cutaway shoulder holsters in soft leather. A small arsenal which no one was aware of, not even Virginia. Magrane frowned: that wasn't strictly correct. He had shown the guns to her once, but that was a long time ago and she had told him to get them out of the house. As far as Virginia was concerned, he'd handed the pistols and ammunition in to the unit armory for safekeeping.

Magrane fastened the wallet and put it to one side while he replaced the floorboard. The nails fitted snugly into their holes and he pressed them home, using the flat of the pliers. That done, he wheeled the barrow back into position and hid the zipper bag inside it where Virginia wouldn't notice it. Picking up the wallet, he let himself into the kitchen.

Closing the door behind him, Magrane called out Virginia's name, gradually raising his voice until it was quite loud. Although there was no reply, he still checked every room in the house to make absolutely sure she wasn't at home. Finally satisfied that he had the place to himself, he went into the guest room to get his clothes and passport.

The guest room: well, that was an ironic description all right, one that just about summed up their relationship. He'd moved in there at Virginia's request shortly after the Army had discharged him from Millbank Hospital. Two people living in separate compartments under the same roof, two people who never spoke to one another unless it was unavoidable. He wondered what Daniel would have made of that, if he'd known.

The Army had retained his official passport when they flew him back from Northern Ireland, but the duplicate was still there under a pile of socks in the chest of drawers. It had been issued by the passport office at Newport and was valid for ten years, which would save Donaldson a lot of trouble. The photograph on page three was his, but the name wasn't. Alec Murdoch: they always gave you a pseudonym with the same initials. Alec Murdoch, the bogus sales representative who'd visited Tel Aviv in September, 1970, when the Home Office had decided to build up a dossier on known Arab terrorists in case Arafat was thinking of extending operations to the U.K. As a result, he and another officer had been sent out to Israel to see what they could learn from the Shin-Beth department.

Magrane reached for the fiberboard suitcase on top of the wardrobe and lifted it down. Although the cheviot suit and brown suede shoes took up most of the space, he managed to find room for a couple of shirts, three pairs of socks and a change of underwear. Tucking the canvas wallet and passport down the sides, he stripped off the borrowed clothes and put on a grey pinstripe. After checking his appearance in the mirror, he went into the bathroom to collect the spare brush and safety razor which he'd left behind when he was posted to Northern Ireland.

The sapphire and diamond ring which Virginia had carelessly left on the bathroom shelf was a legacy from her grandmother. It was insured for two hundred and seventy-five pounds, but a pawnbroker was unlikely to give him more than a hundred and fifty for it. Knowing Virginia, he doubted if she would remember what she'd done with it and a hundred and fifty would certainly come in handy until Donaldson arranged to keep him supplied with money through a dead letter box. Without giving it another thought, he slipped the ring into his pocket, snapped the locks on the suitcase and went downstairs.

Nine fifty-three. Magrane scowled. No point in calling Donaldson just yet. Even if he had caught the first train to Salisbury after travelling down from Inverness on the night sleeper, he was unlikely to be in his office much before ten thirty.

Donaldson walked into his office, saw the crowded filing trays on the desk, read the memo which had been placed on the blotter and knew it was going to be one of those days when every piddling letter was top priority. Striding across the room, he rapped on the communicating door, opened it and poked his head inside.

Colonel Vaughan was standing in front of the wall map looking immaculate in service dress. The number of soldiers at Wilton could be counted on the fingers of both hands, but the officers always wore uniform. The brass maintained it gave the headquarters a martial air, but privately, Donaldson suspected they were far more concerned about preserving their identity in the midst of a host of civil servants.

"You're back then, Robert." Vaughan turned about, greeting him with a faint, superior smile. "Did you have a good journey?"

"Not bad, colonel."

"Good. I saw you on television last night—thought you handled the interview rather well." Vaughan returned to his desk and sat down. "Things have been fairly hectic in your absence."

"So I gather from your memo." Donaldson hovered in the doorway, wondering if he was going to be invited to take a chair. "Something to do with Exercise Sunspot?"

"That's right. The Government doesn't think it would be a good idea to send 3 Para out to Cyprus just now. Things are a bit dicky there and the Foreign Office feels that their presence might be misinterpreted in some quarters. As you can imagine, 3 Para are hopping mad; the exercise is only a fortnight off and they haven't anywhere else to go."

"And you'd like me to find them an alternative training area?"

"If it's at all possible. Stanford, Otterburn and Salisbury Plain are fully booked and they say Barry Buddon is of no use to them. Maybe you can persuade one of the units—" The telephone interrupted Vaughan before he could finish the sentence. "You'd better answer it," he said testily. "Somebody must have told 3 Para that you're back."

Donaldson nodded and withdrew. Lifting the receiver off the hook, he gave his name and appointment.

The caller said, "Relax, it's only me."

"Who's me?"

"Magrane, Andrew Magrane."

Donaldson dropped into his desk chair. "What is this," he snapped, "some kind of hoax?"

"It's no hoax, but you're right to be suspicious. After all, we can't afford to take any chances."

"If this is a joke, the laugh's on you, because I'm about to hang up."

"No, don't do that. You want proof of identity. I'll give it to you. That old man, the one I accidentally killed—"

"David Tulloch? What about him?"

"He had a rifle, a Lee Enfield P14. You won't find that mentioned anywhere in the *Daily Mail*."

Donaldson swallowed. The press didn't know about the rifle because Tamblin had withheld the information. Magrane was still alive then, still at liberty.

"All right, Andrew," he said calmly, "where are you calling from?"

"Now you ought to know better than to ask me that."

"I should?"

"Oh, come on, you're my control, aren't you? Look, if we don't watch our security, this operation will never get off the ground."

Control—security—operation? Daniel was right, Magrane really was crazy. Donaldson cupped a hand over the mouthpiece, leaned forward over the desk and called softly to Vaughan.

"Are you still there?" Magrane asked plaintively.

"Of course I am."

Donaldson transferred the phone to his other hand, opened the top right-hand drawer in the desk and pulled out a memo pad. Racing against time, he wrote: "Magrane on the line, please trace call" and handed the message to Vaughan.

"Is somebody with you?"

"Not anymore, Andrew."

"What's that supposed to mean?"

"The Chief Clerk wanted to see me, but I told him to come back later."

"That's good thinking. However, we need to establish a permanent link. I must be able to get in touch with you at any time of the day or night."

"I see. How do you suggest we go about it?"

"I think you should put an ad in the *Evening Standard*."

"An ad?" Donaldson repeated blankly, making a note that it had to be in the *Evening Standard*.

"Something on the lines of a personal message. You know the kind of thing—For Andrew, please call me on such and such a number and then sign it off with your first name. Incidentally, what is your Christian name?"

Donaldson stared at the spidery notes he'd made and wondered if he'd missed anything. "It's Robert," he said, after a moment.

"All right, Robert, I'll be in touch again just as soon as I see your ad in the *Evening Standard*."

There was a faint click followed by the purring tone. Donaldson hung up, wrote down the earlier part of their conversation as best as he could remember it and then walked into the adjoining office, memo pad in hand.

Vaughan was still talking to the exchange supervisor, but a thumbs down sign told him that he wasn't getting anywhere, which was no great surprise. Obviously Magrane hadn't come through on the military network and there was no way of tracing a long distance call that'd been made without an operator.

"I'm afraid we're out of luck." Vaughan replaced the phone and looked up. "It appears that Magrane dialled straight through to our exchange. He must have got our civil number from directory enquiries."

"What did the operator have to say?"

"Nothing much. She said the caller asked for you by name."

"Did he feed any coins into the box?"

"I don't think so, Robert. Is it important?"

"Well, assuming he was using a private telephone, colonel, it's possible we might be able to locate him if we knew the name and address of his next of kin."

Vaughan stroked his chin and looked thoughtful, something of a rare occurrence for him. "I suppose there's no doubt in your mind that it was Magrane?"

"None at all."

"Did you take any notes?"

"Yes, but I doubt if you can read my handwriting."

"Oh, I'm sure I'll be able to decipher it." Vaughan stretched out a plump hand for the memo pad. "I think I should handle this problem, don't you, Robert?"

"Yes, I suppose so."

"Fine. Perhaps you would be good enough to close the door on your way out?" He smiled condescendingly. "I have a feeling that I shall be spending the rest of the morning on the phone to the Ministry of Defence, but that's no reason why you should be disturbed, Robert."

It proved to be the understatement of the week. Shortly after two o'clock, Donaldson was ordered to pack a suitcase and report to New Scotland Yard where Lloyd would be waiting to brief him.

Apart from the revolving triangular sign set in the pavement outside the building, there was little to distinguish the concrete and glass structure of New Scotland Yard from any other office block in London. The reception area reminded Donaldson of a hotel foyer and was almost as busy. There were four officers behind the desk, not including the sergeant who, before giving Donaldson a visitor's pass, searched his suitcase to make sure it contained nothing lethal. Once he'd filled it in, Donaldson was invited to take a seat in the entrance hall while the sergeant checked to see that he was expected. Five minutes later, a messenger arrived to escort him up to an office on the sixth floor.

Lloyd was sitting on the window ledge, his feet crossed at

the ankles. To his left, sprawled in a swivel chair, was a burly-looking man of about fifty whose broad shoulders and pudgy face gave the impression that he could be as tenacious as a bulldog.

"Commander Ryan—Major Donaldson." Lloyd waved an introductory hand but remained seated on the window ledge.

Ryan half rose from his chair and shook hands, repeating his own name in a muted Lancashire accent, apparently determined that no one should forget it. Donaldson saw that a tubular steel chair had been placed near the desk and assumed that it was meant for him.

"Well now," said Lloyd, "what are we going to do about Magrane?"

"Catch him before he harms anyone else," Ryan growled.

"Quite. And that's where you come in, Robert."

Donaldson met Lloyd's bland smile with a raised eyebrow. "Why me?" he asked quietly.

"I would have thought that was obvious. Magrane is convinced that he has a special relationship with you. What was it he said?—'You're my control, aren't you?' God knows what sort of fantasy he's acting out, but since he has made contact with you, Robert, we think you should build on that. If you can win his confidence, it's possible that Magrane might agree to meet you face to face."

"And then you'd grab him?"

"Precisely."

"Wouldn't it be simpler to circulate his description? I mean, if necessary, you could use the media."

"And drive him underground?" Lloyd shook his head. "Magrane might be mentally unbalanced, but he's cunning and very resourceful. After all, he slipped through our fingers and made it to London in spite of all the odds against him."

"He's here—in London?"

"Magrane owns a house in Harrow." Ryan leaned forward, his elbows on the desk. "We know he was there this morning. According to his wife, he packed some clothes and a few odds and ends. It seems a dress ring valued at two hundred and seventy-five pounds is missing, so he's not likely to be short of a bob or two. We'll turn over a few likely places in Kilburn tonight in case he's gone to ground amongst the Irish community, but I doubt if we'll have any luck.''

"Now perhaps you have a clearer idea of our problem, Robert." Lloyd stretched both arms above his head and yawned. "Magrane has everything he needs to keep a low profile. That's why you must talk to him again.''

"Look, I'm not a psychiatrist.''

"Daniel will be there to hold your hand," Lloyd said swiftly. "The Ministry of Defence have agreed to make him available. He will be leaving from Inverness tonight.''

"I see.''

"And Commander Ryan has found a place for you in Devonshire Terrace. That's in Bayswater. It's nothing fancy— two bedrooms, a kitchenette and a small living room—but you should be comfortable enough. And of course we've arranged for a telephone to be installed.''

"Linked to a tape recorder," added Ryan.

"My word," Donaldson said dryly, "you have been busy.''

"You've got to be one jump ahead just to stay in the game." Ryan produced a visiting card from his vest pocket and pushed it across the desk. "As soon as Magrane has been in touch, you call this number and play the tape back. It doesn't matter what time of day or night it is, somebody will always be here.''

Donaldson picked up the card and studied it. There was no extension listed after the number, which meant that all incoming and outgoing calls bypassed the switchboard. The head man of a county force was a chief constable, but they had a different rank structure in the Metropolitan Police. London was divided into a number of divisions, each one controlled by a commander. There was also a commander in charge of the vice, fraud and serious crime squads. The direct line and the flat in Bayswater were enough to convince him that Ryan was in charge of Special Branch.

There was a gentle knock on the door and both men said, "Come in." A clerk entered the room and handed a folded newspaper to Ryan who passed it to Lloyd. The clerk seemed slightly taken aback, but said nothing. Lloyd waited until the door closed behind him and then turned the newspaper inside out. Presently, his face lit up and, pushing himself off the window ledge, he walked over to Donaldson and dropped the *Evening Standard* into his lap.

The ad was halfway down the left-hand column. It read: ''For Andrew—Please call me on 01-229-8897. Robert.'' If Ryan was concerned about staying one jump ahead, it also seemed that Lloyd was not the sort of man to allow the grass to grow under his feet.

8 . . .

DONALDSON and Daniel of Devonshire Terrace: it sounded like the opening line of a doggerel or one of those tongue twisters drunken drivers were asked to repeat to the police doctor before the Home Office scientists came up with the breathalizer test. Donaldson and Daniel, a couple of amateur Samaritans waiting for a cry for help in the comfort of a Nash-terrace house now converted into flats.

"It's after eleven o'clock," Daniel said quietly.

"So what?"

"So I'm beginning to wonder if Magrane saw your ad in the *Evening Standard* yesterday."

"I don't see how he could have missed it, Bernard." Donaldson turned away from the window to face the psychiatrist who was slumped in an armchair, his feet up on the low coffee table. "Anyway, Lloyd has arranged to have it repeated until we get a response from him."

"I wouldn't bank on Andrew making contact with you again. Believe me, he can be very inconsistent."

Daniel sounded tired and looked it. There were dark circles under his eyes and his lids kept drooping. He was one of those unfortunate people who suffered from travel sickness and it was obvious he hadn't slept a wink on the train from Inverness.

"How long has he been your patient?"

"Almost nine months, but it seems more like nine years. Every time I thought I was beginning to reach him, he retreated into his shell. Whoever supervised Damocles has a lot to answer for. Magrane wasn't the only long-term casualty."

"I thought Sergeant Franklin made a complete recovery?"

"I wasn't thinking of him, Robert. It's Magrane's wife Virginia I'm concerned for. The way things were between them, it's a wonder she hasn't had a nervous breakdown too." Daniel swung his feet off the table and leaned forward to open his briefcase. Extracting a buff-colored file, he opened it and handed a snapshot to Donaldson. "That's Virginia. She's a very nice person as well as being attractive."

Virginia Magrane was standing by a swimming pool wearing a one-piece bathing suit. It was hard to tell if the sun had been in her eyes at the time, but she seemed to be peering into the camera. On the back of the snapshot she'd written "Mrs. Magrane—schoolteacher" followed by several exclamation marks. The edges were dog-eared as if Magrane had been carrying it in his wallet for some considerable time.

"Don't be taken in by the pose, Robert, it's out of character. Virginia is a bit on the prudish side."

"Oh yes? How well do you know her?"

"Probably better than most of her friends. I persuaded Virginia to spend a week up at Strathconan last October during her half-term break. I thought she might have a therapeutic effect on Magrane. But I was wrong. Mind you, her visit did throw a glimmer of light into one of the dark corners of his mind." Daniel broke off to light another cigarette, his seventh in three hours since he'd arrived. "To hear Magrane talk, you'd think she'd led him a dog's life when in fact it was the other way round. According to him, she's had more lovers than Catherine the Great. It was all supposed to have started when he was in Northern Ireland, but it was all in his mind. Do you know what happened when he was discharged from Millbank Hospital and sent home on convalescent leave? While she was out shopping one Saturday morning, he went through the dressing table and burned all her black underwear. He said it was for her own good, and until she stopped behaving like a whore he proposed to sleep in the spare room.

Bloody hell, it was Magrane who bought her the black underwear and she only ever wore it to please him.''

Donaldson wondered if the psychiatrist was being completely objective. His attitude towards Magrane appeared hostile. During the whole of their conversation, Daniel had only once referred to him as Andrew, and somehow that didn't seem right.

''Is that what she told you, Bernard?''

''Yes. And I believe her.'' Daniel mashed his cigarette in the glass ashtray on the coffee table. ''I tell you, Magrane was a disturbed personality before he was sent out to Oman. He wasn't fit to take part in Exercise Damocles. Carr should have spotted that.''

Senior officers had their uses. For one thing, they made convenient scapegoats whenever there was an almighty cock-up, and the same applied to the medical profession. In this case however, the accusation was unfair because Carr was a physician, not a psychiatrist. He was about to ask Daniel if he'd been involved in the selection of volunteers when the telephone rang. He just had time to say, ''Bayswater 8897,'' before the blips cut in. Seconds later, he heard a coin drop in the box and the caller came through loud and clear as he hooked the receiver into the speech amplifier for Daniel's benefit.

''Robert?''

''Yes?''

''It's me, Andrew. You were quick off the mark.''

''You saw the message then?''

''Would I be speaking to you now if I hadn't?''

Magrane sounded annoyed, and Donaldson could have kicked himself. He'd said the first thing that came into his head and consequently they'd got off on the wrong foot.

''I just wanted to make sure,'' he said lamely.

''A security check? Oh well, that's different. Look, before we go any further, I'd like you to do me a favor.''

''Name it.''

''I broke into a house in Balmedie and stole twenty-nine pounds fifty. I don't know who the people are, but they live in Hamilton Close. They'll have reported the burglary by now, so the local police should have their names. Would you make sure they're reimbursed? Okay?''

"Leave it to me, I'll arrange something." Donaldson thought quickly. Lloyd wanted him to arrange a face-to-face meeting with Magrane and this could be the opportunity he needed. It was a little early in the game, but he thought it worth a try. "I'll require your signature on a cash requisition, Andrew."

"Why?"

"Well, you know the Command Secretary, he's the Treasury's watchdog. Every transaction has to be supported by a voucher of some kind."

"I've never known a secret fund to be subject to audit."

Donaldson frowned. Magrane was a lot sharper than he'd bargained for and he wasn't going to fall into a trap that easily. "Times have changed, Andrew," he said smoothly. "All accounts have to be scrutinized now. There are no exceptions."

"I'll take your word for it. Tell you what, give me your address and I'll send you a letter of authorization through the post. How's that?"

Magrane had called his bluff and there was nothing he could do now except give in gracefully.

"I suppose it may satisfy the Command Secretary. Anyway, send it to 298 Devonshire Terrace in Bayswater and we'll see what happens. Incidentally, how are you off for money, Andrew?"

"I'll get by until we can arrange a drop."

A drop? Donaldson shook his head in disbelief. Their conversation was becoming more and more unreal, as if the dialogue had been lifted straight from one of those detective series on television. Daniel too was wearing a martyred expression, like a man with a bad taste in his mouth.

"By a drop, I take it you mean a dead letter box?"

"No, Robert, there's a subtle difference. A DLB is a semi-permanent arrangement, which is unnecessary in our case because we shan't be writing notes to one another. A drop is a one-time collection point. I'm surprised you didn't know that."

"Of course I do, it just didn't seem appropriate. Don't

worry, though, I'll have a scout round and see if I can find somewhere suitable.''

"No," Magrane said abruptly. "That particular ball is in my court. You may prove to be the best control in the business, but I'm not taking any chances. I learned my lesson the hard way in Northern Ireland and nobody, but nobody, is ever going to drop me in the shit again.''

"Tell me what went wrong, Andrew. I don't want to make the same mistake.''

"Another time. This conversation has gone on long enough and we've got to watch our security. I'll call you again in half an hour.''

Magrane broke the connection before he had a chance to come back at him. Angry with himself for having bungled it, Donaldson hung up and rewound the tape. Playing back their conversation, he listened for any wrong phrase or inflection in his voice that might have excited Magrane's suspicion and put him on his guard.

"What did I do wrong, Bernard?" he asked presently.

"Nothing. You handled it very well.''

"You think so? You heard him—he's still calling the tune, not me.''

"Don't rush your fences. That was my mistake. You need the patience of Job to get anywhere with that man.''

"You don't like him much, do you?''

"Who? Me?'' Daniel looked up at him, another cigarette clinging to his lower lip. "No, I'm afraid I don't, but I assure you the feeling is mutual. In case you didn't know already, I'm a Jew. That's one strike against me for a start, but it so happens that Magrane is convinced I'm also a Russian. Now, the way he sees it, there's nothing lower on this earth than a Russian Jew working for the KGB. You should have heard the names he called me whenever he thought I was probing too deep into his private life. I've yet to meet anyone who can match his vocabulary. Reinhard Heydrich—that was his favorite name for me. Oh, I know it was only his defense mechanism at work, but you can take so much, and then the insults begin to get under your skin. I asked Carr to take me off the case, but he wouldn't hear of it. Said that I was a good psychiatrist and that an abrasive approach often paid off. I think he was wrong on both counts.''

"You don't believe that, Bernard, and neither do I."

"Thanks for the vote of confidence.'' Daniel struck a match and lit his cigarette. "The fact is, I've failed him. There's no point in pretending otherwise.''

"Come on, Bernard, stop feeling sorry for yourself and give me some help.'' Donaldson pointed to the telephone. ''We've got another fifteen, perhaps twenty, minutes before he calls again and I'm still groping in the dark. You know the score, he thinks I've been detailed to act as his control. Now what am I going to say if he starts to question me about some operation that's just a figment of his imagination?''

Daniel leaned back in the armchair, his mouth curving in a sardonic smile. "You try to humor him."

"Is that the best advice you can offer?"

"Let me finish, Robert. You try to humor him while I do some quick thinking. Past exercises, operations that happened years ago, briefings for missions that were postponed indefinitely or cancelled altogether; they're all there locked away inside his head and so jumbled together that it's almost impossible to make any sense of them. If he insists on going through with this fantasy, we have to pick the operation that seems the least dangerous, the one we're best able to control." Daniel broke off and glanced towards the telephone as it began to ring. "You see what I mean about inconsistency? Magrane said he would call back in half an hour—that was less than twenty minutes ago.''

Donaldson lifted the phone and the tape started running automatically. A coin pinged in the box and the mechanism whirred like an alarm clock running down, the noise magnified by the amplifier.

Magrane said, "All right, Robert, suppose we pick up from where we left off.''

"Yes, let's do that, Andrew.''

"Good. I'm all set to go just as soon as you give the word. So what's it going to be—Case Black or Operation Damocles?''

Magrane had bounced the jackpot question at him sooner than expected and he looked to Daniel for guidance. The psychiatrist was already on his feet and moving towards him, a notebook held against his chest like a miniature sandwich board. On it he'd written, "Try Damocles—it's safer."

"I don't have to tell you, do I?" Donaldson projected an air of confidence he didn't feel. "You already know the answer. We're going for Damocles."

"That's what I hoped you'd say."

"You did?"

"Well, it's right up my street and you know I can do a good job. However, there are one or two points we have to settle first."

"Such as?"

"The buyers, for instance. You agree there would be a hell of a diplomatic row if we decided to ventilate those people?"

The buyers meant nothing to Donaldson, but ventilate . . . a man was said to be ventilated when you put a bullet through him.

"We certainly don't want a diplomatic row on our hands, Andrew."

"Which means that we're left with the post office, the middleman and the suppliers. I suggest we start with the post office."

"The post office?" Donaldson repeated blankly.

"Great," said Magrane, "that's all I wanted to know."

It happened so fast that he was caught flat-footed. One moment he was talking to Magrane and the next he was holding a dead phone. Nothing had been said about another call and he had a horrible feeling that, unintentionally, he'd set in motion a train of events that would prove impossible for anyone in Special Branch to control.

Rewinding the tape to its original starting point, Donaldson called the number Commander Ryan had given him.

Linda Warwick was on the point of calling Reception to ask if they would send a porter up to room 303 to collect her suitcase when the telephone rang. She wondered if it was Lionel Harkness, but could think of no reason why he should want to contact her again.

A soft, hesitant voice said, "Miss Warwick? It's Mary Klepacz. I know you've got a train to catch, so I won't keep you long."

"Don't give it another thought. I've got plenty of time—the train doesn't leave for another hour yet. What can I do for you?"

"Well, I remembered what you said when you came to see me yesterday morning and I got to thinking . . ."

Linda thought it more likely that Mary Klepacz had remembered the ten-pound note she'd pressed on her and was wondering how she could earn a little more tax-free pin money. The ten pounds had bought a lot of useless tittle-tattle, but Linda had regarded it as an investment for the future. The Army could muzzle Klepacz, but they were powerless to stop his wife talking to the press.

"I don't know if it's any help to you, Miss Warwick, but when Stan returned home last night, he told me that Major Daniel had been called to London."

Daniel? Linda frowned. The name didn't ring a bell. "He's the commanding officer of the hospital, right?"

"No, you're thinking of Colonel Carr. Daniel is the psychiatrist who's been treating Captain Magrane."

"I see. When did he leave for London?"

"Last night, on the sleeper from Inverness. Stan said it was all a bit sudden."

"Well, that's the way they do things in the Army, isn't it? Sometimes it can be all rush."

"Yes, I suppose you're right."

She sounded deflated, which was exactly the reaction Linda had hoped for. The tip seemed promising, but it was advisable not to let Mary Klepacz know that, otherwise she might take it into her head to peddle the same story to every reporter in town. The trick now was to end their conversation in such a way that she was kept dangling on the hook.

"Like you said, Mary, I'm not too sure it means anything, but I'll look into it and let you know what transpires. Okay?"

"Yes. I'm sorry to have troubled you . . ."

"No, really, I'm glad you called." Linda muffled the phone while she held a conversation with herself, and then came back to Mary Klepacz. "That was the hall porter," she explained.

"Oh, well, I won't keep you any longer. Good-bye, Miss Warwick, it's been nice meeting you."

"And you, Mary."

Linda put the phone down. It was possible that Daniel had been summoned to London to attend an official inquiry, but if that was the case, she wondered why the Ministry of Defence were not equally concerned to hear Carr's evidence. Perhaps he was being transferred to another hospital? No, that couldn't be right; if the National Health Service was anything to go by, the medics wouldn't be that quick off the mark. Donaldson . . . she thought it would be interesting to know where he was right now. Reaching for the phone again, she asked the switchboard to connect her with Headquarters U.K. Land Forces at Wilton.

Magrane had lost count of the number of times he'd made a departure from Heathrow. Usually he caught a bus out to the airport from the West London Air Terminal in Cromwell Road, but now that the underground extension was open, he'd been able to catch a through train from Piccadilly Circus. Although the journey took slightly longer, he preferred to go by train because there was less chance of someone remembering his face. The operation had been well-planned and he wasn't expecting any trouble, but it was stupid to take an unnecessary risk. Unlike the train, nobody got on or off the bus once it left Cromwell Road, which meant people were more inclined to take notice of the fellow passengers. Entering the number three terminal building, he walked over to the KLM desk.

The 1420 flight to Amsterdam was fully booked, but he managed to get a seat on the plane departing at 1500 at a cost of forty-four pounds fifty for the round trip. The fare made a hole in what was left of the hundred and fifty the pawnbroker had given him for Virginia's dress ring, but the instant-purchase ticket was a good deal less than he'd expected to fork out for an economy class. He changed seventy-five pounds into Dutch guilders at the branch of Lloyds Bank and then found a seat near W. H. Smith's bookshop where he could watch the security people in action.

Although they were observing all the usual procedures at the baggage counter, he got the impression that it was something of a mechanical process. Certainly they weren't as vigilant as their opposite numbers in Belfast, but here they weren't under constant threat from the IRA, which made a considerable difference. It was academic anyway, because they wouldn't find anything on him no matter how hard they looked. There were only the usual things in his suitcase— pyjamas, shirts, socks, a change of underwear, his wash kit, a spare suit and a pair of suede shoes. And when the Burns Agency people checked the executive briefcase, they'd merely find a collection of brochures which he'd acquired from the Ford Motor Company showroom in Regent Street. Reassured by what he'd seen, Magrane left the bench seat to join the small queue for the KLM flight.

The customs and immigration officer who checked his passport muttered something about the photograph being a reasonable likeness and then turned to the back page, his eyes narrowing thoughtfully as he studied the entries on the exchange control form. There were a few anxious moments, but in the end, Magrane managed to convince him that he wasn't taking more than twenty-five pounds in sterling out of the country and that his firm had arranged the trip at short notice, leaving him no time to get travellers' checks. Following that, the final security check was something of an anticlimax. One of the Burns men ran a metal detector over his body while an assistant examined his hand baggage, after which he was allowed into the departure lounge.

The platform shoes which he'd purchased the previous day from the Oxford Street branch of Marks and Spencer were decidedly uncomfortable, but they had served their purpose. The Bernardelli .25 automatic was a vest-pocket weapon, smaller than the palm of his hand; when broken down into component parts, it fitted snugly into the recesses he'd hollowed out in the heel and instep of both shoes.

9 . . .

DONALDSON thought the response by Special Branch had scarcely been electric. Following his telephone call, it had taken Ryan all of four hours to put in an appearance at the flat in Devonshire Terrace, and even now, after listening to the tape for the second time, he still seemed to lack any sense of urgency. His pudgy face was wrinkled in thought as if trying to solve a problem that would have baffled Einstein.

"Operation Damocles?" he said presently. "Does it actually exist, Robert?"

"Yes. It was the code name of a field trial which was held in Oman in May of last year."

"A field trial?"

"A sort of exercise designed to test new equipment under operational conditions. The trouble is that Magrane is convinced that it was something altogether different. He's got it mixed up with an exercise, or exercises, unknown, or maybe it's something he made up entirely. Lord knows what 'mission' he thinks he's carrying out. Of course, Bernard here is the expert; he can explain his present state of mind much better than I."

Ryan glanced in Daniel's direction. "Can you do that?—in simple terms I can understand?"

"I can try." Daniel pressed his fingertips together and raised them to his lips as if in prayer. "Damocles was a very traumatic experience for Magrane. He was a leader who lost control of the men under his command and the shock was so great that he had a nervous breakdown and became totally withdrawn. For months now, he's been living in a fantasy world. Instead of being a field trial, Damocles has become a real operation that misfired. At one time, he was convinced that this troop had been landed on the Libyan coast from a submarine with orders to assassinate Qaddafi. Of all the exercises and projected operations that are inextricably mixed up in his mind, that particular concept seemed to me to be the least dangerous. That's why I advised Robert to steer him in that direction."

"Qaddafi, eh?" Ryan smiled. "Well, he certainly isn't going to reach Libya on a hundred and fifty pounds."

"Unfortunately, it doesn't look like Qaddafi's his target anymore," Donaldson said quietly. "Otherwise why all the talk about the post office, the middleman and the suppliers?"

"I'm sure I don't know. That's up to you to find out."

"His last call was at eleven forty-five, more than four hours ago."

"So what? He'll be in touch again, won't he?"

"Well, you'd just better pray he doesn't kill somebody in the meantime, because he's talking about ventilating people. Now, that may or may not be pure fantasy, but we know he's a killer and when he does contact me again, I've got to make absolutely sure he doesn't go completely off the rails. To do that, I must have the details of every mission he's ever been briefed for. I can call Tamblin at the Ministry of Defence and set the wheels in motion, but my request won't get very far unless it's backed by Lloyd."

Ryan mulled it over, one hand rubbing his heavy jaw. "I don't think the SAS will agree to that," he said finally. "But I'll tell you what we'll do. If Magrane starts talking about any kind of operation when he's in touch again, you tell him. Tell him that the politicians are having second thoughts and that you'll have to refer the matter to them. And then call us; we'll take it from there." Ryan heaved himself out of the chair and moved towards the door. "That should do the trick."

"Perhaps." Considering Magrane was planning to kill someone, Ryan was a damn sight too casual for his liking. Maybe he was being overimaginative, but it seemed to him that the Special Branch officer was deliberately withholding information from him.

"I'm damn sure it will, Robert." He rubbed his jaw again and looked pensive. "By the way, doctor, what was Case Black?"

"There's no way of telling whether it's merely a figment of his imagination or not," said Daniel, "but it dates back to 1973. You'll recall that, in those days, with the strikes and all, there was a real fear that the country was rapidly becoming ungovernable. Anyway, Magrane got it into his head that he was responsible for arresting certain Marxists in the Trade Union Movement."

"Really?" A slow smile appeared on Ryan's face. "You know something? Maybe you would have done us all a favor if you'd steered him in that direction."

Magrane tipped the bellboy and waited for him to leave the room before sitting down on the bed to remove the platform soled shoes. His feet were hot and sweaty and he could imagine how Virginia's nose would have wrinkled in disgust had she been there. Peeling off both nylon socks, he inspected his feet and was surprised to find that, although sore, they were not blistered. A good soaking would take care of the tenderness, but right now first things first. Collecting the wastepaper basket from beside the dressing table unit, he opened the suitcase and searched through the wash kit for a new razor blade.

The rubber soles he'd glued onto the platform shoes weren't easy to remove and he had to slash them into strips before he was able to peel them off and dig out the square of leather covering each recess. Once that had been done, he tipped the component parts onto the bed and gave them a quick wipe with his handkerchief to remove any traces of fluff left by the cotton-wool packing. Assembling the Bernardelli automatic, Magrane jacked a .25 round into the breach, applied the safety and hid the weapon under the pillow. Satisfied that none of the rubber shavings had fallen onto the carpet, he carried the wastepaper basket over to the window and dumped the mutilated shoes into the Amstel Canal.

Although this was not the first time he'd been to Amsterdam, Magrane had taken the precaution of buying a street plan at the airport. Unfolding the map on the bed, he located the Apollo Hotel where he was staying and then pinpointed the target in the town center next to the Erotica in Speigelweg. Door to door, it added up to a four-mile hike. A taxi was out because the driver might remember his face, but he thought it would be safe enough to catch a number 2-5 tram from Churchill Laan as far as Montplein. From there, it was only a short walk along the bank of the Singel Canal to Speigelweg where Jan van der Pohlmann lived with his common-law wife, Beatrix.

Jan and Beatrix van der Pohlmann—the post office. The SAS had a fat dossier on those two. Both of them had well-to-do middle-class parents whom they'd rejected when they'd embraced the revolutionary cause of the Baader-Meinhof gang. The Dutch police couldn't touch them because there was no law either against publishing an inflammatory broadsheet or running a sex parlor, and it was no concern of theirs that the van der Pohlmanns had close links with the IRA. Harry Gregson had pointed them out to him when they'd followed a couple of Irish buyers over to Amsterdam back in 1971. Or was it 1972? Magrane scratched his head; it must have been 1972 just after he'd completed the language course. That was typical of the Army; they sent you on a two-year course and then assigned you to a job where you never had to speak a word of Russian. Still, it had been very instructive to work with Harry Gregson.

Harry had been an old hand in more ways than one. He'd joined the Special Air Service when it was reformed in the Far East after the war under the guise of the Malayan Scouts. Malaya, Kenya, Cyprus, Aden, Borneo, Northern Ireland—you name it, Harry Gregson had been there. Ironic to think that a man of his experience should end up in a mortuary, put there one night by a mindless twenty-four-year-old in an MGB who'd raced down the King's Road doing seventy, presumably to impress his girlfriend. It just went to show that you never knew when your number was coming up. Magrane smiled. Jan and Beatrix van der Pohlmann didn't know it, but this was going to be the night when they cashed in their chips.

Folding the map away, he took out his wallet to check how much money he had. The pound was worth less than four guilders and with Holland just about the most expensive country in Europe, he was going to feel the pinch. The hotel room would set him back by a hundred and ten and dinner plus a couple of drinks at the bar would probably run to another sixty. That left a hundred and ten to spend in the Erotica where, apart from the steep entrance fee, he and Harry Gregson had been charged four guilders apiece for a bottle of Coke. Maybe he should give dinner a miss? No, the hotel staff might think that was odd and he didn't want to draw attention to himself. Besides, he was hungry. Lifting the phone, Magrane called the restaurant and asked the head-waiter to reserve a table for eight thirty, which he thought would leave him plenty of time to have a bath and take a short nap.

The bath toned him up, but the short nap was a mistake and he woke up sweating half an hour later, the details of the nightmare still vivid in his mind. He could understand the bit where he'd been drowning in his own blood because that had damn nearly happened after the Provos sprang their ambush in the lay-by outside Belfast, but the image of Daniel insisting that he was a very sick man had no foundation whatever. He hadn't felt so well in years . . . Christ, he could use a drink. Dressing quickly, he tucked the Bernardelli into his hip pocket and went down to the lobby. One hour, one dinner and several double whiskies later, he left the Apollo Hotel by the side entrance and hopped a tram at the junction of Churchill Laan and Scheld Straat.

Speigelweg was just as he remembered it, a double row of squat houses with large windows, solid-looking doors and long sloping roofs facing one another across a cobbled alley-way with the Singel Canal at the bottom of the street. The trees had been in full leaf then, but now the branches were bare like witches' broomsticks. The only feature that distin-guished the Erotica from the other houses was the gaudily painted sign above the entrance advertising live sex shows.

A muscle man with a beer-barrel stomach relieved him of fifty guilders at the door, handed over an admission ticket and suggested he might like to have a drink in the bar while he was waiting for the next show which began at ten thirty. The bar was down the hall in a small room at the back of the house. A large power socket below the exhaust fan led Magrane to believe that it used to be the kitchen before the fittings had been removed and the walls and ceiling painted a midnight blue. In keeping with the atmosphere, the lighting was subdued, making it difficult for him to pick his way towards a vacant table in the far corner.

A blonde, topless waitress in a short flared skirt and thigh-length high-heeled boots minced across the room to take his order. Her false bright smile threatened to crack the layer of make-up, but apart from the suspicion of a spare tire around her midriff, her figure wasn't at all bad. As she leaned over him to make herself heard above the piped music, Magrane inhaled a lungful of cheap perfume. Mindful of his previous visit to the Erotica, he ordered a Coke on the assumption they served nothing cheaper. Even so, with a tip, it came to six guilders.

There were nine other men waiting to see the next show, all of them middle-aged except for one whose sallow complexion and spotty face suggested that he was still in his teens. By the time Magrane had smoked his way through a couple of cigarettes, their number had doubled and it was standing room only. Last to arrive were three English couples around his own age and, listening to their conversation, he gathered they were on one of the "bargain break" weekends offered by tour operators in the winter months. The two younger women were obviously nervous and embarrassed, but the eldest of the three looked as if she was getting a kick out of being there.

Twenty-six people packed into a tiny room at fifty guilders a head added up to a lot of money and the Erotica was open from two in the afternoon to 1:00 A.M. There were four performances a day, but not all of them would be as well-attended as the late night show. A man, and more especially a woman, would have to be pretty brazen to walk into a place like the Erotica in broad daylight. Four shows a day, not to mention the bar takings and a percentage of the fee charged by the waitresses when they took a client upstairs. Harry Gregson was right, the van der Pohlmanns were onto a good thing and he would understand why either Jan or Beatrix made a point of turning up to collect the receipts a few minutes after closing time.

Magrane didn't hear any announcement that the next show was about to start, but suddenly everybody began to file out of the bar. The cupboard which he'd noticed under the stairs at the end of the hall offered a good hiding place and, leaving it until the last moment, he tagged on at the end of the queue. The idea was sound enough, but the element of luck essential to the plan was missing. A hostess was barring the way and there was nothing he could do except stay with the herd.

Across the hall, two rooms had been knocked into one to make a small theater. Eight rows of tip-up seats that had seen better days in some flea pit of a cinema had been placed on a raised wooden platform which sloped towards the stage. Midnight blue seemed to be the van der Pohlmanns' favorite color scheme, a monotonous décor only partially relieved by the placards on the walls banning smoking and the use of flash cameras during the performance. Patrons were also forbidden to stand in four different languages and since all the seats at the back had already been taken, he had no option but to sit up front.

Without any warning, the house lights dimmed and to the accompaniment of soft background music piped through the speakers, the curtains parted. The stage props consisted of the bare minimum: a dressing table and stool and a double bed that was soon to be occupied by a tall, thin redhead and the colored girl who was supposed to be her maid. There were only two things to be said in favor of their act; it was over inside twenty minutes and was sufficiently depraved to shock the sightseers. As the house lights came up again, he saw the three English couples get up and leave. It was the opportunity Magrane had been waiting for and he grabbed the end seat in the back row before anyone else could beat him to it.

He sat through two more scenes that were enough to curl the hair and then, as the house lights dimmed for the last act, he slipped out of the room. This time the hall was empty and, edging past the bar, he unlatched the broom cupboard under the stairs and ducked inside.

The minutes slowly ticked away. A door opened and closed and a faint murmur of voices reached him. One belonged to a man, the other, low-pitched and husky, he recognized as the waitress who'd served him in the bar. Presently, he heard footsteps above his head and guessed that she was taking a client up to her room. Some ten minutes later, there was a desultory ripple of applause from the theater and then the audience began to file out of the Erotica.

According to Gregson, the time was fast approaching when either Jan or Beatrix was due to put in an appearance. He hoped it would be Jan because a man was less inclined to do something stupid when confronted with a gun. Magrane reached for the automatic in his hip pocket and waited, the silence growing more and more oppressive as time wore on and nothing happened. Just when it seemed the van der Pohlmanns had broken the pattern, he heard the sound of heavy footsteps as somebody walked past the broom cupboard and entered the bar. The loud gruff voice confirmed his supposition that the newcomer was Jan van der Pohlmann.

The stocktaking in the bar seemed to go on forever, but finally it came to an end. Van der Pohlmann said good night to the hired help, locked and bolted the front door behind them and started back down the hall. As he walked past his hiding place, Magrane stepped out of the broom cupboard and pressed the automatic into his neck. The Dutchman flinched and drew his breath in sharply, making a small hissing sound.

"No noise." Magrane rapped him gently with the pistol to emphasize the point. "You understand?"

"Yes." Van der Pohlmann's voice was low, not much above a whisper.

"Good. Now let's go next door. I want to have a talk with you and Beatrix."

A talk? That was very droll; all he wanted from them was an address. Glancing at the leather pouch the Dutchman was carrying in his right hand, it occurred to him that their bank roll would come in very handy. It would solve the problem of arranging a drop and make him less dependent on Donaldson.

Van der Pohlmann led him into a passageway behind the stage and unlocked the communicating steel door which opened into the adjoining kitchen. When they walked into the living room, Beatrix was curled up on the sofa listening to a tape of Crystal Gayle on the stereo. She hadn't changed a bit, Magrane thought, still as unprepossessing as ever. Her face was long and angular, framed by straight brown hair that fell below the shoulders, and the pair of jumbo-size spectacles merely drew attention to her narrow, spiteful-looking eyes. A shapeless ankle-length dress swamped her stick-thin body.

Suddenly aware that Jan was not alone, she looked up, her jaw dropping.

"Hullo, Beatrix." Magrane smiled fleetingly. "We haven't met before, but my friends in Belfast have told me so much about you and Jan that I feel we're old friends."

Her lips pursed thoughtfully and then the questions came fast, directed at van der Pohlmann in Dutch.

"No, that won't do." Magrane waved the automatic in her face. "We'll talk in English so that I can understand what you're saying to Jan."

"All right. Who are you? What do you want with us?"

"My friends aren't very happy with the service you've been providing lately. They don't like paying over the odds for shop-soiled goods."

"Service? Goods?" Anger showed in her mean little eyes and her voice rose to a shrill note. "What is this imbecile talking about, Jan?"

The Dutchman shrugged his shoulders. "Who knows? I think he is a little mad."

"Like Steiner," said Magrane.

"Who?" Beatrix asked sharply.

"August Steiner, the middleman who's been ripping us off. My friends are anxious that I should meet him to get things straightened out."

"These friends of yours—are they in the same lunatic asylum?"

"Your woman's got a waspish tongue, hasn't she, Jan? Why don't you tell her to shut her mouth?"

"It might be wise to humor him, Beatrix," van der Pohlmann said carefully.

"That's more like it. All I want is a simple answer to a simple question."

"What simple question?"

"One concerning August Steiner. Where's he living these days?"

"Steiner, eh?" Jan threw back his head and laughed. "Now I know you're crazy."

"I'm glad you've got a sense of humor," Magrane said mildly. "I like a good laugh too."

He struck the Dutchman, catching him under the nose with the heel of his left hand. Van der Pohlmann dropped the leather pouch and staggered back, sitting down heavily on the couch, his face registering disbelief as the blood began to course down his chin. Tears welled in his eyes and, searching through his pockets, he pulled out a handkerchief and held it to his injured nose.

"Just give me his address. It's not much to ask, is it, Jan?"

"He's still living in Cologne." Van der Pohlmann inspected the bloodstains on his handkerchief and frowned. "At 78 Glocken gasse."

"You bastard." Beatrix launched herself from the couch and advanced towards Magrane, her eyes glinting with hatred. "Steiner will make you pay for this."

Her lips formed a tight circle and a glob of saliva struck him in the face. Magrane paid no attention to her, though; all he could see was a figure pirouetting in a lay-by, a man being chopped to pieces by a hail of fire from a couple of Kalashnikov rifles that had reached Ireland by way of Amsterdam and the likes of the van der Pohlmanns. If he had any inhibitions about killing a woman, they vanished in that instant. Without the slightest sign of emotion, he squeezed the trigger and shot her through the heart. Pivoting round, Magrane fired again and hit van der Pohlmann between the eyes.

Although each pistol shot had been no more than a sharp crack barely audible above the sound of Crystal Gayle, it was some minutes before his heart stopped thumping and he remembered to tuck the automatic into his hip pocket. The leather pouch was still lying on the floor where Jan had dropped it and, bending down, he opened the clasp and hastily stuffed the bank notes into his jacket. Magrane eyed the telephone on the circular table near the bookcase and wondered if he should risk getting in touch with Donaldson now. He recalled Gregson saying that you could dial straight through to London from Amsterdam, but after a moment's hesitation, he decided it would be safer to use a public call box. Stepping over Beatrix van der Pohlmann, he walked out of the room and closed the door quietly behind him.

Donaldson stirred, turned over onto his right side and reluctantly opened one eye. Seconds later, he was wide awake and scrambling out of bed; he snapped on the lights, grabbed his dressing gown and ran into the living room to answer the telephone.

Magrane was very polite. He said, "I'm sorry to disturb you, Robert, but you know how it can be."

"That I do. I'm your control, aren't I?" Donaldson transferred the phone to his left hand and slipped his other arm into the dressing gown. "And I'm supposed to be available at any time of the day or night."

"You don't sound very happy. Is something the matter?"

"Matter? Do you have any idea what time it is? It's past two o'clock in the morning."

"I've always been a night owl," Magrane said cheerfully, "you'll just have to get used to that. Anyway, I thought you'd want to hear the news."

"What news?"

"About the post office. I've taken it out."

"You've done what?" Donaldson said incredulously.

"Look, I know you're half asleep, Robert, but a word of congratulation wouldn't come amiss. I mean, after all, phase one of Operation Damocles has been completed in record time."

"Well, that's terrific." Donaldson closed his eyes and groped for inspiration. "Listen, Andrew, I think we should arrange a rendezvous. I'd like to discuss our next move with you."

"That's easy. I'm going after the middleman."

"Who's that?"

"Oh, come on, Robert, how many more times do I have to remind you about security?"

"I wouldn't ask if it wasn't important, Andrew."

"Hell, Robert, if you really want to know the answer, look it up in the operation order. You'll find the target listed under phase two."

"Thanks."

"Don't mention it," said Magrane. "I'll be in touch."

Donaldson replaced the phone and turned about, suddenly aware that Daniel had opened the door of his bedroom and was watching him thoughtfully.

"Magrane?" the psychiatrist asked quietly.

"Yes."

"What's he been up to?"

"I think he's killed somebody, Bernard."

"Did he say so?"

"Not in so many words."

"It's just a supposition then?"

"I'd bet my shirt on it. Magrane has taken out the post office; apparently that was phase one of what he conceives Operation Damocles to be. Now he's going after the middle-man."

"Shit."

"You never said a truer word, Bernard. We're in it right up to our necks." Donaldson rewound the tape and then lifted the receiver off the hook. "I think it's about time Lloyd joined us in the cesspool."

10 . . .

MAGRANE checked out of the Apollo at nine o'clock. After paying his bill, he bought a copy of *De Telegraaf* at the desk, then hired a cab to drive him to the Rent-a-Budget-Car firm on Overtoom he'd looked up in the yellow pages. Overtoom was about three and a half miles from the hotel on the far side of the Vondelpark, and that gave him just enough time to leaf through the morning paper. Although he couldn't read a word of Dutch, it seemed reasonable to assume that the name of van der Pohlmann would stand out in the text if their murder had been discovered and reported to the police. Relieved to find that there was no mention of them in *De Telegraaf,* he folded the newspaper away inside the executive briefcase.

It could only be a question of time before their bodies were discovered. The Erotica opened at two o'clock, but the van der Pohlmanns were likely to be missed long before that. Taking the worst case, Magrane thought he could rely on having at least another hour before the police got to hear about it. By then, with any luck, he would be well clear of Amsterdam, heading towards Eindhoven on the motorway.

There was no shortage of funds now. Thanks to van der Pohlmann, he had two thousand eight hundred and ninety-one guilders, the bulk of it stashed away inside the briefcase, the rest in his wallet. Two thousand eight hundred and ninety-one guilders: that was quite a haul, almost seven hundred and thirty-four pounds at the prevailing rate of exchange. Donaldson would be pleased. Or would he? He hadn't been exactly fulsome in his praise on the telephone last night. But he'd met Donaldson's type before, hard-nosed men who found it difficult to say thank you for a job well done. Christ, there was no satisfying some people.

"Please?" The driver glanced over his shoulder twice in rapid succession, the expression on his face posing a question. "Please?"

Magrane felt his stomach drop. "Nothing," he mumbled, shaking his head vigorously. "I was just thinking out loud."

The Vondelpark was on their right and he caught occasional glimpses of it between the gaps in the buildings. This was Overtoom then; no doubt about it.

"Anywhere here will do me," he said.

The taxi driver nodded, flicked the indicator light and immediately pulled into the curb, yet another sign that the Dutchman understood English much too well for Magrane's peace of mind. How much had he overheard? A few griping words about Donaldson, but that wouldn't mean a lot to him. He hadn't said anything about the money, so there was no reason why the driver should remember him. Magrane got out of the cab, paid the fare and then waited until the driver had pulled away before moving on.

Rent-a-Budget-Car was sandwiched between a jeweller's and a dress shop two blocks farther down the street. The front office had potted plants in the window, vinyl-upholstered furniture and wall-to-wall carpeting. There was also a reception counter staffed by an earnest-looking young man in gold-rimmed spectacles who was busy on the telephone and a pert brunette dressed like an air hostess in a red skirt and matching blazer over a plain silk blouse. The girl smiled warmly and greeted him in Dutch.

"I'm sorry," said Magrane. "Do you speak English?"

"But of course. How can I help you?"

He could understand why Amsterdam prospered from the tourist trade when there were girls like her who spoke English as a matter of course and were only too anxious to help a visitor spend his money.

"I have to go to Cologne on business and the train won't get me there on time. I'd like to hire a car from you, but there is a snag."

"A snag?"

"A small problem." Magrane rested both elbows on the counter and leaned forward, displaying his most winning smile. "You see, I don't want to come all the way back to Amsterdam just to return the car."

"That's no problem, sir, we have a branch in Cologne."

The information was not news to him. The branch offices were listed in the yellow pages, but he contrived to appear pleasantly surprised. There were times when it paid to let people think they'd resolved a difficult problem for you. It gave their ego a boost and usually from then on, they would bend over backwards to help you.

"What sort of car were you thinking of—a Volkswagen, an Audi or a Mercedes?" She reeled off the deposit and rental charges for the various models, smiling all the while in case the quotations should put him off.

"How far is Cologne?"

"I think it's a little over two hundred and forty kilometers."

"That's roughly a hundred and fifty miles," Magrane said musingly, "and I have to be there by one o'clock. Perhaps I'd better have an Audi."

"Certainly. There are just one or two formalities." The girl slipped a carbon under the rental agreement and then looked up again. "If I could have your name and address, sir?"

"My name's Murdoch," said Magrane, "Alec Murdoch." He reached inside his jacket and laid the false passport on the counter. "The address is 26 Angel Crescent, Harrow-on-the-Hill, Middlesex, England."

The girl completed the appropriate boxes on the form in a neat hand. "Method of payment," she murmured. "We accept American Express if you wish to charge it."

"I'll pay cash."

The girl nodded and drew a line through credit card. There were more questions concerning his age, physical disabilities and previous convictions for traffic offenses, if any. Apart from their undoubted interest in his money, it seemed to him that Rent-a-Budget-Car wanted to know his whole life story.

"Do you have a current driving license, Mr. Murdoch?"

They had reached the jackpot question and he was going to need all his charm in the next few minutes. He smiled in a way that suggested he never travelled anywhere without it.

"May I see it, please?"

A driving license was one thing he couldn't produce because the Army still had it along with his official passport. Nevertheless, he made a great show of going through all his pockets, the confident expression on his face gradually changing to become increasingly worried.

"I don't seem to have it on me," he said finally. "I must have left the damn thing at home."

The girl frowned. The form had been completed except for his signature on the bottom line and he could see that whatever the company rules might require, she was reluctant to lose a contract. Prompted by his glance, she asked him to please wait a minute while she had a word with her colleague. Following a hurried conversation with the earnest-looking young man, she returned with a broad smile on her face to tell him that they would make an exception just this once.

Thirty minutes later, Magrane was clear of Amsterdam, heading southeast on the motorway towards Eindhoven.

Lloyd turned up at the flat shortly after nine thirty. If he was perturbed by the telephone call from Magrane that Donaldson had taken in the early hours of the morning, he was careful not to show it. In fact, his manner reminded Donaldson of a general who, despite arriving on the scene long after the shouting was over, was determined to deliver a pep talk to the troops which would leave them in no doubt that they were expected to pull themselves together and get on with the job. A bright on-and-off smile preceded his opening remark.

"I gather you're not happy with the way things are progressing, Robert?"

It was the classic Whitehall understatement, and also wholly inaccurate. According to the Oxford Dictionary, progress meant a forward movement, an advance or an improvement, whereas the Magrane affair was going from bad to worse. Happy implied a contented state of mind and Donaldson was a long way from having that.

"I could put it stronger," he said.

"Yes, well, I think you're worrying unnecessarily. I can assure you that no matter what Magrane may have implied, he didn't kill anybody last night. Nobody was murdered here in London, nor in Birmingham, Liverpool, Manchester, Cardiff, Leeds, Glasgow, Edinburgh or anywhere else in the country."

"How about Ireland? He doesn't need a passport to go over there."

"I don't think wild horses could drag him back to Ireland again." Lloyd turned to Daniel for support. "I'm sure you agree with me, Bernard?"

Daniel nodded. "I think it's highly unlikely. He would never talk to me about his experiences in Belfast and whenever I raised the subject, he always shied away from it. However, I did get the strong impression that he wouldn't hesitate to go absent without leave if the Army decided to send him back to do another tour."

"There now, does that set your mind at rest?"

"No, I'm sorry, but it doesn't."

Donaldson strolled over to the window and stood there looking down on the windswept street, annoyed by Lloyd's soothing bedside manner. Like a slipshod builder, he seemed determined to wallpaper over the cracks.

"Look, as far as we know he didn't kill anyone, but that isn't saying much. Magrane talks and acts like a pro and he could have hidden the body or bodies in some place where they won't be discovered in a hurry."

"Bodies?" Lloyd said derisively. "You're expecting more than one to turn up, are you?"

"It's possible." Donaldson turned about to face him. "Magrane said he'd taken out the post office. Of course it could be a one-man business, but that isn't usually the case."

"I think you're letting your imagination run riot."

"That's why I'm here, isn't it?" Donaldson said angrily. "To use my imagination so that we can trap him."

"Actually, we want you to use your initiative, Robert."

"All right, no imagination then, just my initiative, but whichever way you put it, the fact remains we aren't getting anywhere. Andrew is too wily a bird to walk into a trap. If you don't believe me, take a look at this letter that arrived this morning."

The postmark on the envelope showed that it had been mailed in Willesden the day before. Lloyd's face as he read the letter inside was a picture of incredulity. On cheap lined notepaper Magrane had written: "To whom it may concern. This is to certify that the sum of twenty-nine pounds fifty has necessarily been expended on rail fares and subsistence allowance in pursuance of Operation Damocles."

"I take it you've seen this letter?" he asked the psychiatrist.

Daniel nodded.

"Well, what do you make of it, Bernard?"

"In my opinion, it's no more than one would expect from a man who's living in a make-believe world. However, we mustn't underrate him, Magrane can be very cunning."

"And that's exactly why I need a lot more background information," Donaldson chimed in quickly. "I want a complete rundown on Andrew's career, what he's done, where he's been—in fact, everything there is to know about him." Maybe in all this there'd be *some* way to figure out what Magrane's future intentions were.

"How long has he been in the Army, Robert? Thirteen, or is it fourteen years?"

"Something like that."

"Well, of course, I'm not a soldier, but it seems to me you'd have to interview a hell of a lot of people."

Reluctantly, he had to concede that Lloyd was right. It was virtually impossible to compute how many tactical exercises and counterinsurgency operations Magrane had been involved in over a period of fourteen years, and the number of senior officers with whom he'd had dealings could add up to a staggering total.

"As things stand, only Mrs. Magrane, Ryan and one or two of his people, you, me and Bernard know that he's still alive. We want to keep that circle as small as possible, otherwise we'll have the press breathing down our necks." Lloyd snapped his fingers. "That reminds me, Miss Warwick called your office yesterday. She wouldn't leave a message, said it was only a social call, but I'd be careful of her." He reached inside his jacket. "And these two letters arrived for you this morning."

Donaldson noticed that the envelopes had been readdressed to a post office box number, a sure sign that Lloyd was determined no one at Wilton should know where he was staying in London. Of the two letters, one was a bank statement while the other had been posted in Inverness early on Thursday morning. Ripping the envelope open, he found it contained a brief covering note from Linda Warwick on hotel stationery and three pages of typescript. The typescript was the first draft of an article she intended to submit to the *Sunday Times*. The opening paragraph was enough to convince him that Tamblin would have a fit if it appeared in print.

"I think you'd better cast your eye over this." Donaldson smiled faintly. "It looks as though Linda Warwick is about to let the cat out of the bag."

Right from the first sentence it was obvious that there was nothing speculative about the piece she'd written. The confident assertion that Magrane was not the only SAS man who'd received psychiatric treatment at Strathconan was proof that someone on the permanent staff had been talking out of turn. Klepacz seemed the most likely candidate because he was the only civilian to have worked in the hospital.

"If you've no objections, Robert," Lloyd said presently, "I'd like Hugh Tamblin to see this."

"Is that wise? I mean, if he decides to speak to her about it, it could make things worse. I got the impression that Linda Warwick didn't like Tamblin too much."

"You believe she would smell a rat if Hugh got in touch with her?"

"Yes, I do."

"Well, I'll tell him to bear it in mind, but Hugh ought to know what's in the wind." Lloyd folded the typescript in two and tucked it into his inside pocket. "In my view, she's fishing for information and it's best if we ignore her. After all, there's always a chance the *Sunday Times* won't use the story."

"But if they do?"

"Forewarned is forearmed. Hugh will think of a plausible explanation."

"I'd like to sound plausible, too, when Magrane gets in touch with me again."

"But you are, Robert." The on-and-off smile flashed like a warning beacon. "That's why Ryan and I are confident you can pull it off."

Lloyd was moving purposefully towards the hall and, knowing it was pointless to continue the argument, Donaldson accompanied him to the door and let him out. It was the old, old story. Whenever the brass were unable or unwilling to provide any practical help, they gave you a pat on the back and left you to get on with the job. The Home Office was just like the Army in that respect, they even used the same kind of language. But was what they were hiding worth all the people Magrane had killed?

"Hardly satisfactory, was it?" said Daniel.

"Oh, he was very smooth," Donaldson observed sourly, "didn't turn a hair when I showed him that article. Still, he said it—forewarned is forearmed."

"What?"

"I think he'd already seen the story before I showed it to him."

"Are you implying the envelope had been opened before you got it?"

"Knowing Lloyd, I'd say he was unscrupulous enough."

He could see the psychiatrist refused to believe it. Perhaps the idea that Lloyd had been tampering with his mail was a little farfetched, but the envelope had been readdressed in an unfamiliar hand and the postal service had been surprisingly swift, considering the letter had been redirected to a box number in London after it arrived at Wilton. The more Donaldson thought about it, the more he was convinced there was only one way the letter could have reached him in so short a time. Lloyd had suspected that Linda Warwick was on to something and Vaughan had been told to send his mail to New Scotland Yard by special courier.

"You're nearly as bad as Magrane. He was convinced that Carr was deliberately withholding his mail. In his case, it was just another example of his defense mechanism at work; he needed an excuse to explain why his wife had stopped writing to him.''

Donaldson stared at him thoughtfully. ''This was after her visit to Strathconan last October?''

''Yes.''

''And before that, they were writing to each other frequently?''

''Is that a question or an assumption?'' Daniel managed a smile, but it obviously required an effort.

''I'd say it was a deduction. You must have thought they had a stable relationship, otherwise you wouldn't have persuaded her to visit him in hospital.''

''We all make mistakes.''

''I'm not so sure you did. I'm going to see her, Bernard.''

''You can't. I mean, what happens if he tries to get in touch again while you're away?''

''You can always leave the phone off the hook,'' said Donaldson. ''Now suppose you stop prevaricating and give me her address in Harrow?''

Magrane glanced at the clock on the dashboard and smiled. One hundred and forty miles in under two hours was not bad going, but then it was easy to keep up an average of a hundred and fifty kilometers an hour on the autobahn. In another five minutes he would reach the ring road north of Cologne and the moment was fast approaching when he would have to make up his mind one way or the other. The route map, which Rent-a-Budget-Car had supplied with the Audi, showed that the airport was south of the city on the road to Frankfurt, and that was the problem because Glocken gasse was somewhere near the center of Cologne.

The thought of having to double back on his tracks didn't appeal to him. But what was the alternative? To go straight in, locate the target and make the hit? Any fool could do that, but it took brains and careful planning to guarantee a successful getaway after the mission had been accomplished. Experience had taught him it was fatal to go for the shortcut. The assassin who stayed in business was the man who planned every move down to the last detail, but that was only possible with accurate and up-to-date information.

The SAS graded information according to the proven reliability of the source and it was conceivable that van der Pohlmann had deliberately given him a bum steer. August Steiner was known to be living in Cologne, but 78 Glocken gasse could be a false address and he would have to check it against the telephone directory where the lawyer was certain to be listed. Once the target location had been confirmed, he would need to look up the scheduled flights to London because they would govern the amount of time available for the operation. Time and space were always the two most important factors to be considered and it was essential he familiarize himself with the one-way streets in Cologne.

Magrane had only a smattering of German, but he knew what Flughaven meant and he followed the directional signs all the way out to Troisdorf. At the back of his mind he had an idea that Saturday was an early closing day in most German cities and the airport was the one place where he could be sure of obtaining all the information he needed.

11 . . .

THE sun was trying to shine, but it gave out no warmth. A chill wind whipped through the streets of Harrow, cold enough to make a brass monkey feel uncomfortable. Despite the protection afforded by his overcoat, Donaldson was thankful Angel Crescent was only a short walk from the station. Turning into the road where Virginia Magrane lived, he instinctively quickened his stride over the last hundred yards. Opening the front gate, he strode up to the house and rang the bell.

Virginia Magrane answered the door in a pair of faded jeans and a floppy turtleneck sweater. The way she peered at him confirmed the impression he'd got from the snapshot that she was nearsighted.

"My name's Donaldson." He smiled. "I telephoned you earlier this morning."

"Oh yes, so you did." She opened the door wider. "Please come in. It's not a very nice day, is it?"

Donaldson agreed it was decidedly chilly and stepped inside the hall. At her suggestion he removed his overcoat and hung it up on the rack before following her into the sitting room.

"Can I get you a cup of coffee?" She gestured towards a chair, inviting him to sit down. "I'm afraid it's only instant."

"Well, it's very kind of you to offer," he said, "but I had one not long ago."

She nodded and then sat down opposite him, hunched up in the chair as if she was cold. "You're a friend of Andrew's?" she asked.

"To tell you the truth, I've never met him, but Andrew seems to think we have some kind of special relationship."

"You're his superior officer?"

"Sort of." Donaldson took out a packet of cigarettes and offered her one. "I'm trying to persuade Andrew to give himself up."

"And he won't listen to you." Her voice sounded flat.

"No. That's why I need your help."

Donaldson struck a match and she leaned forward to light her cigarette. He noticed that her fingers were stained with nicotine.

"How many times have I heard that line," she said bitterly.

"From Major Daniel?"

"And the police. They were here on Thursday again." Virginia grimaced as if she'd just swallowed a dose of medicine that tasted foul. "I've lost count of the number of times Commander Ryan's called on me. I'm sure the neighbors must think we're having an affair."

Some women were inclined to enlarge upon a story for the sake of effect, but he doubted if that was Virginia's style. He wondered why Ryan had been such a frequent visitor to the house but was reluctant to ask in case she became even more defensive.

"I'd like to win Andrew's confidence," he said, "but I can't get close to him."

"I'm not surprised, he's not the trusting kind."

"So I gathered from Bernard Daniel. He said your husband accused Colonel Carr of withholding his mail."

"Did he tell you I stopped writing to Andrew?" Virginia stubbed out her cigarette in the ashtray with a nervous gesture. "It was his idea. Major Daniel seemed to think my letters were having an unsettling effect on him."

"That must have been rather distressing for you." Knowing what Daniel had told him about their marriage, he realized he was walking on thin ice.

"In some ways it was a relief. Andrew was a different man after he was wounded in Northern Ireland and we went through a very bad patch. He even took to sleeping in the spare room."

She flushed and looked away, embarrassed. For a moment, he thought Virginia was going to dry up, but she gradually recovered her composure.

"Andrew seemed to improve after a while and he was more like his old self. But then he was sent out to Oman and suddenly everything turned sour again."

Donaldson assumed Virginia was referring to Damocles, but as she went into greater detail he learned that she had received a very odd letter from Andrew before the field trial even got under way. It was, she said, a long and rambling account of what life was like in Oman, not only for the local inhabitants but for the men of his troop who he thought were getting thoroughly bored with doing nothing, but then, reading the page-long postscript that followed, she had become thoroughly alarmed.

"I had a horrible feeling that Andrew was heading for a nervous breakdown. He started writing about how his doppelgänger had arrived, the man who had betrayed him in Northern Ireland." Virginia plucked at a loose thread on the sleeve of her sweater, twisting the strand of wool round and round her index finger until the fiber broke off and left a small hole. "He went on and on, literally raving about his imaginary doppelgänger. He was so angry that in some places his pen went through the paper."

"And this was before Operation Damocles started?"

"Yes."

It didn't make sense. The field trial had been carried out under medical supervision and if Magrane had been on the verge of a nervous breakdown, it was inconceivable that his symptoms would have gone unnoticed. It was also unthinkable that he would have been allowed to take part in the trial unless the doctors were satisfied that he was physically and mentally fit to do so. Magrane might have been almost incoherent with rage when he'd written the postscript, but that didn't necessarily mean he was mentally unbalanced at the time.

"Do you still have this letter?" he asked.

"No. I sent it to Major Daniel; he said it might give him a better understanding of Andrew's psychotic condition."

"When was this? After you'd visited him in hospital?"

"No, it was long before that." Her eyebrows met in a frown as she tried to place the date. "Andrew was flown home on the twenty-fourth of May and as far as I can remember they called on me the following day."

"They?"

"Major Daniel and Commander Ryan. I'd met Commander Ryan previously when he came to see me shortly before Andrew was sent home on convalescent leave from Millbank Hospital. You see, the Army was anxious that he should have police protection in case the IRA decided to make another attempt on his life." Virginia found another loose thread in her sweater and began to worry it. "Bernard Daniel tried to warn me what to expect, that I would be upset by the tone of his letters, but I refused to listen to him. Unfortunately, he was proved right."

Magrane had written to Virginia a week later, describing in pornographic detail the various sexual affairs he imagined she'd been having in his absence. The letter had made her physically sick and Daniel had advised her to destroy it. Not surprisingly, she had then readily agreed to the psychiatrist's suggestion that in future the hospital staff should censor her husband's letters with a view to deleting the more offensive passages.

"Some I received were just a mass of obliterations." Virginia finally left the thread alone and clasped her hands together. "I think somebody must have inadvertently told Andrew what was going on, because after a while, all his hatred was directed towards Bernard. I saw that for myself when I was up at Strathconan."

For the first time, Donaldson began to question the kind of treatment Magrane had been receiving. He wondered if Bernard had really been concerned about protecting Virginia or whether he had used her distress as an excuse to censor Andrew's letters. What was it he had said the other day? Past exercises, operations that happened years ago, briefings for missions that were postponed indefinitely or cancelled altogether; they're all there, locked away inside his head. If that was true, it was possible that they had been reluctant to commit Andrew to a proper psychiatric hospital in case he talked to the wrong people. Who did he mean by "they"? Ryan and Lloyd? Christ, he was now beginning to think like Magrane.

"I'm afraid I haven't been of much help."

Donaldson gazed at her blankly for a moment before it dawned on him that he must have been shaking his head. "On the contrary," he said with a quick smile, "you've given me some very useful pointers."

She smiled faintly and glanced towards the clock on the mantelpiece. Taking the hint, he thanked her again, apologized for taking up so much of her time and moved out into the hall. As she let him out of the house, Virginia said he mustn't hesitate to get in touch if he thought she could be of any further assistance, but it was obvious from her tone that she hoped he wouldn't.

Reaching the end of the crescent, Donaldson turned into St. Anne's Road. Prompted by a sixth sense, he glanced back at the house and saw the vague outline of her figure behind the net curtains in the front bedroom. There were no prizes for guessing that it wouldn't be long before Ryan knew he had been to see her.

A number of things suggested that there was a definite alliance between Lloyd, Ryan, Tamblin and Daniel. There was the fact that Virginia had intimated that she'd been introduced to Daniel by Ryan, the inference that from the word go Bernard had been determined to ensure Magrane was unable to communicate freely with anyone on the outside. Fact number two: Lloyd was supposed to be with the Criminal Department in Whitehall, but he'd seemed very much at home in Ryan's office at New Scotland Yard and he'd arranged for Bernard to join him at the flat in Devonshire Terrace. Fact number three: Tamblin was employed by the Ministry of Defence but appeared equally concerned about representing the interests of the Home Office. Lloyd, Ryan, Tamblin and Daniel: a close partnership from which he was excluded.

A partnership? Well, maybe he didn't have a seat on the board, but there were no prizes for guessing who had been elected to carry the can. From the moment he had arrived in

Strathconan, Lloyd had used him as a front man so that he could stay in the background. It was a neat ploy and one that could have been terminated without arousing his suspicion had Magrane been recaptured within two or three days. It was just Lloyd's bad luck that things hadn't quite worked out the way he'd intended.

A call box at the top of Shepcote Road caught his eye and, regardless of the consequences, Donaldson veered towards it. Lloyd had virtually warned him off Linda Warwick, but he was tired of being kept in the dark. It seemed to him that she was the one person who might be willing to throw some light on the Magrane affair.

Magrane left the Audi at the only vacant parking meter on Breite Strasse near the opera house and walked round the corner into Garten gasse. As he'd suspected, van der Pohlmann had given him a false address, but the ruse hadn't worked because August Steiner was listed in the telephone directory. He could understand why the Dutchman should have substituted Glocken gasse for Garten gasse: when forced to lie in a hurry, nine out of ten people always plumped for a name beginning with the same initial letter and usually they had a similar hangup about numbers. In van der Pohlmann's case he'd simply switched the figures around so that eighty-seven became seventy-eight.

Eighty-seven Garten gasse was a three-story block of flats occupied by six tenants whose names were listed beside the appropriate buttons. Magrane frowned. The front door was electronically operated and he didn't like the microphone set in the panel inside the porch. It would allow August Steiner to check the identity of his visitor before tripping the switch.

Magrane glanced at the wristwatch he'd purchased from a jeweller's shop in the precinct at Troisdorf. British Airways flight 745 to London departed from Cologne at five minutes past five Central European Time and that meant he had just over two hours to make the hit and return the Audi to Rent-a-Budget-Car before heading back to the airport. There was one other complication: somewhere along the way he would have to ditch the Bernardelli .25 automatic. He looked up and down the street and, seeing no one about, pushed the button opposite Steiner's name. Several moments later a high-pitched voice grated through the speaker. The words were garbled, but he assumed Steiner wanted to know his name.

"Jan," said Magrane, "Jan van der Pohlmann."

"Bitte?"

"Van der Pohlmann," he repeated and added "schnell, schnell" for good measure while keeping his thumb on the button. After what seemed an eternity, there was a short buzz as the lawyer tripped the electronic switch and, pushing the swing door open, Magrane entered the lobby.

Steiner lived on the top floor and the architect who'd designed the building had evidently thought it unnecessary to provide for an elevator. There was only one way up and, turning right inside the entrance, he climbed the concrete staircase to the top.

The spy hole in the door to Steiner's apartment was another nasty surprise. Magrane could face the other way, but the lawyer was unlikely to release the security chain before he'd had a good look at him. Van der Pohlmann was roughly the same height and build, but there the similarity ended; the Dutchman had had a round, bearded face while his was angular and clean-shaven. His pulse beating faster than normal, Magrane reached into his hip pocket for the tiny automatic and then, having rung the bell, turned his back on the door.

The seconds dragged by, each one seeming more like a minute. Across the landing, he could just hear the noise from the television in the next apartment. And then a chain rattled behind him and he whirled round. The gap was less than six inches wide and only the left side of Steiner's face showed, but at point-blank range, the size of the target was irrelevant. Magrane put three bullets in a tight group above Steiner's left eye, then coolly emptied the rest of the magazine into him as he lay curled up on the floor. Pulling the door closed, he moved swiftly towards the staircase, the crepe soles of his suede shoes deadening the noise of his footsteps. Somewhere in the lawyer's apartment, a woman started screaming.

Magrane was torn between two conflicting desires. On the one hand, he wanted to get out of the building before her cries aroused the neighbors, while on the other, he knew that

if he took the steps four at a time, he could easily miss his
footing and end up with a broken leg. To his sensitive ears,
her shrill voice was still audible from the landing below, but
there was no reaction, either from the tenants on the second
floor or from the two apartments off the lobby.

Garten gasse on a Saturday afternoon was about as lively as
a cemetery and he felt naked, conspicuous and vulnerable.
The woman would almost certainly be calmer now and he
could picture her reaching for the telephone. A lot would
depend on how coherent she was, but he thought it would be
unwise to reckon on more than five minutes before the first
police car arrived on the scene. Five minutes. The Audi was
four hundred yards away and it would take almost that long to
walk to it. Although a loud inner voice kept reminding him
that he was capable of doing the four-hundred-meter sprint in
well under a minute, Magrane refused to panic. As he saw it,
a man walking along a deserted windswept street might or
might not be the object of passing interest, but one who was
running as if his life depended on it was bound to arouse
suspicion.

He turned the corner into Breite Strasse. With still a hundred yards to go, his palms were sweating and a nervous
twitch had developed in his right eye. How did that Ministry
of Transport slogan go? Walk, don't run? Sound advice, but
not so easy to follow when every nerve end was jagged.

Outwardly calm, Magrane unlocked the door, slid behind
the wheel of the Audi and started the engine. Pulling away
from the curb, he continued on down Breite Strasse as far
as Tunis Strasse where he turned right on to the expressway.
In that same instant, a police car passed him going in the
opposite direction towards Garten gasse and a few moments
later he heard the *blee-bah* of another siren in the distance.

The police had been quick off the mark and their intervention changed everything. He had planned to ditch the automatic
before leaving for the airport, but that was out of the question
now. Once the police started looking for eyewitnesses it was
in the cards that some householder might recall having seen
an Audi parked in Breite Strasse, round the corner from the
building. Getting rid of that car had to be his first priority and
it was fortunate that the Cologne branch of Rent-a-Budget-

Car in Eifel Weg was only a ten-minute drive from the expressway. In willing himself to remain calm, Magrane subconsciously tightened his grip on the steering wheel until the knuckles turned white.

Donaldson left the Underground station in Sloane Square and turned into the King's Road. There was an old saying that only fools rushed in where angels feared to tread and he wished now that he hadn't telephoned Linda Warwick and agreed to meet her for a drink in The Duke of York. Lloyd had been right; she was fishing for information and he would have to be very careful. One careless slip of the tongue could be enough to bring the roof down over his ears.

The saloon bar was crowded with Fulham supporters tanking up before the three thirty kickoff, but the lounge next door was practically deserted. Linda Warwick had found a corner table where they could talk in private and, judging by the number of cigarette stubs in the ashtray, it appeared she had arrived well ahead of him. Her face was half-turned towards the window and she seemed deep in thought, but as he approached the table, she immediately looked round and greeted him with a friendly smile.

"I hope I haven't kept you waiting too long?" Donaldson pointed to her empty glass. "Anyway, now that I'm here, let me get you another drink. What will you have?"

"You just stole my line, Robert. Remember Keebleloch? I gave you a rain check."

"I'm saving it for later."

"Later, huh?" She seemed faintly amused. "Well, in that case, I think I'd better stick to tomato juice."

Donaldson collected her glass and went over to the bar. He was tempted to have a whisky but ordered a Carlsberg instead, figuring that in the next half hour or so, he would need to have all his wits about him. Returning to the table with their drinks, he chose to sit opposite her. Sometimes it was possible to tell what a person was thinking from facial expressions, but not with Linda.

"They tell me you're on leave," she said casually.

"That's right."

"Have you run into Daniel yet? I hear he's also in town."

"Really? Where's he staying?"

"I thought you'd know." There was a small puddle of beer on the table and, dipping a finger into it, she traced a neat circle on the polished surface. "Tell you what, Robert, let's quite this stalling and get down to basics."

"Right. Let's talk about the article you sent me. Will it appear in the *Sunday Times* tomorrow?"

"No, the story is incomplete as it stands. I have a feeling that we haven't heard the last of Magrane yet. But I don't have to tell you that, do I?" She looked up, smiling quizzically. "Incidentally, would I be right in thinking you got in touch with me at Hugh Tamblin's suggestion?"

"No, it was entirely my own idea."

"You mean you didn't clear it with PR at the Ministry of Defence?" Linda shook her head. "Oh boy, have you stuck your neck out."

"I'm hoping we can come to a private arrangement," he said quietly.

Linda reared back, her eyes narrowing with suspicion. "Look, you're a nice guy, Robert," she said forcibly, "but I'm a reporter first, last and always. If you're hoping I'll suppress the story, you're in for a big disappointment." She picked up the tomato juice and downed it in one go. "Under the circumstances, I think it's best if we call a halt to this here and now."

"You're leaving?"

"That's the general idea."

Donaldson reached across the table and seized her wrist, gently but firmly. "You don't have to worry about me, I know what I'm doing." He smiled broadly. "At least, I hope I do."

For several moments she stared at him thoughtfully, her tongue making a small clucking noise against the roof of her mouth. Finally, with an almost imperceptible shrug, Linda sat down again. "Okay," she murmured, "but don't say I didn't warn you."

"Suppose we take that for granted and turn to Virginia Magrane? How would you like her address and telephone number?"

"What do you want in return?"

"Everything Klepacz ever told you and a promise not to submit the story until I give the word." Aware that she was about to explode, Donaldson held up a hand, urging her to remain silent and hear him out. "Look, I know what you're going to say, but all you've got at the moment is a short article. I can give you a book."

"A book?"

The cynical note in her voice lacked conviction and he knew Linda was interested. Although it would mean going out on a limb, he sensed the time had come to play his one and only trump card.

"Magrane is still alive," he said. "I have tapes to prove it."

The news left her speechless and she could only stare at him, her eyes growing wide.

"I'll give you a copy of them when I think the time is right. In the meantime, you'll have to be satisfied with Virginia's address and telephone number."

"Do I get it now?" she asked.

"Why not? One of us has to start the ball rolling."

Linda opened her handbag and took out a gold-colored pen and a small black notebook no larger than a pocket diary. After trying out the ballpoint on a beer mat, she looked up expectantly.

"The Magranes have a house in Harrow—26 Angel Crescent. You can reach Virginia on 427-3008." Donaldson lit two cigarettes and handed one to Linda. "Now it's your turn," he said.

"What would you do if I held out on you?"

"Nothing, but you would go down in my estimation."

"Well, don't get into a sweat, Robert. A bargain's a bargain."

There wasn't much Linda could tell him about Klepacz that he didn't already know, but the kind of treatment Magrane had been receiving was something else. If only half the allegations the Pole had made were true, Daniel had a lot to answer for. Apart from scopolamine and Pentothal, the psychiatrist had tried just about every known depressant on his patient. Judging by the number of Nembutal, Mandrax and Seconal pills that Magrane had been given, it would have been a miracle if he hadn't been stoned out of his mind.

"You know what I find curious?" said Linda. "The fact that none of these drugs were used on Sergeant Franklin."

Donaldson frowned. It seemed to him that sinister was a more appropriate word. Psychiatry was a closed book as far as he was concerned, but he found Bernard's methods highly questionable to say the least.

"I wanted to interview Franklin, but of course your Ministry of Defence refused to give me his home address. In fact, you could say they warned me off—in a polite sort of way."

He didn't like the sound of that either. There was any number of ways they could bring pressure to bear on Linda if they had a mind to. Revoking her work permit was only the mildest of them—and right now, he needed what she knew.

"Do you have a solicitor?" he asked abruptly.

"A lawyer? Yes." She looked at him long and hard. "Why do you want to know?"

"Because the way things are going, it might be a good idea if we established a neutral channel of communication."

"You think it's that bad?"

"I have a feeling that neither of us is going to be very popular with certain people," he said guardedly.

Linda opened her notebook again and scribbled down a name and a telephone number. Tearing out the page, she passed it across the table. "You can trust him, Robert," she said. "He's a good friend as well."

Donaldson folded the page in half and slipped it into his wallet. "One more thing," he warned. "Be very careful how you handle Virginia Magrane, otherwise you could find yourself in trouble with the police."

"Thanks, I'll bear that in mind. Now I'll give you a friendly tip. Watch out for Lloyd. I don't know what his job is, but I can tell you he's not with the Police Department of the Home Office."

The jigsaw puzzle was a long way from being complete, but Linda Warwick had just given him two of the missing pieces. The trouble was, he didn't know where they fitted into the picture.

Magrane read the flight information board carefully. So

far, everything was looking good. The departure time for British Airways flight 745 hadn't been altered and unless there was a last minute hitch, the passengers would be called forward at any moment. The plane ticket was inside his breast pocket and he'd already checked his suitcase in at the baggage counter. Leaving his seat in the main concourse, Magrane walked over to the men's room.

Two men standing well apart from one another were using the urinals. Both studiously ignored him, their eyes rooted to the front like guardsmen on parade. Entering one of the cubicles, Magrane bolted the door behind him. The lavatory tank was immediately above the pan, which meant that he didn't have to stand on the seat to reach it. Unfortunately, the bottom of the door was several inches above the tiled floor so that anybody on the outside would see that he was facing the wrong way. Turning about, he performed a simple trunk exercise, one that involved twisting the upper part of his body through a right angle. In that position he was able to raise the lid and lift it away from the tank. Holding the lid in one hand, he took the Bernardelli out of his hip pocket and hid it under the ball cock. That done, he waited two full minutes before replacing the cover. Ripping off several sheets of toilet paper, he then flushed the toilet and left the cubicle to rinse his hands and dry them off under the hot air blower.

With perfect timing he returned to the main concourse to hear that British Airways flight 745 was loading at gate three. The customs and immigration officer gave his passport a cursory examination and waved him through to the departure lounge. Twenty minutes later, the BAC 111 took off for London.

Magrane felt very pleased with himself. Phase two of Operation Damocles—the middleman—had been successfully completed and all he had to do now was report the fact to Donaldson. Leaning back, Magrane began turning phase three over in his mind.

12 . . .

MAGRANE had no problems at Heathrow. Joining the queue of British passport holders, he sailed through immigration and collected his suitcase from the slowly revolving baggage conveyor. Leaving the terminal building, he walked out into the rain and, hailing a cab from the rank nearby, told the taxi driver to take him to the Cumberland Hotel at Marble Arch. With close to six hundred and fifty pounds in his wallet and pockets, Magrane reckoned he could afford to be self-indulgent for once.

So far, the operation had gone like clockwork. There had been one bad moment in Cologne when it had seemed likely that Steiner's woman would rouse the whole neighborhood, but luck had been on his side and he'd gotten away with it. He remembered old Harry Gregson, his guide and mentor, once saying that no plan devised by man could ever be completely foolproof and that one should never discount the element of chance. Gregson had also been of the opinion that without adequate rest and recuperation, a field agent could easily become a liability instead of an asset.

A rest? Magrane frowned at the raindrops on the window. There was no telling what Donaldson would have to say about that, but considering what he'd been through in the past few days, he deserved a spot of leave. Unfortunately, February was a lousy month for a holiday in England. He considered the possibility of venturing again in search of the sun but soon rejected the idea; he would need to be readily available in case phase three of Operation Damocles had to be mounted in a hurry.

Phase three was the big one, the most demanding challenge of all. Steiner and the van der Pohlmanns had had no reason to suspect they were in danger, but after Amsterdam and Cologne, the supplier would know that he was the next target. One thing was certain: getting close enough to be sure of a first round hit would be twice as difficult now. He told himself that there was no point in worrying about it, that things had a habit of working out all right in the end. Problems which at first appeared insurmountable often dwindled to mere molehills on closer examination.

One step at a time: that had been Harry Gregson's motto and it was sound advice. He would check in at the Cumberland Hotel, contact Donaldson after dinner and then recover the Wesson .357 Magnum revolver from the demolition site in Kentish Town. Magrane leaned back in the seat and closed his eyes, satisfied that he had made a wise decision.

Donaldson contemplated the triple-decker sandwich he'd just made and decided they would have to do something about their domestic arrangements. They couldn't go on pigging it like this, living off snacks and eating out of cans day after day. There were a number of good restaurants in the neighborhood and it was only a question of getting themselves properly organized. Lloyd wanted the telephone manned round the clock, but they could get round that by taking turns dining out.

He wondered if he should broach the subject to Daniel now or wait until he was in a happier frame of mind. The psychiatrist had been in a funny mood ever since Donaldson had returned shortly after three o'clock and they'd hardly exchanged more than a dozen words in the last five hours. Had Daniel guessed that he'd met Linda Warwick after leaving the Magranes' house in Harrow? If Bernard had telephoned Virginia, he would know that he'd left before midday and, remembering the article Lloyd had passed on to him that morning, it wouldn't be difficult for Daniel to put two and two together. Alternatively, he could be worried that Virginia Magrane had said too much, especially about the kind of psychiatric treatment Andrew had been receiving. Whatever the reason, he found Daniel a changed man.

Donaldson opened the serving hatch and peered into the living room. Bernard hadn't moved; he was still sprawled on the couch, staring at the television screen as if in a hypnotic trance. The inevitable filter tip was burning away between the fingers of his left hand and four empty beer cans stood on the low coffee table next to an ashtray full to the brim with cigarette stubs.

"Do you feel like a cup of coffee?" he asked. "The kettle is boiling."

The olive branch met with little response. Without bothering to look round, Daniel raised one arm and gave him a thumbs down sign like a Roman emperor at the Coliseum. There was no approving roar from the crowd, only a shrill summons from the telephone. Still clutching the sandwich, Donaldson hurried into the living room to answer it.

Magrane said, "Hullo there, Robert, it's me again, the bad old penny. I bet you'd almost given me up for lost?"

He sounded exuberant and bubbling over with good humor, like some happy drunk who'd already downed one bottle of champagne and was about to start on another. It almost seemed a shame to bring him down to earth again.

"Where the hell have you been?" Donaldson snapped. "I haven't had a peep out of you in nineteen hours. What kind of operation do you think we're running?"

"You can't talk to me like that," Magrane protested. "You've no reason to sound off."

"I've got every reason and every right. I'm your control. Remember?"

"So what—you're not God Almighty."

"I never said I was. I'm just like you, Andrew, one very small cog in a very large machine, but I doubt if you care about my problems." Donaldson raised his voice in mock indignation. "I mean, you field agents are all the same, you think everything's happening at the sharp end and that life on the staff is one bed of roses.''

"My heart bleeds for you," said Magrane.

"Listen, if you think you're hard off, you should be in my shoes. I've got an army breathing down my neck. Practically every government department in Whitehall is anxious to know how the operation is progressing.''

"Well, you can tell them it's going along just fine, Robert, because phase two has been completed.''

"It has?''

"I've put the middleman out of business. You couldn't ask for more than that, could you?''

Without actually saying so, Magrane had made it pretty clear that he expected to be congratulated. Andrew obviously liked being praised; in grade school he'd probably collected more gold stars in his exercise book than any other kid in the class.

"It's like the post office job, isn't it?'' said Donaldson, pretending to be thoroughly bored with the whole business.

"What do you mean?''

"Do I have to spell it out for you, Andrew? The success of your mission is unconfirmed. There's no proof. I've only got your word for it.''

"What did you expect?'' Magrane shouted back. "Should I have dumped their sodding bodies on your doorstep?''

The blips cut in and he caught the tail end of a string of four letter words as Magrane fed another two coins into the box and jabbed the button.

"Christ, you're a difficult man to please, Robert.''

"It's not my fault,'' Donaldson said in a soothing voice. "It's the people up top who are being difficult. They say nothing happened last night, not in London, Glasgow, Liverpool or anywhere else in the country.''

"They want to look farther afield then.''

"In Ireland?''

Magrane snorted in disgust. "Shit,'' he said, "that's the last place on earth I'd choose to go.''

Donaldson took a bite out of the sandwich and chewed it slowly. Was it possible he'd been to Europe and back? Lloyd had led him to believe that Magrane didn't have a passport, but it wouldn't be the first time the Home Office had got their facts wrong.

"How was it on the Continent?" he asked.

"Cold and miserable."

"Where was this, Andrew?"

"How many more times do I have to remind you about security? Jesus Christ, Robert, you're worse than a woman when it comes to gossiping."

"Look, the politicians are beginning to wet themselves. They need to be reassured that everything is going according to plan and I'm afraid your word isn't good enough for them. They want proof. Now, what's wrong with using veiled speech, or is that beyond you?"

There was a long pause and he could hear Magrane drumming his fingers on the coin box as he thought it over.

"Tulips and toilet water," Andrew said finally. "They go together."

Tulips and toilet water. The first part was easy. Holland. But toilet water? Donaldson frowned: did he mean France? No, that couldn't be right—Andrew would have made some reference to either perfume or wine. The phrase "they go together" suggested a neighboring country like Belgium or Germany. Germany—eau de cologne—that had to be it. Magrane had visited Cologne.

"Are you there, Robert?"

"Yes. I was just working out the answer to your conundrum. It's very clever."

"You think so?"

Magrane sounded pleased. There was something about Andrew that reminded him of a friendly puppy who wanted a pat on the back. The only trouble was, he was playing with a rabid dog.

"You've done a great job, Andrew."

"Well, thanks, Robert. It's always nice to know that your work is appreciated." Magrane cleared his throat, apparently embarrassed. "Provided you've no objections, I'd like to take a few days off before we start on phase three."

"You take all the rest you want and have yourself a good time because you certainly deserve it, Andrew. By the way, how are you off for money?"

"I'm sitting on a bankroll. You know those invisible earnings the Board of Trade is always talking about? Well, I've just given the February balance of payments a boost."

It was obvious Magrane wasn't shooting him a line. He had stolen twenty-nine fifty from a house in Balmedie and would have raised another hundred and fifty pounds on Virginia's dress ring when he'd hocked it, but most of that would have been gone by now. Somewhere along the way, either in Holland or Cologne, he'd managed to lay his hands on a lot of money, and that was bad news. Had Andrew been short of cash it might have been possible to arrange a meeting, but as it was, he could please himself about when to get in touch again.

"Before you go," Donaldson said casually, "I think you ought to know that we are running into a lot of flak over phase three. Operation Damocles isn't exactly popular with one or two people."

"Like who, for instance?"

The question almost floored him until he remembered the letter Magrane had written to Virginia while he was in Oman. "Your doppelgänger for one," he said coolly.

A sharp intake of breath told him his long shot had hit the bull's-eye dead center. Seconds later came the explosion, a barrage of hysterical questions punctuated by every known four-letter word in the English language. Magrane paused for breath only when he was obliged to feed two more coins into the box.

"I don't know how or why your doppelgänger is involved," Donaldson told him quietly, "but take it from me, he appears to have a lot of influence in Whitehall."

"The bastard always did."

"Yes, well, you obviously knew him far better than I do, Andrew. That's why I need your help and advice. Between us, we've got to find some way to stop him, otherwise he'll throw a monkey wrench in the works."

The words were barely out of his mouth before Donaldson realized the enormity of what he'd just said. In Magrane's twilight world, stop had a wider definition than that given in the Oxford Dictionary. Unless he put it right, Andrew would seek out the unknown doppelgänger and pump a bullet into his head.

"If we can get together, I'm sure we can lick this problem. If necessary, we can take it to the Foreign Secretary—he's sure to overrule him if we present a good case."

"Maybe."

"There's no maybe about it, we've got to discuss tactics."

"You want to meet me face to face, Robert. Is that the general idea?"

"Yes."

"Okay, I'll think about it and then get back to you. I can't say better than that, can I?"

The question went unanswered. Magrane had hung up.

Daniel continued to stare at the television screen, apparently engrossed even though the volume was turned down so low only a lip reader could have understood the dialogue.

"For what it's worth," he said presently, "you handled Magrane very well."

"You think so?" Donaldson finished rewinding the tape and dialled Ryan's department. "I've got a feeling that I may have frightened him off."

"No, he'll come back for more because you've got him on the hook. He'll agree to a meeting, you mark my words."

A voice in Donaldson's ear said, "7893," and then added, "Norris here, what can I do for you?"

"I have another tape for Commander Ryan."

"From our mutual friend?"

"Who else?"

"All right," said Norris, "I'm ready this end. Let's hear what he's got to say."

Donaldson set the tape in motion, hooked the receiver into the amplifier again and went into the kitchen. Lacking an automatic cutoff, the electric kettle had boiled dry and he unplugged it, switching on the fan to disperse the clouds of steam. Returning to the living room, he had plenty of time to finish the sandwich before the recording came to an end.

After a long silence, Norris said, "What's the significance of tulips and toilet water?"

"It's an oblique reference to Holland and Cologne."

"Do you think he's bluffing?"

"We should be so lucky."

"I see." Norris clucked his tongue. "In that case, I'd better make a few discreet enquiries."

The demolition site in Kentish Town was not unlike some of the streets Magrane had seen in Belfast. The derelict houses were all boarded up and the roads were largely overgrown with weeds and tufts of grass that had taken root in the cracks. The graffiti however was different: "Niggers go home" instead of "Up the IRA," or "No popery here" if the site happened to be on the fringe of a Protestant area.

Inkerman Drive was cloaked in darkness, but Magrane could see a flicker of light beyond the two bulldozers parked on the strip of wasteland near the junction with Sebastopol Gardens, where part of a row of terraced houses had already been demolished. The winos were obviously warming themselves over a fire they'd lit in one of the condemned buildings in Balaclava Road, not far from where he had concealed the Wesson .357 magnum. He wondered if they were the same group of alcoholics he'd seen two nights ago on another lot. Either way, he hoped this wouldn't be the night when some busybody of a social worker or the police took it into their heads to rescue them.

Leaving the bulldozer on his left, Magrane moved across the wasteland towards Balaclava Road. One of the alcoholics, his voice cracked and out of key, was singing a mournful, unrecognizable ballad. His companions started to whine in protest and there was a loud clatter as somebody heaved a brick at him and the song ended abruptly on a high-pitched scream. The babble of voices gradually subsided until they were no more than an unintelligible murmur. Breaking into a house five doors away from the group of vagrants, he climbed the wooden staircase and entered the small bedroom overlooking the back garden.

Magrane felt a shiver run down his spine, and in that same instant there was a sudden flurry of movement in the far corner of the room near the window. Although the light was poor, the rat was close enough for him to see it clearly as it scuttled across the floor in front of his feet to disappear into a large hole in the skirting board. His flesh still crawling,

Magrane walked over to the fireplace and crouched down by the grate. Taking a penknife from his pocket, he inserted the blade between the loose tiles in the hearth and removed them one by one. That done, he reached into the cavity and recovered the brown paper bag containing the revolver, two shoulder holsters and six spare rounds of .357 ammunition in a small cardboard box.

Using a handkerchief, he removed the protective film of oil from the working parts of the Wesson. The smaller of the two shoulder holsters had belonged to the Bernardelli automatic and since it was no longer of any use to him, he put it back inside the hole along with the paper bag before replacing the tiles. Satisfied that it was unlikely to be discovered until the house was finally demolished, Magrane stood up, removed his raincoat and jacket and hung them both on a hook behind the door.

More than two years had gone by since he'd last worn the shoulder holster, but it was still a perfect fit. Designed to his own specifications, the harness consisted of two leather armholes linked together at the back by a thin, adjustable leather strap. Even if a mirror had been available, he wouldn't have had to check his appearance; the Wesson revolver was compact enough to produce no telltale bulge in his jacket.

Magrane reached for his raincoat and then suddenly froze. What the hell was the matter with him? Donaldson had said his doppelgänger was about to throw a wrench into the works, but he had been too stupid to realize all the implications until now. With the resources of the Secret Intelligence Service behind him, Lloyd would have arranged for Donaldson to be kept under surveillance and, knowing his doppelgänger of old, he would certainly have put a wiretap on the flat in Devonshire Terrace.

A nervous twitch developed in his right eye, something that invariably happened when the tension mounted. The wiretap meant that Lloyd had a transcript of every conversation he'd had with Donaldson, but how disastrous was that? He had been very careful not to say too much on the telephone. Donaldson was always fishing for information because Whitehall had obviously told him to make sure he kept a tight grip on the operation. Fortunately, he had never disclosed his future plans to Donaldson. Or had he? The bankroll: he had talked about that and made some flip remark about the February balance of payments. Lloyd had a complete dossier on him and knew that he liked to stay in the best hotels whenever money permitted. No matter how many man-hours it might take, Lloyd would order his people to check out every first-class hotel in London.

Magrane scowled; he could say good-bye to the Cumberland Hotel right now. Obviously he would have to move on, but where to? Another hotel in London—some flea hole like the Coronet in the Euston Road where he'd spent Thursday night? No, even a place like the Coronet would think it odd if he arrived without any luggage. There was no point in turning to Virginia either. For one thing, she was unlikely to lift a finger to help him and for another, Lloyd would have told the spooks to keep an eye on her. What about Molly Gregson then? Harry's wife had always been a bit of a rebel, and after the way Molly had been treated by the Army and the Ministry of Pensions, she had every reason to hate the Establishment.

Molly Gregson would take him in. She farmed a small place near Wrotham in Kent and offhand he couldn't think of a better hiding place. It wasn't ten o'clock yet, so there was bound to be another train to Wrotham from Victoria. One problem had been solved, but others remained. Somehow he would have to figure out a way to warn Donaldson that he was being watched. It was unfortunate that Robert was such a sceptic that he'd probably refuse to believe it unless he was presented with overwhelming proof. Maybe he ought to back off and let phase three go by the board? And hand everything to Lloyd on a platter? Like shit. There had been enough betrayals. Besides, he was depending on Donaldson to resurrect him after the job had been completed.

Magrane slipped his arms into the raincoat, collected the small cardboard box of ammunition and left the house. It was still drizzling with rain and the drinkers sounded rowdier than ever.

13 . . .

A DOUBLE tap on the door roused Magrane from a light sleep and, reacting instinctively, he reached under the pillow, the fingers of his right hand closing round the butt and trigger of the Wesson. The room looked unfamiliar, but then a voice he recognized called to him softly and he relaxed. Withdrawing his hand, he sat up in bed and told Molly Gregson to come in.

"Good morning, Andrew," she said quietly. "Did you sleep well?"

"Like a top." Magrane yawned and hastily cupped a hand over his mouth. "What time is it, Molly?"

"Eight o'clock." She left a cup of tea on the bedside table and moved over to the window to draw the curtains back. "How are you feeling now?"

What on earth did she mean by that? Molly, of all people, ought to know that an SAS man had to be one hundred percent fit in mind and body. He was just a bit tired, that was all.

"Rested," he said. He stared at her back, his eyes narrowing. "I'm not ill, Molly."

"I didn't say you were." She turned round, a hesitant smile on her lips. "But you're not well, are you, Andrew? I mean, you look very rundown to me."

"I've been under a strain," he said carefully. "Surely you can understand that? There must have been times when Harry seemed on edge."

"I didn't see all that much of Harry, he was too busy playing soldiers."

The bitterness was understandable. Magrane had always been puzzled about why Harry had rarely bothered to go on leave when he'd had the opportunity to do so. Even now, somewhere in her early forties, Molly was a very desirable woman.

"I'm not playing at soldiers," he told her. "This is for real."

"Is it?" She moved away from the window. "I wish I could believe that."

"I wouldn't lie to you." Magrane reached out for her and drew Molly towards him. After some hesitation, she sat down on the edge of his bed. "Look, you know I've got to phone Donaldson. If it will set your mind at rest, I'll ask him to have a few words with you. He'll confirm my story."

"You think he will?"

"No, on second thought, perhaps he wouldn't. He's so damn cautious. It would be just like Robert to clam up at the wrong moment." Magrane pushed a hand through his tousled hair. "What can I say to convince you? Officially I am dead, yet here I am in the flesh and despite everything that's happened, the police aren't looking for me. Now surely that ought to mean something?"

"I don't know what to make of it." She looked down at her hands which were clasped loosely together in her lap. "I'm out of my depth, Andrew. I thought people like Lloyd only existed between the pages of a book."

"Harry could have told you different."

"He never talked to me about the SAS or what he did."

"Well, take it from me, he knew what it was like to be dropped in the mire. In our job, it's not only the enemy you have to watch out for; you need to keep looking over your shoulder at the politicians because they're liable to put a knife in your back. I should know, it happened to me in Ireland."

"When was this?"

"Getting on four years ago. In August, 1974."

Choosing his words carefully, Magrane told her about his work with the Special Patrol Force in Belfast. How he had become a bread deliveryman and had eventually succeeded in passing himself as an IRA sympathizer. Told her, too, of the subtle ways the opposition had put him to the test by feeding him false information to see if he was an informer. Of the errands he'd run for the IRA after they had finally accepted him and of the months it had taken him to get close to Sean Loomis, the commander of the Lower Falls battalion. He also tried to explain the anger and frustration he'd felt when his control officer had failed to act on the intelligence data he'd supplied.

"I couldn't understand it," said Magrane. "I was risking my neck to get information out and they just ignored it. That's why I asked for a meeting, I had to find out what the hell was going on. You know what my control officer said? He said there was a real chance of a political settlement and the Army had been ordered to keep a low profile. Two minutes later, the IRA opened up and chopped the poor bastard to pieces. So much for the low profile and the peace negotiations."

"I don't see how Lloyd was involved."

"He was running the Political Intelligence Department."

"And then three years later, he turned up in Oman." Molly raised an inquisitive eyebrow. "Isn't that what you told me last night?"

"Yes."

"Bit of a coincidence, wasn't it, Andrew?"

"Not really, he's one of the best hatchet men in the business. I think he enjoyed telling me that the Cabinet had decided not to go ahead with the operation." Magrane reached for her hand again. "It's a crazy world, isn't it, Molly? I mean, you like Qaddafi. He's done more to encourage terrorism than anyone else you can name, yet when we had the means and the opportunity to give him a dose of his own medicine they suddenly changed their minds and said no."

Magrane scowled. The means and the opportunity had been there all right. Intelligence had known that after making his secret pilgrimage to Mecca, Qaddafi had intended to return home via South Yemen in order to meet the leaders of the

Omani Liberation Army at Mukala, just across the border from the Dhufar province of Oman. Mukala was six thousand feet above sea level and while a night para drop would have been hazardous, at least there would have been no radar defenses to contend with, and after the mission had been completed, they had planned to lie up in the mountains until it was safe for the Puma helicopter to pick up the five-man assault team. And it wasn't just fortuitous that the scientists had decided to hold their field trial in Oman, for without being aware of it, they had been carefully steered in that direction. The presence of the SAS troop in the Dhufar province was the culmination of an elaborate cover plan engineered by the Ministry of Defence.

"Does Virginia know that you're still alive?"

The question caught him on the hop and he thought about it carefully before replying.

"Not officially, but she may have guessed. I went to the house while she was out." Magrane shrugged his shoulders. "Anyway, I doubt if Virginia cares all that much. Our marriage fell apart at the seams while I was in Northern Ireland."

"Poor Andrew." Molly gave his hand an affectionate squeeze and smiled at him sympathetically. "You've really been through the mill, haven't you?"

"No more than you have. Things must have been pretty rough for you since Harry was killed. I don't suppose the Ministry of Pensions were exactly generous, and as Harry wasn't a regular officer, you wouldn't have got much from the Army."

"I manage."

Magrane could see that he had offended her. Molly was a proud woman and she would never admit to being hard up. Harry should have seen to it that she was provided for, but he'd never given a thought for tomorrow.

"Harry was very fond of you, Molly."

"Was he?" she said distantly. "Well, he certainly had a funny way of showing it."

Harry had never really given a damn about her, but Magrane thought it prudent to have Molly believe otherwise. She was aware that he and Harry had been close friends and there was such a thing as guilt by association.

"He was always talking about you, Molly."

"You're very sweet, Andrew." Impulsively, she leaned forward and kissed him on the mouth. "Now drink your tea before it gets cold." She squeezed his hand again and made to get up. "Breakfast in twenty minutes—all right?"

"Fine." Magrane held on to her hand. "You don't mind me staying here for a few days, do you, Molly?"

"No, of course not."

"I promise I won't be any trouble."

"You're welcome to stay as long as you like, Andrew."

He searched her face to see if she meant it and whether he could trust her. What was it Harry had said? Women, they're all the same under the skin; butter them up, give them a bit of what they fancy and you'll have them eating out of your hand. Molly was a good-looking woman, a little on the thin side, but definitely bedworthy; he had Harry's word for that. He drew her close and kissed her in a way no one had for years. Her eyes grew wider and presently her lips parted, and she was neither coy nor resistant when he began to unbutton her dressing gown and ease it off her shoulders.

"Your tea . . .," she murmured.

"It can wait," he said.

Magrane threw the blankets aside and she got into bed beside him, and then he knew that Molly would never betray him to Lloyd. He still had to warn Donaldson, but there was plenty of time for that.

Tamblin was the first to arrive. After paying off the taxi, he walked up and down the pavement outside the flat as if on sentry at Buckingham Palace. Some ten minutes later, a black Rover 3500 drew up at the curb and he left his self-appointed beat to greet Lloyd and Ryan as they got out of the car. After a brief discussion, with Lloyd doing most of the talking, they formed up in single file and trooped inside. By the time they had climbed their way up the spiral staircase to the second landing, Donaldson was at the door to meet them.

Ryan and Lloyd appeared to be empty-handed, but Tamblin was carrying a government-issue briefcase which Donaldson had come to regard as his badge of office; offhand, he couldn't remember having seen the PR man without it. There was the usual chitchat as they filed into the living room. Ryan made some remark about the weather not being too bad for the time of year; Lloyd said he could think of many more pleasant ways to spend a Sunday morning; and Tamblin observed that he'd had to forego his customary round of golf.

"I don't see Major Daniel anywhere." Lloyd sat down in an armchair, giving his trousers a hitch so as not to bag them at the knees. "Where's he got to?"

"He's gone out for a breath of fresh air in the park," Donaldson said casually.

"What a good idea. I assume Bernard holds the fort whenever you go out for a walk?"

The smile was bland enough, but the observation seemed barbed, as though Lloyd were letting it be known that he'd heard about his visit to Virginia Magrane.

"There's nothing wrong with that, is there? Bernard doesn't answer the phone while I'm out, and that's good tactics. I don't want Magrane to get the impression that I'm always at his beck and call."

Lloyd nodded. "Anyway, Robert, it seems events have proved you right."

"What?"

"About Magrane," said Lloyd. "Between midnight on Friday and three thirty yesterday afternoon, two people were murdered in Amsterdam and a third in Cologne. All three were shot at close range with a two-five caliber pistol and from what Magrane said on the telephone, we can assume he was responsible."

"Who were the victims?"

"Jan and Beatrix van der Pohlmann and August Steiner. The van der Pohlmanns ran an establishment called the Erotica which offers live sex shows. They were Marxist revolutionaries, unpleasant people, but scarcely dangerous. The proceeds from the Erotica enabled them to publish an inflammatory political broadsheet. Steiner, on the other hand, was a lawyer. He defended Gertrud Zeishoffer, a member of the Baader-Meinhof group charged with armed robbery in 1971. Later that same year and during the early part of 1972, he was frequently seen in Beirut where he is known to have met George Habbash of the Black September Movement on several occasions. According to the Dutch authorities, Steiner is believed to have been the motivating force behind the student unrest at the University of Amsterdam in 1972, and until December of 1976, it appears he was in the habit of visiting the city about once a month. Steiner specializes in international law and for a time was one of the legal advisers retained by the South Moluccan Independence Movement. The van der Pohlmanns were also supporters of the South Moluccans which is probably how he came to make their acquaintance. They in turn introduced him to Terrence O'Neill and Mauveen Kavanaugh when the IRA sent them to Amsterdam in 1972 to buy arms.''

"Would Magrane know all this?'' Donaldson asked.

Lloyd glanced at Tamblin who immediately opened his briefcase and produced a slim folder. After skimming through the contents, he looked up with a suitably grave expression on his face.

"O'Neill and Kavanaugh were known to Army Intelligence. As a result of a tip-off received from Dublin, two SAS officers followed them to Amsterdam. One was Magrane.''

Donaldson waited, expecting more, but within a few moments it became apparent that was the sum total of Tamblin's information.

"What else is in the file?''

"A few personal details about his background, the various appointments he's held—stuff like that.'' Tamblin leaned forward and passed the folder to him. "We thought it might be of some help to you.''

The profile was brief and consisted of two pages of double-spaced typescript with wide margins. Apart from Magrane's date of birth, religious denomination and next of kin, it contained a résumé of his record of service which Tamblin must have gotten from the appropriate branch of the Adjutant General's Department. Although the material told him a bit more about the man, it was scarcely illuminating, and it was quite evident that the more sensitive details of his military career had been deliberately omitted. Their reluctance to part with any kind of hard information about Magrane was proof that they were still determined to keep him in the dark as much as possible.

"If Magrane didn't have a passport," Donaldson said guilelessly, "how was he able to leave the country?"

There was a heavy silence. Tamblin turned a delicate shade of pink and hooked a finger inside his shirt collar as if it had suddenly become very tight.

"Well, Hugh?" prompted Lloyd.

"I'm afraid there was a slip-up." Tamblin cleared his throat noisily. "Magrane was issued with a duplicate in the name of Alec Murdoch when he went to Israel in 1970 to liaise with their Shin-Beth department. The passport was withdrawn on his return by the unit operations officer who held it in his safe in case it was needed again at a later date. As you'll see from his record of service, Magrane was eventually appointed to the post of assistant operations officer, in which capacity he had access to the safe. At our request, the SAS checked their records last night and it was discovered that he'd removed it and forged an entry in the register of confidential documents purporting to show that the passport had been destroyed. Apparently, this was done just before he was posted to Northern Ireland for the second time."

"That was when he became an undercover agent?"

"Yes."

Donaldson glanced at the folder again. Magrane had been a natural for the job. He was of Irish descent and an experienced intelligence officer, but he couldn't help wondering if Andrew had been pressured into volunteering. If that was the case, he might have stolen the passport as a form of insurance.

"Of course," said Lloyd, "it's a pity none of this came to light before, but these minor slip-ups do occur even in the most efficient organizations."

Despite the protestation, his tone implied otherwise and Donaldson sensed he was thoroughly displeased with Tamblin and everyone else at the Ministry of Defence.

"The immigration people have now been warned to look out for that particular passport, but we're really counting on you, Robert, to flush Magrane out of cover."

"We've no idea who the supplier might be?"

"None whatever. Apart from the fact that the van der Pohlmanns and August Steiner were thoroughly odious people, Intelligence didn't regard them as a threat. In short, there is no third link to the chain that we know of. In fact, it's my belief Magrane will pick up a newspaper one morning and the name of the next victim will simply leap at him from one of the pages. Fortunately, it looks as though he will agree to meet you face to face.''

"And when he does,'' said Ryan, "we'll be there to grab him." Ryan produced a small, oblong-shaped box from his jacket pocket and unwound the length of cord that was looped around the base. "This little gadget consists of a throat mike and a battery-powered transmitter with a maximum range of half a mile in a built-up area. Magrane is certain to run a number of checks to satisfy himself that you're not being followed. He'll probably send you from one public call box to another, but it won't do him any good because you'll be wearing the transmitter next to your skin and we'll hear every word you say to him on the telephone. That way we can keep you under surveillance without making it appear obvious."

"But it won't pick up what he says to me?"

"Unfortunately . . . no. The budget, I'm afraid."

Donaldson picked up the transmitter and weighed it thoughtfully in his hand. The Armed Services and the Police were always the last in line with the begging bowl and, like the Army, it seemed that Special Branch had to make do with second best whenever money was tight. The equipment which Ryan had produced was out of date, which meant that he would have to repeat everything Magrane said if they wanted both sides of the telephone conversation. However, this was only a small point compared to certain other details which Ryan omitted to mention. "Haven't you forgotten something?"

"I don't think so."

"Who are you trying to kid? Magrane has a gun, so naturally your people will be armed. Now that's only sensible, but how do you intend to play it?"

"We won't make a move until you part company," said Ryan. "You have my word on that."

"You won't be in any danger," Lloyd chipped in smoothly.

The glib assurance angered him. Whether or not it was intentional, Lloyd had made it appear he was primarily concerned for his own safety.

"I'm worried about the innocent bystanders," Donaldson snapped. "I don't want a shoot-out."

"That rather depends on Magrane, doesn't it?"

"Given time, I think I can persuade Andrew to give himself up. I mean, that's what we all want, isn't it? Or do you have something else in mind?"

"Like what, Robert?"

"Well, I have a nasty feeling that certain people in high places wouldn't shed any tears if he finished up in the mortuary."

"Perhaps you'd care to enlarge upon that allegation?"

It was an invitation to put his head on the chopping block, but he was tired of being manipulated like a puppet and he wanted Lloyd to know that the shit would hit the fan if Magrane was killed.

"The SAS is a very sensitive organization and I'm willing to bet the Government would be more than a little embarrassed if some of their contingency plans came to light. As the Assistant Operations Officer, Andrew would have had access to those documents."

"Andrew," mused Lloyd. "You're on a first name basis, are you?"

"You know we are."

"Well, mind you don't become too sympathetic towards him. After all, he has killed five people."

"I'm not likely to forget that."

"Good." Lloyd waved a hand, embracing Ryan and Tamblin. "Are there any other points you'd like to raise with us before we go?"

The question seemed innocent enough, but he smelled a trap. Lloyd's hand was still pointing at Tamblin as if he knew exactly what was passing through his mind. It was the old Catch-22 situation. To ignore the bait, to walk away from the trap, would be equally damning.

"Has the press gotten wind of this story yet?"

"You mean the British press?" said Lloyd.

"Yes."

"Is there any reason why they should?"

Lloyd was fencing with him, trying to make him drop his

guard in the hope that he would blurt out the fact that he'd been to see Linda Warwick.

"Has there been a follow-up on that article I gave you?" Donaldson asked ingenuously.

"Not as far as I know. What about it, Hugh?"

"Miss Warwick hasn't been in touch with me," said Tamblin.

"She will. Linda Warwick strikes me as being a very determined young woman. If she thinks we're trying to hide something, I'm the one who's likely to end up with egg on his face."

"I wouldn't worry your head about that, Robert," Lloyd said coldly. "We can take care of Linda Warwick."

Long after they had gone, Lloyd's parting words kept hammering at him. Donaldson wasn't sure what Lloyd had meant by taking care of Linda Warwick, but the phrase sounded ominous. Although they had arranged a neutral channel of communication through her solicitor, he thought it best to get in touch with Linda direct.

Disconnecting the tape recorder, Donaldson dialled Linda's home number and arranged to meet her in Kensington Gardens by the Round Pond at eleven o'clock, figuring that Daniel should be back before then.

14 . . .

THE number had been ringing for a good three minutes, but Magrane continued to hang on, hoping that Donaldson would answer. He told himself it was unreasonable to expect Robert to live by the telephone, but even so a nagging doubt remained. No matter how hard he tried, it was difficult to ignore the possibility that, thanks to Lloyd, Donaldson had backed off and left him in the lurch. Slowly and reluctantly, he replaced the receiver and walked into the kitchen, determined to put a brave face on it because he didn't want Molly to see that he was worried.

The kitchen seemed to be in a turmoil. Some of the breakfast things were still on the table, the sink was full of pots and pans, a saucepan was boiling over on the gas stove, but Molly, up to her elbows in flour, didn't seem in the least bit ruffled.

"Can I lend you a hand?" Magrane pointed to the sink. "I'm no cook, but I could do the washing up."

"It's sweet of you to offer, Andrew, but everything's under control, really it is." Molly flashed him a grateful smile, picked up a knife and deftly trimmed the pastry on the apple pie. "I could do with a drink, though. If you go into the dining room, you'll find a bottle of sherry in the sideboard."

"Right."

"And have one yourself," she called after him. "I think there's some gin left over from Christmas."

The drinks cupboard was pretty bare and he made a note to do something about it. Molly would refuse to take any money, but this would be a tactful way of repaying her hospitality. Finding a couple of glasses, Magrane poured Molly a generous measure of cream sherry and then fixed himself a gin and tonic.

"You were quick," she said when he returned to the kitchen. "You'd make a good barman."

"There's a thought," Magrane raised his glass and winked. "Do you know any publicans round here who might need one?"

"What's the matter, Andrew?" she asked softly. "Didn't you have any luck with your phone call?"

He froze, the glass touching his lips. Molly didn't have Virginia's education, but she was much more perceptive. Virginia would never have guessed that he was worried.

"No, there was no answer."

"I expect Robert has gone for a walk. I daresay he needed a breath of fresh air."

Magrane could have hugged her for joy. Why hadn't he thought of that? Of course Robert would need to stretch his legs—he'd been cooped up there for the past three days.

"I thought I might try again after lunch," he said brightly.

"That's a good idea."

Molly opened the oven and placed the apple pie on the top shelf. She was wearing a short skirt that had long since gone out of fashion and he found himself staring at her legs. Virginia had a better figure, but Molly was warm and loving, not frigid like her. Frigid? Well, that was true as far as he was concerned, but it was probably a different story with lover boy, the gym teacher with the droopy moustache.

"Lunch won't be ready for another hour yet." Molly closed the oven door and straightened up. "So why don't you take your drink into the living room and put your feet up? The *Sunday Express* is on the hall table if you want something to read."

"Are you sure I can't help?"

"Well, I suppose you could lay the table, but there's really no hurry."

Magrane nodded. That was another thing he liked about Molly; unlike Virginia, she didn't want to organize him. "I'll leave you in peace then," he said. "Just sing out when you need me."

"I'll do that," she promised.

The Sunday papers were usually a rehash of the week's news, except for the sporting pages. He noticed that Nottingham Forest was still on top of the First Division, a position they had held since October despite the forecasts of all the pundits. He turned to the front page, scanned the headlines and was about to lay the paper aside when a paragraph halfway down the lefthand column caught his eye.

The crease mark where the newspaper had been folded in half ran straight through the name, but even so it leaped at him from the page and Magrane found it difficult to contain his excitement. Although it would mean a change of plan, he was quite sure Donaldson wouldn't raise any objections. Qaddafi might be the supplier, but compared with this man, he was a nobody. Qaddafi was difficult to reach, but this target was in London, and that was the biggest bonus of all. Lloyd was the one fly in the ointment as far as he could see. It wasn't enough to warn Donaldson about him. One way or the other, Lloyd would have to be neutralized.

Although no two women could have been less alike, Linda Warwick did remind Donaldson of his wife Janet in one respect. Janet had never been one for arriving anywhere on time. His first present to her after they had gotten engaged had been a gold Omega, but the subtle hint hadn't made any difference. As far as she had been concerned, the wristwatch was merely another piece of jewellery. By the time he had completed a third lap of the Round Pond, however, Donaldson was convinced that Linda was in a class of her own.

Tired of walking aimlessly about, he moved to a bench and sat down, wishing to God he'd suggested a different rendezvous. Kensington Gardens: that's what came of seeing too many spy films where two debonair gentlemen in raglan overcoats with bowler hats and furled umbrellas were always meeting one another in some London park to discuss what they ought to do about the poor bloody idiot they'd landed in the shit. Not that he'd had much choice; apart from the art galleries, everywhere else was closed, being Sunday. If God had made the world in six days, it was no wonder he had rested on the seventh; there was probably bloody little else for him to do.

He glanced again at his wristwatch, saw that she was now half an hour late, and decided to make one more lap of the pond before calling it a day. Halfway round the circuit, he spotted her coming towards him from the direction of the Prince Consort memorial. Almost in the same instant, Linda saw him and waved. To appear in a hurry was beneath her dignity, but he noticed with some amusement that she gradually lengthened her stride.

"Hi," she said breathlessly. "What can I say? I'm abject. I surely didn't intend to be late."

"No, of course you didn't." He smiled and fell in step beside Linda, taking hold of her hand as if they had known each other a long time."

"You sounded very mysterious on the telephone, Robert."

"I was being cautious in case Daniel returned unexpectedly." He frowned, unable to remember whether he'd already told Linda that Bernard was sharing the flat with him. "Sometimes I get the feeling he is watching me like I was one of his patients."

"Or his prisoner."

If that was nearer the mark, he wasn't going to say so. "That article you sent me," Donaldson said, changing the subject.

"What about it?"

"Tamblin has it."

"Yes, so I gathered from what you said yesterday."

"He and Lloyd came to see me this morning. I warned Tamblin that you would probably get in touch with him. I said that if you thought the Ministry was trying to hide something, I was the one likely to end up with egg on his face."

"And what did he say to that?"

"He didn't. However, Lloyd told me not to worry, he said that they could 'take care' of you. I could be wrong, but I got the impression he wouldn't hesitate to use the dirty tricks department to fit you up.''

"To do what?" Her voice rose sharply.

"To frame you in some way."

"In other words, I can expect a visit from the law." Linda halted in midstride and gave his arm a savage tug, jerking him round so that they were face to face. "You smarmy bastard," she said in a low voice. "That's what I call playing both ends against the middle. Lloyd tells you what he has in mind and you warn me off because you want to come out of this affair smelling like a rose. I bet he even told you to meet me on some pretext or other so that one of his gorillas could break into my place and plant the necessary evidence. What is it? Pot? Heroin? I bet it's heroin because your wonderful police will want to make sure the magistrate remands me in custody."

"If you really believe I'm capable of that, then you'd better rush into print."

"The *Sunday Times* only comes out once a week."

"So what? I'm sure you can sell the story to another newspaper."

"You must have a low opinion of me."

"Well, it's mutual, isn't it?" he said. "Look, I've told you the score and from now on it's up to you. Believe me, I don't give a damn what you do about it."

Without another word, he turned and walked away from her. A wide gap opened between them. Then, suddenly, Linda ran after him and caught hold of his hand.

"I'm sorry." She licked her lips. "Please forget what I said. I shouldn't have blown my top like that, it was unforgivable."

"You don't have to grovel." He smiled and squeezed her hand. "I'd probably have done the same in your shoes."

"Don't look now," she said teasingly, "but I think I can see a halo showing. What do you say to a drink? The pubs must be open by now."

"There's nothing I'd like more, but I don't want any flak from Daniel." He cupped her chin in the palm of his hand. "Take care now and mind how you go with Virginia Magrane. I think they're watching her."

"I've already seen her."

"When was that?" he asked.

"Yesterday afternoon. Her boyfriend was there." Linda's mouth curved, registering disapproval. "I can't say I admire her taste."

"Poor old Andrew."

"Yes, despite everything he's done, I can't help feeling sorry for him."

Her chin was still in his palm and for no good reason except that he wanted to, Donaldson bent his head and kissed her on the mouth. Linda didn't object, nor did she appear surprised.

Magrane placed his small notebook on the hall table and lifted the receiver off the hook. Although there were butterflies in his stomach, he gave Molly a confident smile, determined to prove to her that he didn't have a care in the world. Slowly and deliberately he dialled 01-229-8897. A few moments later, there was a faint click and then the number started ringing.

"This isn't right, Andrew." Molly stood on one leg and rubbed the other foot against her calf until the itch was stilled. "I don't like eavesdropping on a private conversation."

"But I want you to hear."

"What are you trying to prove?"

"Nothing. I'm just concerned about setting your mind at rest." Magrane slipped an arm round her waist and drew Molly close until their hips were touching. "It's important to me."

"Supposing he's not at home?"

"He will be. Christ, it's the middle of the afternoon."

The ringing stopped and Donaldson said, "8897."

"Robert?" Magrane heaved a sigh of relief. "It's me, Andrew."

"Oh, hullo, I was wondering when you would call."

"We seem to have a bad line." Magrane winked at Molly. "Do you think you could speak up a bit, Robert? I can hardly hear you."

"All right. Can you hear me now, Andrew?"

"That's better, much better." Magrane held the phone between them so that she could hear what Donaldson was saying. "Listen, Robert, I've been thinking over what you said—about our meeting face to face—and I think it might be a good idea. There are one or two problems I want to discuss with you."

"Concerning phase three?"

"What else? You said yourself that we're running into a lot of flak over that."

"Yes, I did. So when do we meet, Andrew?"

"How about tonight?"

"Good idea," said Donaldson.

"Well, here's what you do, Robert. . . ." Magrane opened his small notebook and consulted a list of telephone numbers. "First of all, you make your way over to Edmonton in North London and follow the A10 for Cambridge as far as the intersection with Southbury Road, and you then turn left. Have you got that?"

"Yes."

"Okay. Now you'll see a telephone box on the corner. The number is 01-363-1553. You get there by eight o'clock and I'll call you again."

"You want to make sure I'm clean, is that the idea?"

"Dead right," said Magrane. "Now let's hear you repeat the number."

"It's 01-363-1553."

"Go to the top of the class, Robert."

"Thanks for the vote of confidence," said Donaldson.

Magrane hung up. There was no need to ask what Molly had made of it. The answer was there in her eyes, a sense of profound relief and happiness for him.

"When are you going up to town?" she asked softly.

"I'm not." He slipped his other arm around her waist and hugged Molly to him. "At least not tonight. I thought I'd call Robert from here."

Her face was upturned and smiling and he kissed her. Presently, her mouth opened and she began to brush her knees against his in a slow, tantalizing invitation.

Donaldson got off the bus at the stop before the traffic lights and walked round the corner into Southbury Road. The telephone box was conveniently empty, but London was usually dead on a Sunday night, especially in winter, and Edmonton was no exception. Although Ryan had had plenty of time to get his people into position, there was no sign of them in the immediate neighborhood, which was fair enough provided the transmitter didn't go on the blink, provided too that he remembered to switch it on. Donaldson checked to make sure the button was pushed forward and then entered the box.

Some mindless vandal had slashed one of the directories into ribbons with a sharp knife and had put his boot through several panes of glass, but the telephone was still intact. Having satisfied himself that the instrument was in working order, Donaldson lit a cigarette and settled back to wait.

The minutes dragged by. Eight o'clock came and went with no word from Magrane. A man out walking his dog stopped by the box and gave him an odd look, but moved on again once the animal had left its mark. Some ten minutes after he'd disappeared round the corner, a couple of teenagers strolled by in the opposite direction and then dived into a shop doorway farther down the road. Just as Donaldson was beginning to think that he'd been sent on a wild goose chase, the telephone suddenly rang. Before he could lift the receiver, the ringing stopped, only to start again a few seconds later. He caught it, this time.

Magrane said, "Is that you, Robert?"

"Of course it's me," Donaldson said irritably. "What the hell kept you?"

"You can blame the GPO for the delay—their system is all cocked up. I got an engaged signal five times in a row and then when I did get through, the bloody line went dead. That's progress for you; we'd be better off with a megaphone."

"We'd be a whole lot better off if you got to the point."

"You know something, Robert? I wish I hadn't bothered to call."

There was a long silence during which he realized that Magrane was waiting for an apology. Whether he owed him one or not was beside the point. It had taken a lot of time and effort to arrange a meeting and he couldn't afford to let Andrew hang up on him now.

"I'm sorry," said Donaldson. "Only it's bloody drafty in this box."

"No need to apologize, Robert," Magrane said contritely. "These last few days can't have been easy for you."

Donaldson tried not to laugh. There were moments when he thought Andrew was absolutely priceless.

"I mean, I know Lloyd of old."

"Who?" Donaldson was conscious that his voice was hoarse with surprise.

"I'm talking about Lloyd, my doppelgänger, the bastard who loused things up in Northern Ireland when he was Director of Political Intelligence. He pulled the plug on me again in Oman in May of last year. But I guess you know that."

His ears hadn't deceived him then. Magrane had named his bogeyman and it wasn't a hallucinatory figure. It was conceivable that he was referring to another Lloyd, but that would be too much of a coincidence, especially as Linda Warwick had said that Lloyd was not with the Police Department of the Home Office. He fingered the transmitter under his jacket and wondered how he could prod Andrew into telling him the whole story without Ryan's people being any the wiser. Although they could only hear one side of the conversation, he would need to phrase his questions very carefully.

"I don't think I've got all the details," he said slowly. "Maybe you'd better go over them again?"

"I'm not with you. Do you mind rephrasing the question in English?"

"I want you to repeat the whole thing, Andrew."

"Seems to me we're wasting time, Robert, but you're the boss. But I just wish you wouldn't insist on this double-checking all the time."

It was a variation of an old theme, with Qaddafi as usual the target, but for once Magrane was surprisingly lucid and rational. There were no emotional outbursts and while his story was undoubtedly fantastic, it carried a ring of truth. The Foreign Office would never have gone along with a plan to assassinate Qaddafi at Mukala, but that didn't mean the operation hadn't existed on paper. It was an option that could have been floated round Whitehall and taken seriously enough for somebody to make a contingency plan and brief Magrane. The more Donaldson thought about it, the more he was convinced that that somebody had to be Lloyd. It would explain how he had managed to involve Special Branch in the affair. They were the Corporation garbage crew. Whenever the SIS fouled its own doorstep, they were invariably called upon to help clean up the mess.

"He's probably got you bugged, Robert."

"What?"

"Do I have to spell it out for you?" Magrane said with a trace of impatience. "Lloyd will have arranged to put a wiretap on your flat the moment he saw the ad in the *Evening Standard*. Look, I know you only gave your phone number, but the post office will always disclose the name and address of a subscriber to the police. Ever heard of a Commander Ryan?"

"Yes."

"Well, he and Lloyd are as thick as thieves, and that makes it awkward for us because I've just discovered that the primary target is here in England."

"Are you going to tell me who it is?"

"Who else?" Magrane sounded pleased with himself. "Just ask yourself one question—who's behind the supplier?"

"The manufacturer?"

"Precisely."

It had been a complete stab in the dark, yet it appeared he had said the right thing and Magrane evidently thought they were on the same wavelength.

"Listen, I'm sorry to have dragged you all the way out to Edmonton, Robert, but I had to warn you about Lloyd and your telephone isn't secure."

"I take your point, Andrew, but what happens now?"

"You go back home."

"I thought we were going to meet?"

"Not yet. I'll call you tomorrow, okay?"

"Whatever you say."

Donaldson waited for Magrane to hang up and then replaced the receiver. Pressing the microphone closer to his throat, he said, "That's it, the party's over. Magrane won't come out to play. If you can hear me out there, I'd appreciate a lift home."

Somebody did hear him. Shortly after turning the corner

into Great Cambridge Road, a car drew up beside him and the nearside rear door was flung open. Ryan invited him to get in and almost before Donaldson had time to close the door, he leaned forward and told the driver to move on. In the very next breath, he asked what Magrane had had to say for himself.

"He went on about his doppelgänger, said he'd undoubtedly put a wiretap on my phone." Donaldson smiled. "Of course he was only guessing, but all the same, it's ironic."

"Oh, he's a right clever little bugger is Magrane," Ryan said acidly. "He's up to more tricks than a wagonload of monkeys."

"I don't think Andrew was having me on when he said the next target was here in England."

"England." Ryan snorted in disgust. "That's a fat lot of help. What are we supposed to do—watch every embassy and guard every visitor to this country?"

"No, I think we should look for a VIP who's just arrived, somebody who could loosely be described as the manufacturer."

"Of what?"

"Of arms," said Donaldson. "Look, this is how Magrane's Operation Damocles seems to stack up: the IRA is buying arms from Steiner, the middleman. But Magrane can't go after the IRA because of the political repercussions, so he takes out the middleman, first paying a visit to the people who store the arms—the post office—Jan and Beatrix van der Pohlmann. Phase three is to kill the one who's been supplying them to Steiner, whoever that is, but now he's suddenly switched to the 'manufacturer'—the person making the arms in the first place. And that manufacturer is in England."

"I don't know of anybody who would fit that description."

"Well, maybe I'll get a chance to worm it out of him. At least we're still talking to one another."

"When is he going to call you again?"

"Sometime tomorrow."

"Tomorrow." Ryan produced a handkerchief and blew his nose loudly. "It wouldn't surprise me if I was in bed with a dose of flu by then. This bloody weather will be the death of me. Sleet, wind and rain one moment, sunshine the next— contrary like a woman."

Donaldson edged away from Ryan until there was a respectable distance between them. "About Magrane," he said casually, "I presume your people are looking for him?"

"We're checking all the hotels and rooming houses, but so far we haven't come up with anything. He probably registered under a false name."

"I have a feeling he's found a friend to take him in. When Andrew phoned me this afternoon and again tonight, he wasn't using a public telephone."

"Are you sure of that?" Ryan asked.

"I didn't hear him feed any coins into the slot and he was on the line for a good twenty minutes."

"He could have broken into an office somewhere in London." Ryan blew his nose again.

"Unlikely, wouldn't you say?"

"Perhaps his wife might be able to help us. She must know who his friends are."

From the way he paused and glanced at him, it was obvious that Ryan was hoping for an answer, but Donaldson refused to be drawn. There was no way he could give an opinion unless he'd met Virginia Magrane, and Ryan knew it.

"I don't suppose he put a name to this doppelgänger of his, did he?"

"What do you think?" Donaldson said quickly.

"I think Magrane is a nut case."

Ryan turned away from him and stared out of the window, seemingly deep in thought. He came to life again when they pulled up outside the building in Devonshire Terrace, but only to wish Donaldson good night.

15 . . .

MAGRANE stirred, heard a creak outside the door as if somebody had trodden on a loose floorboard, and was instantly awake. He groped under the pillow for the Wesson revolver and, unable to find it, suddenly realized that he was in Molly's bedroom. Before he had time to move, the door was thrown open and two shadowy figures rushed into the room. A flashlight played on his face, half blinding him. Molly screamed and sat up in bed, and then somebody found the switch inside the door and the room was flooded with light.

There were three of them, not two, and they knew their business. They stood in a semicircle, just far enough away from the bed to be out of reach. Two were armed, their handguns pointed at his chest. The third man was holding a large flashlight, swinging it loosely in his right hand as if intending to use it as a truncheon. They were silent, their frozen immobility suggesting that they were waiting for someone to tell them what to do next. And then Ryan entered the room.

"Well, Andrew," he said quietly, "we've caught up with you at last."

Molly gave a sharp intake of breath and she clutched the

bedclothes to her chest. There were goose pimples on her arms and she was shivering.

"Who are these men?" she whispered.

"We're police officers." Ryan took out a handkerchief and sneezed into it. "I think you had better show Mrs. Gregson your warrant card, Sergeant Norris. It may set her mind at rest."

The stocky blond man with the flashlight reached inside his jacket and held up a small blue folder.

"I know what you're thinking, Andrew, but it won't do you any good." Ryan wiped his nose and put the handkerchief away. "The house is surrounded."

"I'd be surprised if it wasn't."

"Then I take it you're going to be sensible?"

Magrane nodded and got out of bed. Norris handed the flashlight to the thin, hawk-faced man on his left, produced a pair of handcuffs from his hip pocket and signalled Magrane to turn about and face the wall. Moving in behind him, he grabbed hold of Magrane's right arm, twisted it behind his back, manacled the wrist and then cuffed it to the other hand.

"Aren't you going to allow me to dress?"

"All in good time, Andrew." Ryan turned to Molly, a solicitous expression on his face. "I'm sorry about this, Mrs. Gregson," he said, "but I'm afraid I'll have to ask you to get dressed."

"For Christ's sake, leave her alone," Magrane shouted angrily. "She hasn't done anything."

"No need to lose your rag, Andrew. All we want from Mrs. Gregson is a statement."

Magrane scowled. Ryan was a chameleon, hard and uncompromising one minute, courteous and restrained the next. Right now, butter wouldn't melt in his mouth. He felt a hand on his elbow and tried to shake it off, but Norris refused to let go. Authoritatively and firmly, he steered him out on to the landing, where they stood to one side while Ryan went ahead and opened the door to the spare bedroom. Presently, the thin, hawk-faced man joined them and, taking hold of Magrane's other arm, he helped Norris lead him into the small back room. Glancing over his shoulder, Magrane noticed that the fourth officer had stayed behind to guard the stairway, presumably in case he decided to make a break for it.

"Is this yours?" Ryan pointed to the raincoat hanging in the wardrobe.

Magrane nodded; there was no point denying it.

"You're travelling light, aren't you, Andrew?"

"I didn't have time to pack."

"I wonder?" Ryan glanced at the hawk-faced policeman. "What do you think, Sergeant Quinn?"

"I don't believe Captain Magrane arrived here empty-handed, sir."

"Neither do I. You and Norris had better turn this room over."

"With or without a search warrant?"

"Don't be stupid, Andrew." Ryan placed a hand on his shoulder and forced him to sit down on a chair. "Of course we've got a search warrant. You don't think I'd stick my neck out, do you?"

Quinn whipped the sheets and blankets off the bed, dumping them on the floor. The pillows followed suit, exposing the Wesson .357 magnum and leather wallet.

"That's dangerous." Quinn picked up the revolver, broke it open and ejected the shells into his palm. "Bloody dangerous."

"Would this be the bankroll you mentioned to Donaldson?" Ryan examined the wallet, removed the wad of notes and counted them. "Four hundred and eighty-five pounds," he said presently. "Quite a tidy old sum for a man who's travelling light."

Magrane said nothing. His eyes were on Norris, willing the sergeant not to look inside the porcelain vase on the window ledge after he had finished going through the chest of drawers. There was a hundred and fifty pounds tucked inside it, money that would have been a surprise present for Molly if he'd had his way.

"What have you done with your passport, Andrew?"

"It's in my jacket in the other bedroom."

Ryan looked at Quinn and jerked a thumb towards the door. "Go and get it, will you, Les? And the rest of his things."

"What about Mrs. Gregson?"

"I hope she's downstairs being interviewed by Chief Inspector Attwood. Christ, she ought to have finished dressing by now."

Magrane waited until Quinn had left the room and then launched himself from the chair. Norris heard him coming and whirled round, his right arm scything through the air to deliver a forearm smash to the head. The karate blow failed to connect, however, and going in under it, Magrane butted him in the stomach. Slammed against the chest of drawers behind him, Norris buckled at the knees and sank down on his haunches, gasping for breath. Magrane went down with him and was still trying to get up off the floor when Ryan grabbed him from behind in a bear hug. Dropping down on one knee, he rolled over on to his back, pinning Ryan underneath him. Somehow he managed to break the arm lock across his chest, but it didn't get him very far. As he staggered to his feet, Ryan grabbed hold of one ankle and then Quinn dropped the clothes he was carrying and drove a fist into his chest. The punch caught him under the heart and suddenly the floor was tilting crazily and he could feel himself sliding into unconsciousness.

A dark veil had descended, but it was only temporary. Somebody was holding a cold compress against his neck and then two pairs of hands lifted him up and sat him down in the chair.

Ryan said, "You're not going to give us any more trouble, are you, Andrew?"

There was no menace in his voice. If anything, Ryan sounded weary, as if the whole business had gotten on top of him and he'd had enough of it.

"Don't worry, I know when I'm beaten." Magrane looked down at his feet, hiding a smile of triumph, because the diversion had worked and Norris had overlooked the flower vase on the window ledge. "I'll come quietly."

"I'll believe that when I see it." Ryan caught his breath, searched his pockets for the handkerchief, and sneezed loudly before he could find it. "I should be home in bed," he complained morosely. "This cold will be the death of me."

"Can I rely on that?" said Magrane.

"We all know you're a comedian." Norris held up a pair

of trousers in front of him. "Now let's see if you can be an acrobat."

"I've always wanted a valet," said Magrane.

Quinn and Norris got him into the pants, pulled on his socks and hammed his feet into the suede shoes. He thought they would unhandcuff him so that he could slip his arms into the shirt and jacket, but instead they merely draped a blanket round his shoulders and led him downstairs.

Quinn opened the front door and they went on down the path. Two plainclothesmen were hanging about in the lane outside the house where three cars were parked in line ahead. As they walked towards the Ford Granada in the center, other police officers began to materialize from the surrounding fields. In a perverse sort of way, Magrane felt flattered that Ryan had thought it necessary to deploy so large a force to arrest him.

Norris opened the left-side rear door of the Granada, pushed him into the car and scrambled in beside him. Ryan had a few brief words with the assembled officers and then he, Quinn and the driver joined them. The lane ended in a cul-de-sac and with little room for maneuver, there was a certain amount of confusion between the drivers before they managed to get the cavalcade facing in the right direction. Once they had gotten themselves sorted out, they drove through Wrotham, and, turning left on the A20, headed towards London.

Ryan said, "What, no questions, Andrew?"

Magrane sighed. "All right, I can see you're dying to tell me."

"Tell you what?" countered Ryan.

"Who turned me in."

"Give you one guess."

"I don't have to guess," said Magrane. "It's got to be Virginia."

Everybody laughed as if he had made a very subtle joke, but Magrane was damned if he could see the funny side of it.

Donaldson caught a Circle Line train from Bayswater, got out at St. James's Park and walked down Broadway to New Scotland Yard. All around him, people were hurrying to get to work on time, but his job was finished, or at least he assumed it was, otherwise Lloyd would not have sent for him. Lloyd had been singularly uncommunicative on the telephone, this despite the fact that the tape recorder had been disconnected at his request. Thinking about it, Donaldson came to the conclusion that Lloyd didn't trust him. Well, it was mutual.

A messenger was waiting for him in the entrance, clutching a visitor's pass that had already been made out in his name. Once satisfied as to his identity, he escorted Donaldson up to Ryan's office on the sixth floor, handed the pass over to Lloyd and then withdrew.

Ryan was suffering, his face decidedly flushed, his eyes red-rimmed and streaming. His nose resembled a piece of raw beefsteak and the wastepaper basket was half-full of used tissues from the box of Kleenex on the desk. In contrast, Lloyd was the picture of health and obviously enjoying himself.

"Well now, Robert." Lloyd smiled and rubbed his hands together. "I expect you can guess why you are here."

"You've apprehended Magrane."

"Indeed we have. Commander Ryan arrested him in Wrotham at three o'clock this morning."

"Congratulations," said Donaldson.

"You don't sound exactly overjoyed, Robert."

"Perhaps it's because I find the whole thing a bit of an anticlimax."

"I doubt if we would have picked him up quite so soon but for you." Lloyd glanced to Ryan for confirmation. "Isn't that so?"

Ryan nodded. "It was that last phone call of his that unlocked the door." His voice was hoarse, like a rasp. "If your hunch was right and Magrane had used a private telephone, I knew he had to be staying with an old friend, someone he trusted completely."

"And Virginia Magrane supplied the answer?"

"She gave us the names of three officers. One was serving in Malaysia, another had retired and was living in South Africa and the third was the widow of his guide and mentor, Harry Gregson."

"So what happens now?"

"Well, you've done your job, Robert. As of now, you're

free to return to Wilton whenever you wish.'' Lloyd flashed him another on-off smile. ''Naturally I shall be writing to Colonel Vaughan to express our appreciation.''

''And Magrane?''

''Oh, he'll be returned to Inverness where he will be charged by the local police, but I doubt if he will stand trial for murder. Andrew is obviously insane and it would be administratively more convenient for everyone concerned if he were simply detained in Her Majesty's Pleasure. I imagine he will end up in Broadmoor or some other similar institution.''

Donaldson wondered what sort of story they planned to give the newspapers. As if reading his mind, Lloyd handed him a copy of the draft press release which had been lying in Ryan's pending tray. To anybody not aware of the facts, it was a very full and frank statement, one that reconstructed Magrane's movements after he had come ashore near Balmedie and explained in some detail the circumstances leading to his arrest at Vale End cottage near Wrotham. There was no mention of the van der Pohlmanns or August Steiner. Evidently, as far as Lloyd was concerned, Magrane had never left England.

''Where are you holding Andrew?'' Donaldson asked quietly.

''Bethnal Green,'' said Ryan. ''My old stamping ground.''

''I'd like to see him.''

''I don't think that would be a very good idea, Robert,'' Lloyd cut in smoothly. ''In his present mood, it's quite possible that he will attack you, and we can't have that.''

''He's violent?''

''It took three of us to subdue him,'' said Ryan.

''In other words, you mean he's not fit to be seen by anyone, other than a doctor.''

''Watch it,'' Ryan growled. ''I won't have you casting slurs at my officers.''

''On second thought, maybe it would be a good thing if Robert did see him,'' Lloyd suggested tactfully.

''I've got news for you,'' said Ryan. ''There's only one place I'm going and that's home to bed.''

''What about Sergeant Norris? Couldn't he go with Robert to Bethnal Green?''

''He's got a lot of paperwork to catch up with.''

"Somebody else then."

Lloyd was insistent, his manner brusque and uncompromising. Ryan glared at him, snatched a tissue from the box of Kleenex and blew his nose noisily.

"Do you think my people have nothing better to do than chauffeur Donaldson around?"

The question, it seemed, was purely rhetorical. Before Lloyd could answer it, Ryan buzzed for the civilian clerk, told him to order a car from the motor pool and then sent for Sergeant Quinn.

It was the longest and slowest five miles that Donaldson could remember. Quinn wasn't in a talkative mood, the driver didn't know any shortcuts and the traffic was log-jammed from Whitehall as far as Tottenham Court Road. They made better progress once they turned into New Oxford Street, but even so, every red light seemed to be against them all the way to Bethnal Green Road. Forty minutes after setting off, they pulled into the small yard behind the police station. Obviously Ryan had warned the station sergeant to expect them, otherwise there would have been another frustrating delay while the local police checked with the Yard to see if it was okay for him to see Magrane.

Andrew was stretched out on the bunk, staring up at the ceiling. As they entered the cell, he stood up and faced them with a lopsided smile, one more rueful than defiant.

Donaldson said, "Hullo, Andrew, how are you feeling?" It seemed an odd way to greet a man he'd never met face to face before, but the telephone had forged a bond between them, and in that sense they were scarcely strangers.

"I'll survive." Magrane pointed a finger at Quinn and the young police constable, both of whom were standing behind him. "Did you ask for an escort, Robert, or did they insist you have one?"

"I don't think I'm allowed to see you alone—there's some rule about a police officer having to be present."

"Too bloody right there is," said Quinn.

"What I've got to say to you is personal. It concerns a lady and I don't want them to hear."

"How about it?" Donaldson turned to face Quinn. "Can you bend the rules this once?"

"Not on your life."

"Five minutes; that's all I'm asking for. Look, you can lock me in the cell with him, stand outside the door and watch us through the spy hole. Where's the risk in that?"

"I've got my pension to consider," said Quinn. "If anything should happen, it'll go down the drain."

"Look at it this way. Ryan fixed it so that I could see Magrane. He didn't say that you had to hold my hand while I talked to him."

Quinn thought it over and then nodded. The young police constable looked dubious, opened his mouth to say something, but thought better of it and remained silent. As the door closed behind them, Magrane raised two fingers to show what he thought of the police.

"Five minutes." Magrane sat down on the bunk. "We don't have much time, do we, Robert?"

"Not a lot."

"So what's the score?"

"Come again?"

"What does Lloyd intend to do about you and me?"

"I'm returning to my desk job at Wilton."

"That figures."

Magrane waited, an anxious smile on his face, one that seemed to ask, "What about me then?"

"Hasn't Ryan told you?" Donaldson said quietly.

"No, he just said, 'We've got you now, Magrane, got you dead to rights' over and over again."

Donaldson found it hard to believe him. To have deliberately kept Andrew in the dark would have been more than Ryan's job was worth. If there was any substance to the allegation, a good barrister would nail him to the cross. Andrew had simply refused to listen to Ryan; that was the most likely explanation.

"I understand you'll be returned to Inverness and charged with murder."

"Whose?"

"Tulloch's and that male nurse."

"Joseph?"

"Yes."

"What about the van der Pohlmanns and August Steiner?"
In his anxiety, Magrane's mania for security had gone by the
board and the cloak of anonymity had been stripped from the
"post office" and "the middleman."

"Lloyd didn't say anything about them."

"No, he wouldn't." Magrane jumped to his feet and paced
up and down the cell. "It won't come to a trial, Robert.
They'll have me certified and put away."

It would have been easy to dismiss the accusation as the
convoluted thinking of an unbalanced mind but for one thing.
Lloyd had put it more delicately when he'd said it would be
administratively more convenient if Andrew was detained in
Her Majesty's Pleasure, but it amounted to the same thing.

"Well, I want my day in court, you hear, Robert?" He
halted in midstride and turned to face him, his eyes glinting
dangerously. "I want the world to hear what those bastards
did to me. If I'm insane, they pushed me over the brink with
their barbs, sleepers and downers. Christ, Daniel had me
doped up to the eyebrows. You ask Klepacz, he'll tell you."

"There'll be a trial, Andrew."

"Like hell there will. Lloyd and Ryan can't afford to let
me go into the witness box. You know why?" He tapped his
forehead. "Because I've got enough ammunition stored in
here to blow those two to kingdom come and back. If they
have their way, they'll lock me in a padded cell and throw
away the key."

"They can't circumvent the law, Andrew. You'll appear in
court, have no fear of that."

"If I do, they'll make sure I'm represented by a crummy
barrister. I mean, I can't afford to hire the best. I'll have to
take what I'm offered by legal aid."

"Nobody is going to railroad you," Donaldson said impatiently. "If necessary, I'll see to that."

"How?"

"There's always the newspapers."

"Yeah? What makes you think the press will take any
notice of you?"

"I know one reporter who might and that's all we need."
Donaldson went through his wallet, found Linda's card and

handed it to Magrane. "Take it from me, once that young woman gets her teeth into something, she won't let go."

Magrane sat down again, his face transformed by a lazy smile, like a cat who'd got at the cream. "Beautiful," he murmured.

"Our time must be about up," Donaldson reminded him gently.

There was no reply. The vacant smile was fixed as if he'd gone into a trance.

"Andrew."

"What?"

"Our time is about up. Is there anything you want before I go?"

"What?" he repeated vaguely and then smiled again. "Well, I'm dying for a smoke. Could you leave me couple of cigarettes?"

"Of course I can." Donaldson retrieved Linda's card and tossed a packet of Benson and Hedges on to the bunk. "How are you off for matches?"

"I'm okay." Magrane gave him a thumbs up sign. "There's no need to look so downhearted, Robert," he said cheerfully. "We're not beaten yet."

Donaldson nodded gravely, walked over to the door and gave it a thump with his fist to let Quinn know that he was ready to leave. He thought Magrane was back in cloud cuckoo land again.

16 . . .

Magrane smiled to himself. There was no getting away from it, Donaldson was quite brilliant. All that crap about getting the newspapers interested in his case had merely been a blind, a clever excuse for him to produce the calling card. Linda Warwick—Worplesdene Gardens—South Kensington—telephone 01-589-46372. The important details were imprinted on his mind, just as Donaldson had intended. The flat in Devonshire Terrace was a busted flush and Linda Warwick was the new contact, the go-between he'd had to find in a hurry. Even cleverer was the fact that the calling card had been Robert's way of letting him know that phase three of Operation Damocles was still on.

If there had been any doubt in his mind, it had been dispelled by Donaldson's parting question. What was it he'd said? "Is there anything you want before I go?" Could there have been a more pointed or subtle remark than that? For a moment he'd been tempted to say, "How about the keys to the cell?" but had sensed that that kind of flip retort wouldn't go down too well. Robert was a good man; unfortunately, he lacked a sense of humor.

Magrane swung his feet off the bunk and sat up. Phase three was going to be stillborn unless he did something about it. Ryan had had several hours in which to make the necessary arrangements to have him transferred to Inverness, and whatever the mode of transport, the police were bound to move him from Bethnal Green before the day was out. Given any choice, he would have preferred to wait until nightfall before making a bid to escape, but time wasn't on his side. He pushed his cuff back to look at his wristwatch, momentarily forgetting that they had removed it along with his tie. The tie he could understand, because it was a potential weapon, but he couldn't think of one good reason why they should have taken the wristwatch.

He looked towards the door, drawn to it by a faint, uneven noise in the corridor outside. Two men walking out of step, one taking shorter paces than the other, as if he were carrying something. A tray? Yes, that was probably it; his stomach told him that lunch was about due. Fried food from the canteen and a cup of tea, the man walking slowly in case it slopped over into the saucer. He heard them stop outside his cell and then a key was inserted in the lock and the door opened outwards.

The sergeant entered first. Magrane hadn't seen him before, but although his hair was beginning to go grey in places, his bearing and physique suggested he knew how to take care of himself in a roughhouse. The officer who followed him into the cell carrying a lunch tray looked young enough to have just graduated from police cadet. Of the two, the sergeant was obviously the more dangerous. Dipping into the pen pocket of his jacket, Magrane produced a cigarette, stuck it between his lips and then patted his other pockets as if looking for a box of matches.

"Would either of you two happen to have a light?" he asked politely.

The sergeant shook his head, the police constable shoved the tray at him, said, "Here, hold this," and reached inside his trouser pocket. Magrane heaved the tray at the sergeant, turned sideways and, pivoting on his right leg, kicked the younger man in the stomach. The police constable cannoned into the bunk, went over backwards, struck his head against the wall and was unconscious before he hit the floor. The sergeant was still clawing baked beans out of his eyes when

Magrane chopped a forearm smash into the left side of his neck, dropping him where he stood.

There was no time to think out the next move. The element of surprise was no longer on his side and there was nothing for it but to bulldoze a way through every obstruction in his path. Magrane ran out into the corridor, wheeled left and raced towards the main entrance. Although a blanket had been draped over his head before arrival, on Ryan's orders, he knew that they had driven into a small courtyard at the back of the station. Once inside the building, the blanket had been removed and Norris had led him down a narrow passageway into the main hall where the desk sergeant had recorded his arrival in the occurrence book. Undoubtedly, the back yard was the best avenue of escape and he persuaded himself that it was merely a question of retracing his steps.

Two police officers were talking to an elderly man in the main hall. Apparently unaware of the disturbance in the cell, all three turned to gawk at him as he swiftly changed direction and made for the passageway on his right. The desk sergeant was the first to recover his wits. Yelling at the top of his voice to summon assistance, he vaulted over the counter, knocked the constable aside and hared after him. In that same instant, a slender woman officer stepped out of an interview room to see what all the noise was about and blundered straight into Magrane. Grabbing her by the arm, he whirled the woman off her feet and sent her flying towards the sergeant. Unable to retain her balance, the woman went down on all fours, collided with the sergeant and gave a muffled grunt as he fell on top of her. They were still lying in a tangled heap on the floor when Magrane yanked the side door open and ran out into the back yard.

A plainclothes officer reversing a Ford Escort into a vacant parking space saw him coming and, shifting into first gear, jumped the car forward to block the way. Stalling the engine, he tried to scramble out of the car, but he wasn't quick enough. Magrane grabbed hold of the door, slammed it against his left leg and then dragged him out of the car, butting him savagely in the face as he did so. Bleeding from the nose and mouth and in no condition to offer any resistance, the police officer collapsed at Magrane's feet and rolled over onto his side.

The keys were still in the ignition and, sliding into the car, Magrane slammed the door, depressed the clutch and cranked the engine into life. He took off fast, the rear wheels spinning to leave black skid marks on the pavement before they found purchase. Locking the wheel hard over, he shot through the gates and, completing the U-turn, headed towards Bethnal Green Road. Nothing was going to stop him, not the stop sign at the top of the street nor the oncoming bus approaching from the right. Tires screaming in protest at the sharp turn, he cut in front of the bus and, weaving in and out of the traffic, managed to beat the lights at the next road junction.

Uppermost in his mind was the knowledge that within a matter of minutes the vehicle registration number of the Ford Escort would be radioed to every police car in the neighborhood. Obviously he would have to abandon it—and soon—but what then? He was flat broke and lost somewhere in the East End of London. Magrane clenched his teeth, willing himself to keep calm. So what if he didn't have any money? Once he found a telephone he could call Donaldson by reversing the charges. Robert would help him, that was his job.

A signboard attached to a lamp standard informed him that he was in Globe Town. He went on over the Grand Union Canal and turned right on Grove Road where another sign told him that he was approaching Mile End. Glancing at the speedometer, Magrane saw that he'd covered less than two miles. Two miles in something like five minutes, and that after driving like a maniac. Flicking the indicator, he turned into a side street and parked the car in a vacant space at the curb.

Magrane looked into the rearview mirror, saw that the road behind was clear and got out of the car. He was about to lock the door when he noticed the raincoat lying on the back seat. Ducking inside again, he grabbed it and slipped it on. Harry Gregson had often said he had the luck of the devil, and he was right. Going through the pockets as he walked away from the Escort, Magrane found a packet of cigarettes in one and a handful of loose change in the other amounting to just under a pound.

Magrane walked back to the main road and turned left towards Mile End. Five minutes later, he strolled into the Underground station on the corner of Bow Road.

• • •

Donaldson finished packing and left the bedroom, closing the door behind him. The living room where he had spent so many hours waiting for Magrane to telephone seemed strangely empty without Daniel. He thought it curious that Bernard should have left without saying good-bye or leaving a note to explain that he had a train to catch and couldn't wait any longer. Odd, too, that the tape recorder should have vanished along with Daniel, but of course Ryan would have seen to that.

No tape recorder, no story; he'd really sold Linda Warwick a pig in a poke. Donaldson wondered how she would take it when he broke the news to her. Knowing Linda, she would probably think he'd taken her for a ride, and with some justification. They might have struck a bargain, but he had been aware all along that he would never be able to deliver his end of it. There was no reason why she should ever know that. In seizing all the tapes, Ryan had given him the perfect way out, but he would tell her all the same. That was the trouble with having a conscience. Lifting the receiver, he dialled Linda's number.

There was no reply and he put the phone down, uncertain whether to hang on and try again later or write her a note. There was a lot to be said in favor of a letter. For one thing, he could present his side of the story without fear of interruption and for another, he wouldn't have to answer any embarrassing questions off the cuff. On the other hand, it was a pretty sneaky way of getting himself off the hook, one that went against the grain. In the end, the telephone solved the problem for him with a strident summons. Answering it, Donaldson found he had a very bad-tempered Lloyd on the line.

Without any preamble, he said, "If you're thinking of leaving, Robert, forget it. Chief Inspector Attwood and Sergeant Norris are anxious to have a few words with you and, believe me, you've got some explaining to do."

"What about?"

"Magrane—he's escaped from Bethnal Green Police Station."

"When did this happen?"

"Less than an hour after you had your little heart-to-heart talk with him."

"Before or after the press release?"

There was a long pause. When Lloyd finally did get around to answering the question, he was almost incoherent with anger. "Can't you guess?" he snarled. "Have you ever known Magrane to make things easy for us? Of course he escaped after we had released the news of his arrest."

"Christ," said Donaldson.

"You'd do well to pray," Lloyd said grimly. "You're going to need all the help you can get before Attwood is through."

The phone went down with a bang, terminating the conversation before he had a chance to come back at Lloyd. Donaldson replaced the receiver, picked up his suitcase, carried it back into the bedroom and dumped it on the bed.

Magrane left the Underground at Temple and walked along the Victoria Embankment past Somerset House and on over Waterloo Bridge. Although Ryan was in possession of his small black notebook with the list of telephone numbers, the location of every call box was firmly imprinted in his mind. Turning into Villiers Street, he found the one above Watergate Walk, picked up the phone and dialled 01-589-46372.

The number rang, but there was no answer either from Donaldson or Linda Warwick. It wasn't too difficult to guess what had happened. The police weren't fools. Donaldson had been the last person to see him so naturally they would want to question Robert and the girl too. If Lloyd and Ryan had anything to do with it, the interview would last all day. They might even find themselves spending the night in Bethnal Green Police Station.

Magrane frowned at the handful of change he had left. Forty-seven pence: enough for a cup of coffee and a sandwich. Forty-seven pence: and Molly was sitting on a bundle and didn't know it. Sooner or later, Ryan was bound to conclude that he would be forced to turn to Molly for help, but with a bit of luck there was a chance he would beat him to the punch. Forty-seven pence: and the standard charge for a three-minute, operator-connected service was seventy-two.

There was only one thing to do; he would have to reverse the charges. Lifting the receiver, he dialled 100 and got the operator.

He counted off the seconds, chafing at the delay. What was the operator doing, for Christ's sake? Maybe there was some sort of industrial dispute and she was on a slowdown? Sweet Jesus, that's all he needed. A cool, pleasant voice said, "You're through, caller" and his anger suddenly evaporated.

"Molly?" he asked quietly. "Are you alone?"

"Andrew? Is that really you, Andrew?"

Magrane closed his eyes. Stupid bitch, who did she think it was? Hadn't the operator already told her that before she accepted the call?

"Of course it's me," he said impatiently. "Now tell me, are you alone or not?"

"Yes."

"Yes, what?"

"I'm quite alone." Molly hesitated, and then said, "Where are you? Have the police let you go?"

"Not exactly, that's why I need your help."

"My help?" she said warily. "I don't understand."

Magrane pinched his eyes. Molly was apprehensive enough already, so how was he going to explain things without alarming her even further? I've escaped to prove my innocence? Could there be anything more corny than that line? Corny or not, it was the only explanation he could try on her.

"You do understand, don't you?" he said presently.

"I think so."

Tiny beads of perspiration gathered on his forehead. Molly was still doubtful and he wondered what else he had to do to convince her.

"Look," he pleaded, "once the newspapers get hold of the story, Lloyd won't be able to sweep everything under the carpet. They will have to put me on trial whether they like it or not. That's all I want. It's not much to ask, is it?"

"No. I suppose it's the least you deserve, Andrew."

"Then you'll help me?"

"How?"

Magrane sighed with relief and wiped the sweat from his forehead. It was the one-word answer he'd been praying for.

Striving to remain calm and collected, he told Molly about the hundred and fifty pounds he'd concealed in the porcelain vase on the window ledge of the spare bedroom.

"You want me to bring the money to you?" she asked.

"Yes."

"All right, Andrew. Where shall I meet you?"

Magrane hesitated. He needed a place that was usually crowded, somewhere he could merge into the background.

"How about John Lewis's in Oxford Street? We could meet outside the restaurant."

"When?"

"Can you make it by four thirty?"

"I don't see any reason why I shouldn't," she said.

It sounded too good to be true. Magrane just hoped Molly wouldn't let him down when it came to the crunch.

Attwood and Norris were as different as chalk and cheese. The chief inspector was a thin, reedlike man with a small black moustache and a mournful air that Donaldson thought more suited to a pallbearer. Norris, on the other hand, didn't fit the mental picture he'd formed from talking to him on the telephone. Instead of a quiet, rather slow-thinking man, Donaldson found himself confronted with a blond athlete who looked as if he would be at home in a boxing ring.

"I expect Mr. Lloyd will have told you why we're here," Attwood said primly.

"I gather I've got some explaining to do," said Donaldson.

"Well, you were the last person to see Magrane before he escaped." Attwood pressed his fingertips together to form a church steeple. His facial expression became even more solemn, something Donaldson would have thought impossible had he not seen it with his own eyes. "And you did go out of your way to persuade Sergeant Quinn to leave you alone in the cell with him."

"I didn't have to twist his arm."

"I'm not saying you did."

Attwood was all sweetness and light, so reasonable that Donaldson knew it had to be an act. Norris was obviously cast in the role of the heavy who would start to lean on him when Attwood gave the nod. The sergeant was standing in front of the TV, rocking up and down on his heels as if raring to go. His presence soured the atmosphere in the living room.

"This personal matter that Magrane wanted to discuss with you? It didn't concern Mrs. Gregson, did it?"

"No, that was just a blind so that Quinn wouldn't hear what he had to say about your guvnor."

"Commander Ryan?"

"And Lloyd. He alleged they were determined to have him committed to a mental hospital."

"What's wrong with that?" Norris demanded loudly. "He belongs in a loony bin."

"Let me tell you something about Magrane," Donaldson said in a level voice. "There are times when he's as sane as you and I. For instance, I believe him when he says there are a lot of people in Whitehall who would be very embarrassed if he went into the witness box."

"Well, what do you know?" said Norris. "Magrane's condition must be contagious. We've got another nut on our hands."

Attwood ignored the outburst. "Like who, for instance?" he asked.

"Lloyd, for one. Between 1974 and 1977, he was responsible for running at least two SAS operations."

"That's a very wild allegation. The Home Office has never had any dealings with the Special Air Service."

"I'm not denying that. Lloyd isn't a civil servant in the Police Department, he's with the Secret Intelligence Service, and they certainly do have a close working relationship with the SAS."

"Balls," said Norris.

Donaldson shook his head. "Magrane is a very inquisitive person. You can bet your bottom dollar that when Andrew was made assistant operations officer, he read every top secret document in his custody from cover to cover. That's why you people can't afford to put him on trial for murder. You're frightened he will shoot his mouth off if he elects to give evidence."

"I'm just an ordinary policeman," Attwood said mildly. "It's up to the Director of Public Prosecutions to decide whether or not he goes to trial."

"Oh, come on," Donaldson said irritably, "you must think I was born yesterday. How can you be an ordinary copper when Ryan is head of Special Branch?"

"And the DPP?"

It was very apparent that Attwood was trying to give the impression that the suggestion was preposterous, that in asking the question, he was merely humoring him.

"It wouldn't be the first time that political considerations were taken into account."

"I see. What else did Magrane say to you?"

"Nothing," said Donaldson.

"Really? Are you telling me you'd no idea what he had in mind?"

The telephone pinged once and then started ringing; Attwood frowned at Norris and jerked his head, signalling him to answer it.

"He didn't give you a hint of any kind?"

"No."

"Who else do you suppose he would turn to for help apart from yourself?"

Donaldson hesitated. That damned calling card. He should never have shown it to Magrane. Given his twisted way of thinking, it was possible Andrew had decided that Linda Warwick was a contact.

"He won't come near me, that's for sure."

"I don't think you're being completely frank with me," said Attwood.

"You can think what you like. I haven't the faintest idea what Magrane will do."

"I have." Norris put the phone down and faced them with a broad grin. "He's asked Mrs. Gregson to meet him outside the restaurant in John Lewis's at four thirty."

Norris went on to say that it was smart of her to get in touch with the local police straight after his call, but Donaldson wasn't paying much attention. He sat there in the armchair, thinking about Magrane and pitying him. He couldn't help feeling that somehow all of them had betrayed Andrew in one way or another.

"We'll be going then."

"Yes." Donaldson looked up, frowning at Attwood. "What am I supposed to do in the meantime?"

"You wait here and twiddle your thumbs," said Attwood.

Donaldson glowered. Like hell he would. As soon as they had departed, he would go and see Linda Warwick. He thought it was time he mended a few fences.

17 . . .

MAGRANE pushed the cup of coffee to one side, propped his elbow on the table and cradled his chin in the palms of his hands. He read the front page of the *Evening Standard* again, a slight frown appearing on his forehead. He thought the vendor, who had crayoned "SAS Killer Escapes" on the billboard beside the newspaper stand ought to be prosecuted for false advertising. The escape was mentioned all right, but only in a couple of sentences hastily inserted under "Stop Press"; the lead story concerned the train of events leading to his arrest at Vale End cottage near Wrotham. To all intents and purposes, the account was a work of fiction bearing little or no relation to the truth. The reporter had done his best with the press release, but it still smacked of Lloyd.

He looked up and stared through the café window at the John Lewis department store across the street. It was foolish to underestimate the opposition. Ryan wasn't a flat-footed oaf with his brains in his boots. What on earth had made him think he could beat the head of Special Branch to the punch? Ryan would have alerted the Kent police to watch Molly within minutes of learning that he'd escaped from Bethnal Green. If the police were really smart, they could have a tail on Molly right now, and without being aware of it, she could lead them straight to him.

Magrane wavered. He needed the hundred and fifty pounds, but was it worth the risk? This was the make-or-break situation. If he went ahead and kept the appointment and the police were waiting for him, phase three of the operation would go down the drain. Yet without the money he was hamstrung. Donaldson couldn't help him there, because he was being held for questioning. Robert had been vulnerable from the word go and he should have gotten rid of the calling card before they picked him up. Had he done so, Special Branch wouldn't have gotten on to Linda Warwick quite so soon. Ryan would have to let them go in the end, but not before his people had bugged the flat in Worplesdene Gardens. Perhaps Robert would be smart enough to give the flat the once-over, but that was yet another risk he couldn't afford to take.

D-Day was less than forty-eight hours off, and there was no way he could make the hit without a rifle and ammunition. It was really up to Robert to provide him with the tools to do the job, but he couldn't expect any help from that quarter, not with Ryan and Lloyd watching Donaldson like hawks. Where could he get a gun then? If push came to shove, he could always break into a Territorial Army drill hall, although it would have to be somewhere nice and quiet, like the one in Loughborough.

He could see the drill hall clearly in his mind's eye, a red-brick building about half a mile south of the town center on the road to Leicester, the caretaker living next door in a small house that backed on to the park. Ironic to recall now how he had kicked against being posted to the T.A. What was it the Adjutant had said to him when he had reported back after convalescent leave? ''You may think you're fit for duty, Andrew, but we know better. A year with the Territorial Army will do you the world of good. It's an interesting job and you'll see a lot of the country.'' He had, too, travelling the length and breadth of England to deliver the same old lecture over and over again.

The drill hall in Loughborough would be a pushover provided he had the means to get there. One way or another, he had to raise some money. Magrane glanced at the department store again and decided he would have to look elsewhere for it. Leaving the café, he set off at a brisk pace towards Oxford Circus.

There was just twenty-seven pence left in his pocket. Faced with the same predicament, Harry Gregson would probably have found himself a dark alleyway, lain in wait and then mugged the first person who entered it. Magrane knew he couldn't be that indiscriminate. If he was going to resort to robbery with violence, the victim would have to be somebody who wouldn't trouble his conscience. Turning into Regent Street, he strode purposefully past Dickens and Jones, Liberty's and Hamley's toy shop and then wheeled into Brewer Street behind the Regent Palace Hotel.

He tried a couple of shops in Old Compton Street which sold girlie books but decided to give them both a miss, ruling out the first because he didn't fancy his chances with the staff and the other because it was too popular with the middle-aged dirty raincoat brigade. Halfway along Frith Street he found just the place he was looking for, a small intimate cinema with a sign above the door which said Members Only.

The usual soft porn was on display in the foyer, imported glossy magazines from West Germany, Denmark and Holland with long-legged girls dressed in rubberwear and leather on the front covers. The floor was carpeted in bright orange and the walls were a surrealist nightmare of black, silver and gold streaks of paint. The box office was a small counter covered in white vinyl. The young man seated behind it raised his eyes from the book he was reading, took one look at Magrane and, sizing him up, began to feel for the buzzer under the counter. He was still groping for it, still smiling nervously, when Magrane shopped a fist into his neck and knocked him cold. Catching him as he started to fall out of the chair, Magrane lowered him carefully to the floor, grabbed a handful of notes from the till and walked out of the cinema. There was no commotion behind him and nobody ran after him, but even so, his heart stayed in his mouth until he reached Shaftesbury Avenue when he began to breathe a little easier.

One problem had been solved, but others remained. A car: that was his next priority. To steal one he would need a screwdriver to jimmy open the vent window and a length of cable to bypass the ignition switch, items which could be obtained from any hardware store. Entering Piccadilly Circus via the subway outside the London Pavilion, Magrane joined the small queue at the booking office and purchased a ticket to Rayners Lane.

Donaldson paid off the taxi outside 22 Worplesdene Gardens, walked up the short flight of steps to the front door and pressed the buzzer to flat number three. Some moments later, there was a faint whirring noise followed by a sharp click as Linda Warwick tripped the electronic switch. Pushing the door open, he stepped inside the hall, uncertain what kind of reception he would get.

New York had evidently left its mark on Linda. In addition to a double Yale lock and a security chain, the door to her flat was also bolted top and bottom. Unlocking it was like opening a bank vault. Presently her face appeared in the gap between door and jamb, her mouth forming a perfect circle as if she were about to give a low whistle.

"Oh, it's you," she said.

Her voice was completely neutral, neither cool, friendly nor surprised. Taking the chain off the hook, she opened the door wider.

"You'd better come inside."

The invitation sounded a bit ominous, a preamble to "I want to have a few words with you."

Donaldson removed his raincoat and hung it up on a peg in the hall. "I expect you can guess why I'm here," he said.

"You think you owe me an explanation, is that it?"

He nodded and followed her into a room that seemed crowded with furniture even though it was spacious.

"I can't let you have the tapes." Blunt and to the point, that's me, Donaldson thought. Jump in with both feet and get it over with and remember to duck when she heaves the flower vase at you. "It's true Ryan seized them before I could record a duplicate track, but I would probably have welshed on the deal even if he hadn't taken them."

"What is this?" she said. "Confession time?"

"Something like that."

"Well, I'm not about to give you absolution, Robert." She frowned. "As a matter of fact, I might even bury a hatchet in your skull, metaphorically speaking."

"Thanks," he said dryly.

"Aren't you going to threaten me with a libel suit? That's how censorship works in this country, isn't it?" She shook her head, seemingly perplexed by the whole business. "Boy, if we had your libel laws in the States, the *Washington Post* would have printed one story on Watergate and that would have been it. Nixon would have ridden out the storm and finished his term in office."

"It's possible that Magrane will get in touch with you," Donaldson said abruptly.

"What?" She stared at him, her eyes almost popping out of her head. "Did I hear you right?"

"I saw Andrew about an hour before he escaped from custody. He was convinced that Lloyd meant to have him certified, that he knew too much to be put on trial. I said the press wouldn't allow the authorities to get away with that."

"I must be dense—"

"He thought I was just whistling in the dark, so I showed him your card."

"Terrific." Her voice was barely audible and he suspected that she had a pretty shrewd idea of what was in store for her.

"Daniel once said to me that Magrane believes what he wants to believe, that he'll bend the facts to suit his fantasy. That is why I have a nasty feeling he thinks I've advised him to use you as a go-between."

"Why, for God's sake?"

"Because he's convinced Lloyd has put a wiretap on my telephone, and of course he's right in a crazy sort of way."

"I think I need a drink." Linda left her chair, went into the dining alcove at the far end of the room and crouched in front of the sideboard. "How about you?"

Four thirty was a little early in the day for him, but he thought it priggish to say so and, instead, settled for a whisky and soda.

"Cheers," she said.

"Cheers." Donaldson raised his glass. "Perhaps I'm being unduly alarmist. The police are confident they'll nab him."

"Do they know where to find Magrane?"

Donaldson nodded. The jersey wool dress was a distraction; it clung to her figure, emphasizing every contour.

"But you have your doubts?"

"Magrane is a very resourceful man; he's proved that time and again."

"So what am I supposed to do?"

Take a holiday, he thought, go away and lie low until it's over. Sound advice, but he doubted if she would accept it. "Your telephone could be temporarily out of order."

"No way." She shook her head vehemently. "I need it too much, it's my bread and butter. Anyhow, I can't see Lloyd agreeing to that."

"He doesn't know about it."

"You mean you haven't told him?" One eyebrow rose in disbelief.

"Not yet, and with any luck I won't have to."

"You shouldn't go out on a limb for me, Robert."

It was another way of saying, "I'm a big girl now, I can look after myself." Watching her over the rim of his glass, Donaldson wondered if she could.

"I don't want you getting into trouble on my account."

"The shoe's on the other foot," he said. "You're the one who's in a fix and I'm responsible."

Linda smiled. "You certainly have a yen for sackcloth and ashes," she said.

"Never mind that. You just take care, you hear?" He swallowed the rest of the whisky and set the glass down on the occasional table beside the armchair. "If Magrane does telephone, don't keep it to yourself."

"What are you trying to do?" she asked. "Scare the pants off me?"

"Magrane is a killer; if you say the wrong thing to him, he might get the idea that you're a police informer." He stood up and moved towards the hall. "And I don't want anything to happen to you, Linda."

"I'm touched."

"So don't open the door unless you know who it is."

"I never do," she assured him solemnly.

"And don't go out alone at night."

"I might as well get myself to a nunnery."

"You'd be a lot safer and I'd be a whole lot happier if you did."

"Hey, I'm not used to this." She reached out and touched his face. "It's been a long time since anybody felt they had to protect me. You know what?" She smiled. "I think I like it."

Her mouth was very inviting and he kissed her, experiencing a warm glow that stayed with him as he walked through the rain to the Underground station in South Kensington.

Lloyd was sitting in an armchair near the television, a glass of whisky at his elbow. He seemed very much at home in the flat, which confirmed Donaldson's suspicion that it was the SIS and not Special Branch who paid the rent. For some moments neither said a word, but Lloyd's cold, appraising stare warned him what to expect.

"Where have you been?"

The inevitable and obvious question posed in an icy, suspicious tone.

"I popped out to get some cigarettes," said Donaldson.

"And I've been waiting more than twenty minutes."

"It's a good thing you had your own key then."

"The nearest tobacconist is just round the corner from here."

"They didn't have my favorite brand."

"Don't try to be funny with me," Lloyd snapped. "Attwood told you to stay put."

"He also told me to twiddle my thumbs." Donaldson helped himself to a drink, thinking he was going to need one before Lloyd was finished with him. "That's why I didn't take him seriously."

"I see. You knew Magrane was still at large and might therefore try to get in touch with you, but you decided to leave the telephone unattended because you needed a packet of cigarettes. Is that how they do things in the Parachute Regiment?"

The withering sarcasm got under his skin, just as he supposed Lloyd had intended. "You know damn well it isn't," Donaldson said angrily.

"No, you wouldn't last five minutes with them if you were that stupid. Correct me if I'm wrong, but I think you knew Magrane wouldn't keep his appointment with Mrs. Gregson."

"It occurred to me that Andrew might have second thoughts about it."

"And that's what prompted you to call on Linda Warwick?" Lloyd waved a warning hand. "Don't bother to deny it, Robert, I know you met her yesterday morning by the Round Pond in Kensington Gardens."

"You've had her watched?"

"As of Saturday evening. Does that surprise you?" Lloyd smiled and shook his head. "It shouldn't. You might have guessed that Virginia Magrane would get in touch with us after you left her house at twelve o'clock. Since you didn't arrive back here until past three, I was curious to know where you'd gotten to in the meantime. Remembering how you had reacted to her letter earlier that morning, I wondered if you had been to see Linda Warwick. And of course you had."

"So what are you going to do about it?"

"I could arrange for her to be deported. It wouldn't be very difficult."

Donaldson finished his whisky and left the glass on the sideboard. Lloyd wasn't bluffing; he held all the cards and always had, right from the first moment he'd met him up at Strathconan. Headquarters Land Forces had been ordered to provide a sacrificial goat in case anything went wrong and Vaughan had picked him. And why? It would be nice to think it was simply because he'd been available at the time, but there had been more to it than that. With the benefit of hindsight, he knew it was more than likely that Vaughan had thought he was naïve enough to be taken in by Lloyd and Tamblin. That was the thing that really stuck in his gullet.

"I wouldn't do that if I were you," Donaldson said quietly. "Get rid of her and bang goes your best chance of recapturing Magrane. You see, Andrew believes that I want him to keep in touch with me through Linda Warwick."

There was a long silence and then Lloyd said, "You'd better tell me what you have in mind."

It had been raining steadily for the past two hours and the

road was a gleaming black ribbon in the headlights. There was very little traffic about, but that wasn't the reason Magrane had avoided the M1. Driving a hot car on the motorway was just asking for trouble because it was too well policed; giving it a wide berth more than doubled the odds against being picked up.

Magrane took his eyes off the road to glance briefly at the fuel gauge and saw that it was below the quarter-full mark. At a rough estimate, there was enough left in the tank for another seventy-odd miles, providing the car lived up to the manufacturer's specification of thirty-four to the gallon. He could make it to Loughborough all right and travel south again as far as Northampton, but after that he would have to change cars. Even if he were willing to risk it, there would be no point in stopping at a filling station, not when the owner had fitted a security lock on the tank.

Odd that a man should be so careful in that respect, yet so careless in others. The owner had remembered to lock his door when he'd parked behind the building near the Odeon Cinema in Rayners Lane, but had forgotten to check the others. Three out of four left unlocked: how stupid could you get? Magrane frowned: what the hell was he beefing about? He ought to be grateful there were idiots like him around. Owners like him made thieving easy.

Ten to eight, and an orange glare on the horizon that had to be Leicester. Less than twenty miles to go then. Magrane pursed his lips: best to find a lay-by and kill an hour. It wouldn't do to arrive in Loughborough and find the drill hall crowded with part-time soldiers. He'd look a proper fool trying to hold a platoon of hairy-arsed paratroopers at bay with a screwdriver. Humming a tuneless dirge to himself, Magrane eased his foot on the accelerator.

18 . . .

THE call box was roughly a mile from the drill hall. Leaving the engine running, Magrane went inside, found the telephone directory and opened it to the letter B. Slowly and methodically, he ran a finger down each column looking for the name of the caretaker, finally coming to a halt at Bartlett, E. Bartlett; he repeated the name to himself, thinking it was a good thing he'd stopped to check because he could have sworn Ted's surname was Bartram. Closing the directory, he placed it back in the bin, left the box and drove on down the road.

Ted Bartlett would be getting on to sixty now, a short tubby man with a monk's fringe of hair and chronic asthma. He'd met Ted when the caretaker had been helping out in the bar of the officers' mess and he seemed to remember that one of the T.A. subalterns had also pointed out his wife to him, but he was damned if he could recall her face now. Not that it mattered; it would be Ted who answered the door when he called.

His memory for a face might be at fault, but he knew just where to look for the military signboard. Spotting it in the hedgerow some twenty-five yards before the entrance, Magrane doused the headlights and shifted into neutral. Coasting into the forecourt, he steered the car into the space between the caretaker's house and the drill hall where it would be hidden from the main road, and then cut the engine.

The drill hall was closed for the night but, to his relief several lights were showing in the house. Although the Bartletts were unlikely to offer any serious resistance, he figured the screwdriver he'd purchased from a hardware store in Rayners Lane would clinch the issue and persuade them to be cooperative. Careful to make as little noise as possible, Magrane got out, closed the door behind him and walked across the yard in the rain.

The television was going full blast and, getting no reaction at first, he rang the bell again and kept his thumb on the button. Presently he heard footsteps in the hall and a grumpy voice said, "All right, hold your horses, I'm coming."

The letter box rattled and, knowing he was being watched, Magrane said, "No need to be alarmed, Ted. It's only me—Major Donaldson."

"Major who?" Bartlett grunted.

"Major Donaldson. Surely you remember me? We met when I was up here with the Para recruiting team about a couple of years ago."

"Donaldson," Bartlett repeated vaguely. "Oh yes, I remember you now."

As far as Magrane knew, Bartlett had never met Robert, but he wasn't surprised that the caretaker pretended otherwise. When confronted by a stranger who claimed to know them, it was a fact that most people professed to remember the face even if they couldn't put a name to it.

The door opened a fraction. Giving it a shove with his shoulder, Magrane forced his way into the hall and pointed the screwdriver at Bartlett's throat.

"You're not going to give me any trouble, are you, Ted?" he asked softly.

"No." The caretaker swallowed nervously. "No, I can see I wouldn't stand a chance against you."

"You're dead right. Who else is here?"

"Only Jean, my wife. She's in the sitting room."

"I'd like to meet her," Magrane said politely.

"Must you? She hasn't been well lately."

"I'd still like to meet her."

Bartlett nodded glumly and, backing off down the hall beyond the staircase, opened a door on his left. The noise from the television was such that it was some moments before the sallow-faced woman in the armchair became aware of them. Even then, she failed to grasp the significance of the screwdriver in Magrane's hand and it wasn't until he pulled the plug out of the socket and plunged the screen into darkness that it finally dawned on her that something was wrong.

"Ted?" Her voice was little more than a whisper. "Who is this man? What does he want?"

"Well, it's like this, Mrs. Bartlett," Magrane said calmly. "I've been ordered to collect certain items of equipment and your husband has the keys to the drill hall and the armory." He smiled at the caretaker. "Isn't that so, Ted?"

"Yes."

"Good. Have you got them on you?"

"No, I keep them upstairs in our bedroom."

Magrane studied him thoughtfully. "Do you know who I am?" he asked.

"Yes." Bartlett licked his lips. "You're Major Donaldson."

"No, my name's Magrane, Andrew Magrane."

Two pairs of eyes widened. Bartlett caught his breath and wheezed. His wife stared at him, her mouth open.

"That's right; I'm the SAS killer the police are looking for. You bear that in mind, Ted, when you're upstairs getting the keys. I mean, you don't want Jean to come to any harm, do you?"

"No."

"That's what I thought." Magrane jerked a thumb towards the door. "Off you go then, Ted, and don't take all night. If you're not back inside two minutes, I might get the wrong idea."

He didn't shout at Bartlett. There was no need to. The media had hung a label round his neck and it was evident they believed he was ruthless enough to kill anyone who stood in his way.

Bartlett left the room, his head bowed as if carrying a heavy burden on his shoulders. Suddenly the years told and he looked an old sixty. Magrane glanced at the framed snapshot on the mantelpiece and found it hard to believe that the slim, upright, fresh-faced corporal in battle dress and forage cap was one and the same man. Corporal Ted Bartlett, Royal Engineers circa 1940; the young warrior just back from the beaches of Dunkirk. Thirty-eight years later the gladiator was pear-shaped and suffered from asthma.

"I suppose it happens to all of us in time," he said.

"Pardon?"

The woman was staring at him, a wary expression in her eyes as if she feared he had taken leave of his senses. It would be a waste of breath to explain that these last few days had been an intolerable strain, as bad as anything he'd experienced in Northern Ireland. She would never understand what it was like to work undercover with everyone against you, nor would she wish to know. There were thousands like her up and down the country, people who were wrapped up in their own little worlds, comfortable, secure, content to let someone else do the dirty work as long as it didn't affect them. A floorboard creaked in the hall and he wheeled round to see Bartlett holding a bunch of keys aloft.

"I've got them."

"So I see," Magrane said coldly. "Have you got a flashlight?"

"There's one in the hall."

"All right, let's go." Crisp and decisive, that was more like it, he thought. It was no good being introspective with the Bartletts; they had to be constantly reminded that he was calling the tune.

"You lead the way, Jean and I will follow."

"It's still raining," Bartlett protested.

"So what?" said Magrane. "You'll survive."

They left the house, Magrane unlocking the door before pulling it shut behind him. Bartlett hurried across the yard, his wife close on his heels and complaining because she was wearing carpet slippers and her feet were getting wet. Her behavior didn't surprise Magrane. From past experience, he had learned that in a crisis the mind was often preoccupied with the trivial. Halting in front of the drill hall, Bartlett tucked the flashlight under one arm while he sorted out the right key and opened the door.

A narrow passageway stretched before them. The training hall was on their left, and to the right a concrete staircase with a metal handrail led to the lecture rooms and officers' mess on the floor above. The armory was situated directly opposite the entrance at the far end of the passage beyond the accommodation stores. Magrane remembered one of the T.A. officers assuring him that although it would take a wheelbarrow-load of plastic explosive to blow a hole in the steel door, the armory was also protected by a sophisticated electronic defense system.

"Hold it, Ted," he said curtly. "Stop right there, don't move another inch."

"Why not?"

"Don't play the innocent with me." Magrane punched him in the back. "You know damn well there's an infrared fence between us and the door. We break it and the alarm rings in the local police station and the TV cameras inside the armory are activated. Once they see our faces on their monitor screen, they'll know it wasn't set off by accident. Am I right?"

Bartlett nodded. "A good thing you reminded me," he said lamely. "I'd forgotten all about the master switch."

"Are you sure nothing else has slipped your mind?"

"I don't think so."

"The system hasn't been modified since I was here two years ago?"

"No."

"Certain of it, are you?"

"I'm positive," said Bartlett.

The master switch was concealed behind a panel set in the wall which Bartlett opened by rotating a dummy fire alarm in a clockwise direction. Reaching inside the compartment, he neutralized the infrared intruder system and then unlocked the armory. As the steel door swung back on its hinges, the overhead fluorescent lights automatically came on.

Although aware that several units shared the drill hall, Magrane was surprised at the number of weapons held in the armory. Sterlings, General Purpose Machine Guns and FN Self-loading Rifles were chained together in racks positioned against the walls to form a hollow square. Apart from the small arms, ten Carl Gustav antitank projectors lay packed in wooden chests down the center of the room. Beyond the counter facing the entrance, individual cleaning kits in square-shaped, tobacco-sized cans were neatly stacked on the shelves of a metal filing cabinet. Opening half a dozen cans, Magrane removed the pull-throughs and handed them to Bartlett.

"What am I supposed to do with these?"

"Can't you guess?" Magrane said quietly.

Pull-throughs were three-foot lengths of cord with metal weights at one end and two loops for cloth and wire gauze at the other. As far as Bartlett was concerned, they were only good for cleaning the barrel of a rifle. It simply didn't occur to him that they could serve another purpose.

"They're for Jean."

"What?"

"I want you to tie her up." Magrane waved the screwdriver under Bartlett's nose. "Look, Ted, I don't like the idea either but it's got to be done. I can't afford to take any chances, you understand."

It was obvious that Bartlett didn't and he wondered if he should take him into his confidence. If Bartlett knew what was at stake, if Ted could be made to see that phase three of Operation Damocles would bring lasting peace to Northern Ireland, then perhaps he wouldn't be quite so unhappy about it? Magrane pushed a hand through his tousled hair. No, that wouldn't do. To convince him, he would have to disclose the identity of the target and Ted couldn't be trusted to keep his mouth shut. The local police were bound to contact the Metropolitan Police and once Lloyd knew who he was going after, Ryan would seal off the area and that would be it.

"The knots," he snapped, "they're too loose. Make them tighter."

Magrane wished the woman would stop snivelling. Did she think he enjoyed seeing her humiliated, that he was some kind of sadistic freak? Christ, surely she must realize that he didn't have any option.

"That'll do," he said irritably. "Now you can unchain the rifles."

"I can't," said Bartlett. "I don't have the keys. The unit commanders keep them."

"Don't try to put one over on me, Ted. You're not smart enough."

"How many more times do I have to tell you?" The veins stood out on Bartlett's forehead. "I don't have the sodding keys."

"All right, Ted, calm down. I'll take your word for it." Magrane opened the armorer's locker, went through his tool kit and found a hacksaw. "This should do the trick."

"No chance."

"Well, we'll know that soon enough, won't we?" Magrane passed the saw to him. "Once you get going with this."

"Those links are thicker than my little finger."

"Then you'd better put your back into it."

Magrane folded his arms and leaned against the wall. The links weren't made of tungsten and there were plenty of spare blades in the tool chest. Nothing was going to stop him; if necessary, he would tell Ted to cut through the trigger guard. So what if it did make the rifle look unsightly? The mechanism wouldn't be impaired and that was all that mattered.

The grating made by the hacksaw set his teeth on edge. It was worse than squeaky chalk on a blackboard or the dentist's drill boring into a cavity. How much longer was Bartlett going to take, for Christ's sake? Judging by his present rate of progress, anybody would think he was using a nail file on the bloody chain. Virginia was always filing her nails; sometimes he thought she did it just to annoy him because she knew he couldn't stand the noise.

Time was running on, the minutes multiplying faster than he cared to think about. The police were pretty thin on the ground in Loughborough, but there was always a chance that one of their prowl cars might pull into the forecourt, especially if the driver felt like having a smoke. If one of the constables then decided to stretch his legs, he could be in trouble. Magrane smiled: that would hardly be a new experience for him.

"Hoo-bloody-ray." Bartlett pulled the severed chain through a dozen trigger guards and stood up, a sullen expression on his beet-red face. "There you are," he said, "you can take your pick."

"Well done, Ted." Magrane patted him on the shoulder.

Old soldiers liked to be praised and Bartlett was no exception. "I don't know what I would have done without you."

Ironic, but true all the same. No matter how unwillingly, Bartlett had done his bit and now the rest was up to him. Moving down the line, Magrane examined the rifles with a critical eye, looking for a weapon that belonged to a marksman. The good shot always kept his rifle in immaculate condition, the foresight blackened, the working parts clean and slightly oiled. Seven down from the right, he found one which measured up to his standards.

"You've picked a good 'un there," Bartlett said grudgingly.

Magrane knew he had, at least as far as external appearances were concerned. He just hoped that the owner of this particular rifle possessed normal vision, otherwise there could be an almighty cock-up. There would be no opportunity to adjust the sight and that meant he wouldn't know whether the damn thing was firing low, high, right or left until he squeezed the trigger and saw the bullet strike. At a range of a hundred yards, however, he was unlikely to miss the target and, with any luck, he'd have enough time to correct the point of aim and make sure of it with the second round.

"Are they still using the same old ammunition depot, Ted? The one behind the drill hall?"

"Why bother to ask when you already know the answer?"

"I was only checking. The last time I was here, somebody told me the estimates committee had just given their approval for a larger one."

Magrane laid the FN rifle on top of the counter and opened one of the drawers underneath. Although several units shared the drill hall, he knew there was only one key to the ammunition depot and that, for security reasons, it was kept in the armory where it was protected by the electronic defense system. Drawing a blank with the left-hand drawer, he tried the one in the center and found the key tucked inside the arms register.

"The routine never changes, does it, Ted?" Magrane handed the key to Bartlett and picked up the screwdriver again. "You go first," he said.

Although it was fairly dark outside and his eyes had become accustomed to the artificial light in the armory, Magrane spotted the depot while they were still some distance away. Its shape was unmistakable. A square brick building, its design owed a lot to the aboveground air-raid shelters that had been put up during the war. As they drew nearer, Bartlett's flashlight picked out the double yellow lines of the No Parking area and the inevitable signs prohibiting smoking and naked lights within twenty-five meters of the bunker.

Bartlett unlocked the steel door and went inside. With unerring instinct, he shone the flashlight on the boxes of 7.62mm stacked in the far right-hand corner. Lifting one from the top, he removed the wooden lid and ripped open the tinfoil liner. The ammunition was packed in cartons, each one containing fifty loose rounds.

Muttering to himself, he prised one free and gave it to Magrane. "You've got enough there to start a war."

"Or stop one," said Magrane.

"How?"

"By serving notice on the Kremlin that you intend to draw the line." Magrane froze, suddenly realizing that he'd said far too much. "Come on," he muttered, "it's time we were going."

Bartlett declared that he would never get away with it but from the lack of conviction in his voice, it was clear that he was just making the right noises. The moment they were back inside the armory, he crossed his wrists behind him, anticipating that Magrane would tie them. Bartlett was only being sensible, but it was obvious that his wife despised him for it.

Magrane said, "I'm sorry I have to do this to you, Ted."

"So am I."

"I'll phone the police tomorrow morning and tell them to release you both."

"That's big of you," Bartlett said bitterly.

Magrane shrugged and spread his hands regretfully. Then, picking up the self-loading rifle, he walked out of the armory, locking the door behind him. As he moved down the passageway, he thought he could hear the woman screaming, but then the noise ceased abruptly and he supposed Bartlett had told his wife to save her breath. Leaving the drill hall, he dumped the rifle and ammunition on the back seat of the car and went back inside the house.

The caretaker was the wrong shape and size, but Magrane thought the knitted blue tie which he found hanging in the wardrobe would improve his appearance. Going into the bathroom, he opened the linen cupboard and found a clean towel before helping himself to Bartlett's shaving gear and facecloth. Satisfied he now had everything he needed, he went downstairs and switched off the lights in the living room and hall to give the impression that the Bartletts had gone to bed. That done, he released the catch on the front door and left the house.

It was difficult not to feel elated and he had to remind himself that he wasn't out of the woods yet, not by a long sight. Finding another car was the next problem and once that had been solved, he would have to get in touch with Donaldson. That Lloyd would be able to eavesdrop on their conversation was a distinct advantage. Providing he played his cards right, he could hoodwink the lot of them.

Completing a reverse turn in the yard, Magrane drove out into the main road and, turning right, headed towards Leicester. The time was eleven thirty and it was still raining but not nearly so heavily.

Donaldson opened one eye. A low hum came from the television, but the screen was blank. Swinging his feet off the couch, he sat up and peered at the wristwatch, amazed to see that it was past two o'clock. Still feeling bone tired despite the prolonged catnap, he switched the set off and headed for the bedroom. The telephone started jangling before he was even halfway there and a faint hope that the caller had dialled the wrong number evaporated the instant he lifted the receiver.

In a brittle voice, Linda Warwick said, "It seems you were right about Magrane, Robert."

"You've spoken to him?"

"A few minutes ago. We had the weirdest conversation. I didn't understand half of it, especially when he started talking about cut-outs and deep cover. However, for what it's worth, he did give me a message that appears to make sense in a crazy sort of way. Have you got a pen or pencil handy?"

"Yes."

"Well, first of all, he wants a large scale map of the

Knightsbridge area and then you're to obtain a detailed plan of 58 Princes Gate from the Borough Surveyor's office. Okay?''

Donaldson scribbled the details on a pad and read them back to Linda.

"Does 58 Princes Gate ring a bell with you?" she asked.

"Not offhand."

"Better hold on to your hat because that's the address of the Libyan Embassy in London."

"I don't like the sound of that," he said uneasily.

"There's more to come. Magrane says that he's got all the necessary equipment for the job, but you've got to provide the backup."

"What backup?"

"Search me. Perhaps he'll enlighten you when he calls at twelve o'clock tomorrow."

"Tomorrow?"

"I mean today—this morning—oh, what the hell. . . ." She swallowed nervously. "Will you be here to take his call?"

"Of course I will. Look, would it help if I came round now?"

"No, it's sweet of you to offer, Robert, but I'll be all right, really I will. I've just taken a couple of sleeping pills."

There was a long pause while each waited for the other to say something, and then, just as he was about to tell her that he would check with Special Branch to make sure they were watching the flat, Linda suddenly wished him good night and hung up.

Donaldson stared at the message on the memo pad. The Libyan Embassy certainly tied in with Magrane's conception of Operation Damocles, but all the same, he had a nagging suspicion that Andrew still had a few surprises up his sleeve. Lifting the receiver again, he called Lloyd.

19 . . .

MAGRANE glanced at the speedometer, saw the needle was hovering at sixty and immediately eased his foot on the accelerator. London was less than twenty miles away now and unless he took it slowly, he would hit the North Circular Road long before the first trains and buses started running. Although he'd avoided the main roads after swapping the car for an Austin Maxi in Leicester, the journey south had taken far less time than he'd expected, even allowing for the wide detour through Uppingham. Slowing down to under thirty miles an hour, Magrane kept his eyes open for a suitable spot to pull off the road and hole up for a couple of hours. Ten minutes later, he found just the place he was looking for: a narrow dirt road on the left that wound through a copse thick with holly trees. Reversing into a clearing, he cut the engine and switched off the lights.

Magrane rubbed his jaw, feeling the stubble. After phoning Linda Warwick to leave a message for Donaldson, he'd stopped at Grafham Kimbolton and had a quick shave in the town's public lavatories which obviously hadn't been close enough. He would need to give the beard another scrape before the day was out, but a clean shave was the least of his worries. Right now, there were more important things to consider.

Long before the population of London was up and about,
he would have to find a temporary hiding place for the FN
self-loading rifle and carton of 7.62mm ammunition. Much as
he disliked the idea of using the same derelict house in
Kentish Town where he'd stored the handguns, a suitable
alternative failed to spring readily to mind. That was the
trouble with not having a detailed map; you hadn't a clue
where to look. He made a mental note to buy a copy of
Nicolson's Street Finder as soon as the newsstands were
open.

Magrane stretched both arms above his head and yawned.
He was tired, bone tired, and he wasn't thinking straight; his
mind was jumping around like a grasshopper. He should be
thinking about the car, not the map. Clearly, it was essential
he ditch the vehicle a long way from the derelict house in
Balaclava Road, otherwise the Austin could lead the police to
the rifle. He could drive out to the suburbs and leave the car
in a quiet side street where it would probably remain unnoticed
for some considerable time. Either Kenton or Wembley would
do; he was equally familiar with both. Perhaps Wembley
would be better; it was farther away from Harrow.

He fished a crumpled packet out of his raincoat pocket and
lit a cigarette. As soon as he had abandoned the car, he would
use the Bakerloo Line from Wembley Central to get back into
London, by which time the snack bars ought to be open and
he could get something to eat. Money wasn't a problem; he
still had eighteen of the twenty-two pounds he'd grabbed
from the till yesterday.

So far so good. What next? The Bartletts? No, they would
have to wait until he'd completed his reconnaissance of Princes
Gate. If Donaldson was to be convinced that Qaddafi's man
in London was the target for phase three, it was vital Magrane
know the neighborhood like the back of his hand; that was
only good thinking. But what would the opposition be doing
in the meantime? Or had they already taken preventative
action? His escape from Bethnal Green Police Station would
be in all the headlines today and if there had been a demand
for it, the Ministry of Defence would probably have released
his photograph, especially if Lloyd had thrown his weight
behind the press. Did it matter all that much if they had?

Magrane angled the rearview mirror towards him and smiled into it, suddenly grateful to Daniel because, thanks to him, his face had changed out of all recognition in the last nine months. Looking on the bright side, there might even be a hidden bonus in the publicity; the police could be inundated with false sightings, and if he was any judge of human nature, the hoaxers would have a field day.

Magrane opened the ashtray and stubbed out his cigarette. Three forty-five: time for an hour's shuteye. Leaning back in the seat, he closed his eyes and within a matter of minutes was fast asleep.

Less than twenty-four hours had passed since Ryan had taken to his sickbed and not surprisingly he still looked under the weather. His nose and eyes weren't quite so red, but his face was the color of dough and there were obvious signs that a hacking cough had kept him awake all night. Donaldson couldn't make up his mind whether Ryan had turned up at the office at Lloyd's request, or out of a sense of duty, or because the Magrane affair had now become such a hot potato that he was afraid to leave anyone else in charge. It was probably a combination of all three, but whatever the prime motive, he thought Ryan might just as well have stayed at home considering how little he had contributed thus far. Not that Chief Inspector Attwood was exactly a ball of fire. He had found himself a niche in the far corner of the room and was busy taking notes, so diligent about it he gave the impression his future career depended solely on his ability to produce a complete record of who said what and to whom.

Lloyd had been doing most of the talking, which was not unusual. Seated as far away from Ryan as the office would allow, he was concentrating his attention on the large-scale map and the architect's plan of 58 Princes Gate, both of which had been pinned to a large piece of hardboard that took up the whole of one wall.

Lloyd said, "This discussion isn't getting us anywhere." He looked round the room, his jaw set at a pugnacious angle as if daring anyone to contradict him. "I think it's time we decide what we are going to do about Magrane. Now, we could warn the Libyans to be on their guard, but I don't want to do that unless it's absolutely unavoidable. Diplomatic relations are not exactly cordial as it is and I can imagine Qaddafi's reaction if he learned that an SAS officer was planning to assassinate his ambassador in London. In short, we've got to stop Magrane without the Libyans becoming aware of what's going on.''

''Is 'A' Division to be kept in the dark as well?''

It was the first time that Ryan had strung more than two words together and his sudden intervention came as a surprise. Up till then, he'd confined himself to an occasional monosyllabic grunt.

''In case it's slipped your mind, they are responsible for protecting the embassies.''

Lloyd turned a frosty smile on him. ''Well, obviously 'A' Division must be briefed to double the number of men on duty at 58 Princes Gate, but it's got to be done discreetly. They will have to wear plainclothes and we don't want them parading up and down the pavement like a bunch of guardsmen from Knightsbridge Barracks.''

''They're going to be loitering in Exhibition Road, queuing up at the Albert Hall and strolling about in Hyde Park, are they?'' Ryan glared at the murky sky outside the office. ''In this weather? If the Libyans don't notice them, Magrane certainly will.'' He picked up a copy of the *Daily Express* lying on his desk and held it aloft like some member of Parliament waving a paper to catch the Speaker's eye. ''Magrane was a suspicious bastard to begin with, but now that his face is in every newspaper, he's going to be twice as difficult.''

''It's not a very good likeness,'' Lloyd observed mildly.

Donaldson agreed with him, up to a point. The picture looked like an enlargement of a passport photograph, one that had been taken several years ago when Magrane had been bright-eyed and bushy-tailed. In his opinion, it bore only a passing resemblance to the Magrane he'd met in Bethnal Green Police Station yesterday. Nevertheless, Ryan was right; the publicity was going to make him doubly cautious.

''I can't understand why the Ministry of Defence released it,'' Ryan grumbled.

"They didn't have any option," Lloyd said tartly. "The press was clamoring for a photograph and Tamblin would have been laughed out of court if he'd insisted that Magrane had to remain anonymous in the interests of security. Anyway, I won't complain if all this exposure cramps his style."

"It's certainly cramping ours." Ryan coughed twice in rapid succession and then paused to catch his breath. "God knows how many people haven't already phoned in to say that they've seen him. We've got squad cars chasing Magrane all over London."

"I hope you've got something in reserve. We'd all look pretty silly if we were unable to respond to an emergency in Princes Gate."

"Somehow I can't see Magrane walking up to the front door of the embassy."

"Neither can I," said Donaldson, "especially as he told Linda Warwick that he has all the necessary equipment for the job."

"Whatever that means." Lloyd glanced in Ryan's direction, one eyebrow raised to invite his opinion.

"I assume he's referring to a firearm of some sort, but I don't see how he could have obtained one."

"Perhaps he has a private arsenal."

"You mean 'had'," Ryan said irritably. "We've been over his house in Angel Crescent with a fine-tooth comb and the cupboard's bare. He started out with two handguns. We've got the Wesson .357 magnum revolver and the West German police found the .25 Bernardelli automatic in the men's room at Cologne airport."

"And we know that none of the gunsmiths in London were broken into last night," Attwood chipped in helpfully.

"What about the rest of the country?" asked Donaldson.

"We haven't heard anything."

"Have you asked?"

"No, I didn't think it was necessary." Attwood smiled. "You see, we know there was less than a pound in the raincoat that had been left on the back seat of the Escort Magrane stole from the police station. He wouldn't get very far on that, would he?"

"Let me ask you a question," said Donaldson. "How

many cars were stolen in the London area last night, how many houses were broken into and how many people got mugged? You take it from me, Magrane isn't short of money, he's mobile, and by now he's probably got a rifle.''

"I agree with Robert," said Lloyd. "It's a mistake to underestimate him."

Attwood held the smile, but it began to look a mite sick. It looked even sicker after Ryan told him that that would teach him to think twice before jumping in with both feet.

"Of course, we don't *know* that the ambassador is the target. It's possible he may have someone else in mind, like the Head of Chancery, for instance, or one of the First Secretaries." Lloyd left his chair to take a closer look at the maps. "Even if we assume that Magrane does have a rifle, I don't see how he can hope to pull it off. None of the principal offices in 58 Princes Gate are overlooked, so he won't achieve anything if he does break into another house somewhere in the immediate vicinity of the embassy. Still, he has asked for the map and the architect's plan which would indicate that he intends to meet you, Robert."

"Not necessarily. Andrew could get all the information he needs by question and answer."

"Then you'll have to lead him on. Perhaps we can lay a trap for him." Lloyd stroked his chin. "Harrods is no distance away."

"Harrods?"

"Why not? There's a good chance Magrane would believe it if you said you had information that the ambassador and his wife were planning to visit Harrods at such and such a time. I admit it's a bit of a long shot and you'd have to play it very much by ear, but I think it's worth trying."

"Maybe."

"You have reservations?"

"Let's say I have a feeling he's taking us for a ride. This is the first time that Andrew has asked me to do something positive for him. Up to now, he has always kept the initiative and been able to dictate events." Donaldson shrugged his shoulders. "I could be wrong, but this sudden reversal strikes a false note with me. I can't help wondering if he hasn't got some other target in mind."

Lloyd didn't say anything—he didn't have to—the sceptical expression on his face showed exactly what he thought of the suggestion. Donaldson frowned: possibly he was attaching too much significance to the time delay, but he thought it odd that Magrane hadn't got in touch with Linda Warwick sooner. He'd been very quick to contact Molly Gregson, telephoning her less than an hour after he'd escaped from Bethnal Green. But what if he had tried to call Linda earlier and she had been out? Andrew was capable of putting his own interpretation on her absence. Nothing was too improbable for him; he was paranoiac enough to assume that Ryan had pulled her in for questioning. He was also clever enough to proceed on that assumption and turn it to his advantage.

". . . and of course there's the Russian trade delegation. They're a possibility."

Donaldson looked up, annoyed that he'd only caught the tail end of the conversation between Ryan and Lloyd.

"But I can guarantee Magrane won't get within a mile of Congress House." Ryan started coughing again. Tears welled in his eyes and he pounded a fist against his chest. It was hardly a remedy that any self-respecting doctor would have prescribed, but it seemed to do the trick. "Anyway," he wheezed, "they're flying back to Moscow around lunchtime tomorrow."

Lloyd was about to say something when there was a knock on the door and Sergeant Quinn put his head inside the room.

"What do you want, Sergeant?" Ryan scowled. "Can't you see we're busy?"

"Yes, I know, sir, but I thought you'd want to hear the latest about Magrane. It seems he made a call about half an hour ago. At first the Duty Inspector thought it was just another crank trying to take the mickey out of the police until he said there were two people locked inside the armory of the T.A. Drill Hall up at Loughborough."

"And?"

"It wasn't a hoax." Quinn glanced at the slip of paper in his hand. "According to the local police, he's stolen an FN self-loading rifle, serial number XJ156970, and fifty rounds of 7.62mm ammunition."

"What about the people who were locked in the armory? Do we know who they were?"

"Yes." Quinn glanced at the scrap of paper again. "They're a Mr. and Mrs. Bartlett. Both of them are pretty shaken by the experience but they'll be okay. Bartlett is a caretaker employed by the T.A. and I understand he's still being questioned by the CID. They may have something for us in an hour or so."

"All right," said Ryan. "Keep me informed."

Quinn nodded and withdrew. There was a brief silence and then Lloyd weighed in, describing in general terms how he thought Donaldson should handle Magrane when he telephoned at noon. Even now, no one, not even Lloyd, was wholly convinced that a high-ranking official in the Libyan Embassy was the primary target, but with time running out, they had to act on what they had—and act fast.

Magrane heaved a sigh of relief as the train started moving again. It had been stuck in the tunnel somewhere between Archway and Highgate for more than five minutes and the unexpected delay had stretched his nerves to the breaking point. Donaldson was expecting him to call at twelve o'clock and this was one occasion when he couldn't afford to be late. Now that Donaldson was no longer operating from the flat in Devonshire Terrace, almost overnight he had become less available and therefore less dependable.

Less dependable? That was ridiculous; Robert had always been there when he needed him. Robert had the patience of Job and he'd wait for the call. Nodding to himself, Magrane left his seat and moved towards the door. Moments later, the train drew into the station and shuddered to a halt. The doors opened and, stepping out onto the platform, he turned left and hurried towards the exit.

He told himself there was bound to be a telephone box in the station, and he was right. There were six in an alcove beyond the newsstand, but none of them were of any use to him because some officious idiot in the GPO had seen fit to remove every door so that it was impossible to hold a private conversation. Swearing under his breath, Magrane headed for the stairway leading to the station yard above.

He considered stopping someone to ask the way to the nearest phone booth, but it would be just his luck to accost a stranger who didn't know the area. Halting at the top of the steps, he pulled the copy of *Nicolson's Street Finder* out of his raincoat pocket and opened it at page 47. Within seconds elation replaced despondency as he spotted a post office in Highgate High Street near Waterlow Park.

Waiting for a break in the traffic, he crossed Archway Road and turned into Jackson's Lane, his stride gradually becoming shorter and shorter as he climbed the hill.

20 . . .

LINDA Warwick reread the article she had just finished typing and then, her face a picture of frustration, she wadded the original and two copies together and hurled the ball of paper into the wastebasket.

"How many does that make it?" Donaldson asked quietly.

"Who knows? I've lost count." Linda fumbled with a book of matches and lit a cigarette. "Does it matter?"

"No." He smiled. "And you've made your point—I've got the message."

"What?"

"Whenever Janet said, 'Does it matter?' I knew I'd gone too far and it was time to back off. It was a sort of warning shot across the bows."

Donaldson fell silent. He didn't want to talk about his wife, at least not now. Janet had died of leukemia, her body slowly wasting away until, just before the end, she'd weighed less than five stone. Sixty-eight pounds of skin and bone with matchsticks for arms and legs, her face so aged that it was difficult to believe she was only twenty-six. That was four years ago, but the memory of her ordeal was still fresh and it still hurt.

"How long have you been at Wilton?"

Donaldson looked up, grateful to Linda for the change of subject. "About eighteen months. It's a two-year posting."

"And then where will you go?"

"Back to regimental duty, hopefully with 3 Para."

"Why the third battalion?"

The questions were coming fast and she even contrived to sound interested. He liked her for that.

"No special reason," he told her, "other than the fact that I've always served with them."

"And you feel at home?"

"Yes."

"I envy you. I wish I could find a niche."

"Don't you like it over here?"

"Sure I do, but sometimes I get a little homesick for New York." Linda stubbed out her cigarette with a quick nervous gesture. "How does that old saying go? The grass is always greener on the other side of the fence?"

There was a wistful expression in her eyes and he felt a sense of impending loss. He wanted Linda to know that he would miss her, but he never got around to expressing it in so many words. The telephone saw to that.

"That will be Magrane," she murmured.

"Yes."

"He's late."

"He always is." Donaldson lifted the receiver. "That's one area where Andrew is consistent, he's never on time."

"I heard that," said Magrane.

"So?"

"So I'm sorry I kept you waiting, Robert." Magrane cleared his throat. "Did you get the maps I asked for?"

"I've got them here in front of me." Donaldson caught Linda's eye and winked. "As a matter of fact, I was studying the architect's plan when you called and I figure we've got problems."

"How come?"

"Well, for one thing, the building is pretty secluded and none of the principal offices are overlooked."

"That confirms my impression. I had a look at the place earlier this morning. The question is, what do we do now?"

Donaldson frowned. Their conversation wasn't going quite

the way he'd expected. Magrane sounded tired and listless, as if he was looking for any excuse to back off.

"We keep our fingers crossed and just hope that Linda's information is correct."

"What the hell are you talking about, Robert?"

Donaldson wished he knew. They had reached a deadlock, and to break it, he'd said the first thing that had come into his head. Glancing in Linda's direction again, he saw her staring at him, completely motionless as if in a hypnotic trance. Her mouth was slightly open and both hands rested on the portable. The typewriter gave him an idea, not brilliant, but the best he could think of on the spur of the moment.

"Linda happens to be a free-lance journalist." He paused, allowing Magrane time to digest the information. "I suggested she get in touch with the press secretary at Princes Gate to ask when our friend would be available for an in-depth interview. It seems he has a very full week in front of him. In fact, looking at his program, I think Linda is going to be out of luck unless he agrees to fit her in after he returns from Harrods."

"When's this?"

Magrane surprised him by his eagerness to swallow such an improbable story. It wasn't like him at all; usually he was a lot more cagey.

"Robert?"

"What?"

"I asked you a question."

"Sorry. I was looking at this program to see if I could find the registration number of the Mercedes our friend will be using."

"You needn't bother," Magrane said crisply, "I already have it."

"You do?"

"I don't know why you're so surprised. After all, it's in the Damocles file."

"Oh, really?"

"The number is 59845. There now, does that satisfy you?"

"Yes."

"Then, for Christ's sake, answer my question."

"There's no need to fly off the handle," Donaldson said

mildly. "Our friend is visiting Harrods tomorrow. He's scheduled to leave Princes Gate at ten fifteen. I don't have to tell you what it's like driving along the Brompton Road. If his car isn't stuck in a traffic jam, it'll only be moving at a walking pace. Now, there's a house up for sale in Ovington Gardens and I figure you'll get a clear view of the main road from the attic."

"Don't think me ungrateful," Magrane said courteously, "but I always make it a rule to find my own site. Anyway, shouldn't you be thinking about other things?"

Magrane was back in form again, secretive and obscure, so obscure that at first he didn't know what to make of the question, but then the penny dropped and he remembered the message Andrew had left with Linda.

"If you are referring to the backup," he said, "that's all taken care of. Before you know it, you'll be sunning yourself in—"

"I don't want to hear," Magrane cut in.

"I take your point."

"It's about time you did, Robert, because your security stinks." Magrane chuckled. "Still, I should worry, this is the last time we'll be using this telephone, because tomorrow morning you're going to be waiting for me in Hans Crescent with a blue van."

"A blue van?"

"That's right, a blue van, and you're to park outside number 184 Hans Crescent. If you're not there by nine o'clock, I'll assume that phase three is off."

Magrane repeated the address, said that it was just behind Harrods and then hung up. Taken by surprise, Donaldson slowly replaced the receiver and turned to face Linda.

"I think we're home and dry," he said.

"You think?" Linda pursed her lips. "Does that mean you're not sure?"

"Well, you never know where you are with Andrew. He's cunning one moment and so incredibly naïve the next that it's almost unbelievable. The trouble is, I can't make up my mind whether he was being naïve or cunning when he swallowed that story about the Libyan ambassador. There's something wrong somewhere . . . God, I wish I could put my finger on it."

"He gave you a rendezvous, didn't he, Robert?"

"Yes."

"So what's the problem?" Linda rested both elbows on the desk and leaned forward. "Look, you've done your bit. Surely the rest is up to Lloyd?"

It was another way of saying every man to his trade, and she had a point. Lloyd was the professional intelligence agent, a man with a brain tortured enough to play chess in three dimensions. If anyone was mentally equipped to determine a hoax from the real thing, it was he. Compared with Lloyd, he was a rank amateur.

"You're absolutely right," said Donaldson. "I'll simply pass the message on and leave everything to him."

Magrane left the call box and strolled into Waterlow Park to follow a paved footpath that meandered past the duck pond and deserted tennis courts to the wrought-iron gates at the bottom of the hill. Donaldson had given him a few anxious moments and at one stage he'd had a nasty feeling that Robert thought he wasn't serious about the Libyan ambassador, but in the end, everything had come right. Harry Gregson always used to say that time spent on reconnaissance was seldom wasted and Harry was dead right. He would never have been able to give Robert the number of the Mercedes if he hadn't gone to Princes Gate. That it might not be the one used by the ambassador was immaterial. Lloyd would soon discover that the car belonged to the embassy and that would be enough to point him in the right direction. He could rely on Lloyd to order Ryan to move his people into the Knightsbridge area and that would leave the field clear. Passing through the gates at the bottom of the hill, Magrane ignored the cemetery facing him and, turning left, entered the original burial ground on the east side of the park.

The cemetery had been neglected and was an eyesore. Some attempt had been made to keep the grass down on either side of the gravel path, but behind the narrow trimmed border it had been allowed to grow waist high and encroach upon the graves. The trees looked as if they hadn't been lopped in years, and ten yards in from the path, saplings and evergreen bushes formed an impenetrable jungle. In spring and summer, the undergrowth would almost certainly be choked with cow parsley, bindweed and clumps of stinging nettles.

Some two hundred yards from the main gate, Magrane branched off to the left and went on down the hill, passing family vaults, Victorian mausoleums and weathered statues entangled with ivy. The memorial he had come to see was on a level piece of ground just before a sharp right-hand bend in the track.

On top of a grey marble plinth, cast in bronze, the massive head and bearded face of Karl Marx stared into the far distance, his forehead bulging and deeply lined. Carved on the plinth, bold letters inlaid with gold leaf exclaimed: "Workers Of All Lands Unite," while below the commemorative plaque to Jenny von Westphalen, beloved wife, Henry Longuet, Helena Demuth and Eleanor Marx, daughter, was another piece of wisdom which read: "The Philosophers have only interpreted the world in various ways. The point is to change it."

Magrane looked up at the bust of Karl Marx and smiled wolfishly. He was going to change the world all right. Tomorrow morning around eleven thirty, when Vladislav Nikolaevich Zimin came to Highgate Cemetery to pay his respects to the man who'd written the *Communist Manifesto*. Zimin: now there was a name to send a shiver down the spine. If you read the *Sunday Express* on the twelfth of February, he was the president of the Iron and Steel Workers Union and a member of the Soviet trade mission, but if you had access to Top Secret Intelligence files, you knew he was a Lieutenant General in the KGB and one of the leading lights in the First Chief Directorate. Italy, Lebanon, Angola, Ethiopia, Rhodesia: you name the trouble spot and there in the background, busily stirring up the shit, would be at least one officer from the First Chief Directorate. Every revolutionary organization, from the Japanese Red Army on one side of the globe to the IRA and the Baader-Meinhof gang on the other, could rely on Zimin for encouragement and material support in one form or another.

Zimin: he could remember the photograph in the dossier with total clarity, a short dumpy man in a baggy pinstripe suit whose features resembled those of Khrushchev. Zimin: the fanatical bureaucrat and three-time recipient of the gold star medal as Hero of the Soviet Union, who was now his target for phase three. Zimin: the manufacturer. Oh, the Russians were going to raise a stink about this one and Whitehall would have Lloyd running in circles. The thought that Lloyd would probably end up with his head on the chopping block pleased Magrane enormously.

Magrane glanced to his right. There was a clear field of fire in excess of a hundred yards, which meant that Zimin would be in full view for at least two minutes before he reached the memorial. That would give him plenty of time for an aimed shot, provided he could find a suitable position. Turning his back on Karl Marx, Magrane stared at the building across the way beyond the plane trees and the railings that enclosed the cemetery. It looked grey and forbidding like some nineteenth-century factory or warehouse. Drawing nearer, he saw the guttering and drainpipes were painted dark blue. A hospital? The map on page 47 of the *Street Finder* showed one in the vicinity, but the red cross symbol had led him to assume it was on the far side of Dartmouth Park Hill. Whatever it was, the building definitely had possibilities. He moved nearer still, forcing his way past an overgrown bush. It was only then that he noticed the construction site farther down the hill.

He could see that the bricklayers had already completed one three-story block of flats, but a high wooden fence obscured his view of the lower floors and from where he was standing it was impossible to tell whether anybody was working inside the shell. The fire escape caught his eye and he looked up at the flat roof. Nobody would spot him up there behind the parapet, and there was a loophole in the near corner to allow the rainwater to drain off into the gutters below. The range and elevation couldn't be better either, though the acute angle plus the bend in the track would reduce the field of fire and Zimin would be out of sight until the last moment. Nevertheless, it seemed he had a choice of fire positions, for unless appearances were deceptive, either the grey stone building or the block of flats would serve his purpose.

Deciding he would need to view the target area from a different standpoint, Magrane returned to the path, made his way back to the entrance and doubled back through the park.

Outside the gates, he turned right and went on down Dartmouth Park Hill.

First appearances were deceptive. He could forget the grey stone building. It was part of Whittington Hospital and too many things could go wrong if he attempted to take over one of the rooms backing on to the cemetery. Hospitals were like railway stations; people were always coming and going, and the last thing he needed was a bunch of hostages on his hands.

The building site was a much more attractive proposition. As far as he could see, nobody was working inside the completed shell and although the compound would be locked at night, he would have no trouble climbing over the fence. Once inside, he could use the fire escape to get up on to the roof. He would have to telephone Donaldson before Zimin arrived, but that wouldn't be a problem; the works office was just inside the gate and, provided he was dressed the part, he could pass himself off as a subcontractor. All he required was a pair of overalls and a large toolbag, both of which could be obtained from a do-it-yourself shop. Convinced that he had seen enough, Magrane moved on.

It was his intention to catch a Northern Line train from the Underground station in Tufnel Park but, noticing that *Star Wars* was showing at the local cinema, he suddenly changed his mind and went inside. So far, nobody had paid the slightest attention to him despite the fact that his face had been in all the newspapers, but now that he had time to kill, he decided it would be stupid to press his luck too much.

There was no sign of the drinkers and Balaclava Road was as quiet as the grave. Hoping it would stay that way, Magrane broke into the derelict house where he had left the rifle and made his way up to the small bedroom overlooking the back garden. Although it wasn't a particularly dark night, there was insufficient light for the kind of fiddly job he was faced with and, opening the big canvas toolbag he'd bought earlier that evening, Magrane took out a small bicycle lamp.

He swept the beam over the floor looking for fresh scuff marks in the dust and, finding none, trained the lamp on the wall, spotlighting a large hole in the plaster near the corner.

Reaching inside the cavity up to his shoulder, his outstretched fingers encountered the foresight and then closed around the barrel of the FN. Careful not to knock the rifle against the wall, he lifted it out and laid it down on the canvas bag. As he had previously charged the magazine with twenty rounds, there was no need to retrieve the rest of the ammunition and he left the carton where it was.

Magrane knelt beside the rifle, removed the loaded magazine and, pressing the release catch behind the receiver, broke the weapon open like a shotgun and extracted the bolt and operating assembly. Apart from stripping the extractor and firing pin, only a qualified armorer was allowed to go any further as far as the Army was concerned, but he had other ideas. With the aid of a small screwdriver, he pried the retaining pins loose and pulled the butt out of the housing behind the pistol grip. Placing the pair of blue overalls on one side, he packed the component parts into the canvas toolbag, together with the lamp. That done, Magrane stripped off his raincoat and jacket and, removing his tie, unbuttoned the shirt at the neck. Wasting no time, he pulled the overalls on over his pants and hastily donned the jacket and raincoat. Satisfied that he hadn't forgotten anything, he picked up the toolbag and left the house to catch a train from Kentish Town to Highgate.

Three quarters of an hour later, Magrane was safely inside the building compound on Dartmouth Park Hill.

21 . . .

MAGRANE got to his feet and slowly straightened up. He felt dead tired and his body ached all over. Not so very long ago, he would have slept like a top on the concrete floor and never even felt the cold, but now he appeared to have suddenly become old before his time. Stretching both arms above his head, he yawned loudly and then turned about to face the open window.

Although the street lights were still on, it was no longer dark and the first buses were running. In perhaps less than an hour, the building site would be crawling with construction workers. The thought galvanized him into action and, grabbing the canvas toolbag, Magrane left the room where he'd spent the night and made his way up to the roof via the fire escape.

There had been a heavy downpour sometime during the early hours of the morning and several puddles lay on the flat roof where the rainwater hadn't drained away. Choosing a relatively dry spot by the parapet, Magrane removed his raincoat and sat down to open the toolbag. His fingers seemed to be all thumbs and he spent some minutes rubbing his hands together to restore the circulation before he attempted to reassemble the self-loading rifle. As soon as a sense of touch had returned, he picked up the butt, forced it into the housing behind the pistol grip and pressed the retaining pins home with the aid of a screwdriver. Inserting the bolt and operating assembly into the receiver, he closed the body, replaced the loaded magazine and pulled the cocking handle back to chamber a round.

Checking to make sure the change lever was on safe, Magrane carefully placed the rifle to one side and took out his shaving gear. Dipping the brush into a puddle of water, he lathered his face with soap and then gingerly scraped off the beard. The blade was dull, but despite nicking himself in a couple of places, Magrane was convinced he felt much more alert for having shaved. That chore completed, he packed the shaving kit away in the toolbag, leaned back against the parapet and lit a cigarette.

His stomach rumbled, an audible reminder that in the last twenty-four hours he'd had to make do with a couple of cheese sandwiches and a cup of coffee. One thing was certain; if he was hungry now, he was going to be ravenous before the day was out. Still, he thought, that was a small price to pay for the privilege of eliminating Vladislav Nikolaevich Zimin. Of course, his cup would have been filled to overflowing if he had been allowed to take a crack at Qaddafi, but that was like asking for the sun and the moon.

Qaddafi: now there was a man who had more lives than a cat. If it hadn't been for Lloyd, they would have nailed him when he stopped off at Mukala to visit the Omani Liberation Army after making a secret pilgrimage to Mecca. And there was that missed opportunity in Tripoli when they had been all set to ambush him as he left the Presidential Palace on his daily visit to the mosque. On that occasion they had actually got into the inflatable assault boat and were about to shove off from the Oberon-class submarine when the operation was cancelled. Lloyd couldn't be blamed for that one because it had happened long before he came on the scene. Magrane stubbed out his cigarette with a nervous gesture. Maybe at some distant date in the future, it would be a case of third-time lucky? Like hell it would: there never had been and never would be any shortage of faint hearts in Whitehall. Magrane frowned: he must be getting old, because his memory was going too. The submarine had surfaced off Kyrenia, not Tripoli, and after they had infiltrated through the beach defenses, his SAS patrol had been supposed to blow up the radar station on Mount Heraklion. The exercise had been arranged by Cyprus District and Headquarters 16 Parachute Brigade. Exercise? Well, the directing staff may have thought it was, but as far as the SAS was concerned, it was a dress rehearsal for Operation Damocles.

Magrane looked up at the sky; the light had improved enough so that he ought to be able to see the target area. Careful to keep his head below the parapet, he crawled towards the gutter in the corner and lay flat on his stomach. The aperture above the gutter was about six inches in diameter and, peering through it, he found he had a clear though oblique-angled view of the Karl Marx memorial. By a process of trial and elimination, he also discovered it would serve as a loophole for the rifle, provided he adopted a fire position some three feet back from the wall. The height of the building coupled with the narrowness of the aperture restricted his field of fire, but this disadvantage was largely outweighed by the fact that the loophole would conceal the muzzle flash of the rifle.

Magrane crawled away and returned to his former position. Making himself as comfortable as possible, he settled back to wait out the next few hours.

There was a double yellow line outside 184 Hans Crescent and Donaldson wondered how long it would be before the Ford Transit van caught the eye of a traffic warden. According to Attwood, Special Branch had taken action to warn them off, but he could recall at least a dozen instances where things had gone wrong because, somewhere along the line, one of the Chiefs had failed to brief the Indians properly.

The blue van was something of a Trojan horse, with Attwood and Norris concealed in the back ready to grab Magrane when he approached the vehicle. At least that was the theory, but he doubted if it would be put to the test. That Andrew intended to send him to another rendezvous in due course had been obvious to Donaldson the moment he saw there was a telephone box outside 184 Hans Crescent. He suspected Lloyd and Ryan were convinced the final rendezvous would be somewhere in Knightsbridge because they wanted to believe that Magrane had swallowed the bait. And there they differed. The more he thought about it, the more he suspected that Andrew had deliberately sent them on a wild goose chase. Magrane had made no attempt to use veiled speech when arranging the rendezvous. In fact, now he came to think about it, Andrew had broken every rule in the book seconds after warning him to watch his security. Magrane had been inconsistent in the one area where he was normally consistent and somehow that didn't ring true. But it was too late now to do anything but sit and wait for Andrew's next move.

The operation had started at seven o'clock, when it was still dark. By the time they arrived in Hans Crescent, Ryan had already thrown a cordon around the area enclosed by Exhibition Road, Knightsbridge, Sloane Street, Cadogan Gardens, Draycott Avenue and the Brompton Road. There had been the usual flurry of whispered code words after the observation parties provided by the Special Patrol Unit had established themselves on the rooftops soon after daybreak, but ever since then the radio had been silent, apart from the background mush. Curious to know if anything was happening, Donaldson reached behind his head and opened the sliding panel in the partition.

"What's going on?" he asked.

Norris turned the volume down on the radio. "Not a lot," he said cheerfully. "Our guvnor wants to organize a house-to-house search, but Lloyd thinks we should wait until there are more people about."

"He has a point," Attwood said grudgingly. "Magrane would soon spot us if we started the ball rolling now."

Donaldson glanced at his wristwatch. If Andrew really was lying in wait for the ambassador, then Lloyd was probably wise to delay the search. On the other hand, if he left it any longer, the Special Patrol Unit would be pushed for time. Andrew had been led to believe that the ambassador would leave Princes Gate at ten fifteen and he was unlikely to hang about if half an hour later there was no sign of the Mercedes.

"How many men does Commander Ryan have at his disposal?" he asked.

"Thirty-eight," said Attwood, "excluding Norris and myself."

Lloyd had definitely cut it too fine. It was almost nine o'clock and thirty-eight men would never be able to search an area the size of Knightsbridge in under two hours.

Donaldson reached behind him to close the sliding panel and then froze. "Hullo," he murmured, "we've got trouble."

"What kind of trouble?" said Norris.

"A little man with a yellow band round his hat."

Donaldson pointed to the traffic warden who was coming towards them and then got out of the van to meet him. The friendly smile on his face failed to do the trick and the traffic warden didn't want to know when he tried to explain that the police had given him permission to park in Hans Crescent.

Magrane arched his back and rubbed the base of his spine. For close to three hours, he had been sitting in exactly the same position and, not surprisingly, his pelvis ached like hell. Waiting for the balloon to go up was always the worst part of any operation, but he consoled himself with the thought that it wouldn't be long now. An hour and a half at the most and then Vladislav Nikolaevich Zimin would come striding down the gravel path to keep an appointment with destiny. An hour and a half? Robert would need all of ninety minutes if he was going to shake off Lloyd before driving out to Highgate. Anxious not to show himself above the parapet, Magrane crawled across the roof and then went down the fire escape. Nobody saw him leave the empty building and, hurrying across the compound, he rapped on the door of the site office and went inside.

Two men were huddled together over a large drawing board that took up the length of one wall. Magrane thought the taller of the two was probably an architect, largely because he was wearing a fairly presentable suit and a pair of shin-high Wellington boots that were spotlessly clean. His companion was also in a suit, but it looked baggy and well-worn and there was enough mud on his boots to fill a small window box. Neither man took the slightest notice of him.

"Mind if I use your phone?" Magrane jerked a thumb over

his shoulder. "My truck won't budge an inch. I reckon the half-shaft is gone bust."

The smaller man twisted round to face him, his eyes narrowing. "Are you from Sedgewicks?" he snapped.

Magrane nodded. It seemed the only safe thing to do.

"Have you brought our steel window frames?"

"They've already been unloaded." Magrane looked him straight in the eye. "One of your blokes has got the invoice."

"Good. Let's hope you've delivered the right size this time." The clerk of works turned his back on him and returned to the drawing board. "I've just about had a bellyfull of Sedgewicks."

Uncertain whether he had permission to use the telephone, Magrane went ahead anyway, and lifting the receiver, dialled the call box in Hans Crescent. The switching mechanism clicked, there was a slight pause and then the busy tone came through loud and clear. It was the one thing he hadn't bargained for and so totally unexpected he lost his self-control and ripped off a string of profanities as he slammed the phone down.

"Having trouble?"

He looked up, suddenly aware that the architect was frowning at him, his face registering disapproval. "The line's busy." Magrane smiled weakly. "It always is. I'll have to try again in a couple of minutes."

"There's no call for that kind of language, is there?"

"Sorry."

He managed to sound contrite, but it was an effort, because deep inside he was burning with anger. He had met people like the architect before, pompous and sanctimonious, the kind of individual who deserved a good boot up the arse.

"Haven't I seen you somewhere before?"

"Probably," said Magrane. "I've worked for a lot of suppliers in my time."

The architect grunted disparagingly and immediately lost interest in him. Magrane stared at the block of flats through the window, hoping and praying that nobody would find the rifle while he was away.

The girl was young, around nineteen or twenty, and had

the gift of gab. By Donaldson's reckoning, she had been chattering away on the telephone for the best part of twenty minutes at somebody else's expense. She had rung her friend, given the number of the telephone box, hung up, then waited for whoever it was to call back.

Twenty minutes. He wondered if Andrew had tried to contact him during that time, wondered too how he would have reacted to the unforeseen delay. He would certainly have been very angry, but Donaldson didn't believe the setback would deter him. Once he had made up his mind to do something, there was no stopping Andrew. He had taken out the post office, eliminated the middleman and now he was going after the manufacturer. It was as simple as that.

The manufacturer: Donaldson felt his stomach lurch. The van der Pohlmanns had run a kind of post office and August Steiner could loosely be described as a middleman, but by no stretch of the imagination could the epithet of manufacturer be applied to the Libyan ambassador.

That Magrane had deliberately set out to hoodwink them was no longer in doubt. The ambassador was part of his deception plan and thanks to him, they had fallen for it. There was only one consolation; even if he had remembered the code word and appreciated its significance, it wouldn't have made an awful lot of difference. Ryan would have held his people and the Special Patrol Unit in reserve instead of deploying them on the ground, but they would still be waiting for Magrane to call the tune. Perhaps he ought to explain things to Lloyd and suggest that it might be a good idea to call off the house-to-house search? He glanced again at the box and saw that at last the girl had left. A few seconds later, the telephone began to ring in the empty call box.

Magrane bit his lip. What the hell was Robert playing at? The number had been ringing for what seemed an eternity and unless he was deaf or had gone to sleep, he must have heard it by now. Close to despair, he was about to replace the receiver when there was a loud click and he heard a familiar voice on the line.

"Robert?" Magrane turned his back on the two men and mumbled into the phone. "It's me—Andrew."

"Yes, Andrew. Where are you?"

Donaldson sounded tense but that was understandable. Robert had been left in limbo for several hours.

"I'm broken down in Highgate."

"I can't hear you."

Reluctantly, Magrane raised his voice. "I said I'm stranded in Highgate, next door to Whittington Hospital."

"Whittington Hospital? Where exactly is that?"

"In Dartmouth Park Hill. How soon can you get here?"

"I don't know, but I'll leave straightaway."

"No, hold it a minute." Magrane racked his brains. The two men would hear every word he said and he had to find some way of warning Donaldson about Lloyd that wouldn't arouse their suspicion. "Look," he said presently, "it's no use bringing your van, it's not powerful enough. You'll have to find another vehicle. Lloyd won't like it, but he doesn't have to know, does he?"

"I take your point," Donaldson said quietly.

"Good. I hoped you would." Magrane put the phone down and turned to leave. "Thanks," he said tersely.

The architect looked up. "Everything under control?" he asked.

"It is now," said Magrane.

Donaldson left the box on the double and scrambled into the van. As he did so, Norris whipped the sliding panel open. Anticipating him, Donaldson said, "You'd better get on the blower to Ryan. We're in the wrong place—Magrane's in Highgate."

"Whereabouts?"

"Somewhere very close to Whittington Hospital." Switching on the ignition, he cranked the engine into life and revved up. "Can one of you tell me the way to Dartmouth Park Hill?"

"Jesus Christ, the cemetery!" Attwood yelled above the noise, "That's where we'll find him. Vladislav Zimin is going there this morning to lay a wreath on the Karl Marx memorial. Zimin's got to be the target."

"Forget the explanations," Donaldson shouted back, "just show me how to get there."

Attwood jumped out of the van, ran round to the front and got in beside him. "You'd better make for Marble Arch," he said breathlessly. "I can direct you from there."

Donaldson nodded, pulled out from the curb and, turning right, headed for the Brompton Road. Headlights on full beam and blasting a continuous warning on the horn, he cut across the oncoming traffic and joined the stream moving towards Hyde Park Corner. There was a forty-mile-an-hour speed limit on Park Lane, but there was no need for Attwood to point out that it didn't apply to them. Ramming his foot down hard, he managed to get up to sixty before the usual log jam at Marble Arch forced him to slow down. Rounding the island, they went down the Edgware Road and turned into Old Marylebone. The A1 to Highgate was only two and a half miles away, but despite going through every red light, it still took them over fifteen minutes to reach the junction.

Lloyd forced himself to remain calm. It was no use fretting about the traffic, because there was nothing they could do about it. In any case, even if the roads had been clear, it wouldn't have made the slightest scrap of difference. By the time Norris had called in, Zimin had already left Congress Hall and was on his way to Highgate Cemetery. There had been a few nailbiting moments—there really would be hell to pay if Zimin popped off—but now the operations room at New Scotland Yard confirmed that a police car was in position in Swain's Lane waiting to intercept Zimin when he arrived at the cemetery. Lloyd was persuaded there was no real cause for alarm.

It was a comforting thought to cling to as his car sped through Pentonville. Unfortunately, Lloyd had reckoned without Zimin's bullheaded obstinacy.

Magrane stared through the loophole, his eyes riveted on the bend in the track. It could only be a matter of minutes now before Zimin appeared in view and then his task would be completed and it would be up to Donaldson to get him out of the country. What was it Robert had said? "Before you know it you'll be sunning yourself in the Bahamas?" No, that couldn't be right—he'd cut Robert off before he had a chance to tell him. Bermuda would be nice at this time of the year, or Jamaica; in fact, almost anywhere in the West Indies would suit him down to the ground. On second thoughts, perhaps Rio de Janeiro would be better. There was no extradition treaty with Brazil and that meant Lloyd wouldn't be able to drag him back to England if the situation turned sour and Donaldson couldn't straighten things out with the Foreign Office.

Magrane rubbed his forehead and wondered how it was that he could be sweating when it was such a cold and blustery day.

Right from the moment Control had ordered them to drop what they were doing and get over to Swain's Lane, Police Constable Edwards had had a premonition that this just wasn't going to be their day. He'd said as much to Police Constable Ives and, by God, he'd been proved right. The other Russians had been quite amenable when he'd explained that he couldn't allow them inside the cemetery, but not Zimin. Comrade Zimin was being very difficult and while Edwards couldn't understand a word of Russian, it was pretty obvious that it was going to take more than a mere bomb threat to hold Zimin back, especially when it was way over in Dartmouth Park Hill.

In no time at all, it had become very clear to him that Mr. Comrade-bloody-Zimin was in no mood to listen to anyone as lowly as a police constable and he'd sent Ives back to the car to summon help from the station. Edwards had thought it possible that Zimin would be prepared to listen to an Inspector; he'd heard the Russians set great store by protocol, but from the resigned expression on Ives's face and his frantic gestures, it seemed they were out of luck. Edwards sighed; he might have known the Inspector wouldn't be available when he was needed. Any other time, you couldn't turn round without him being there behind you, but right now, judging by the way Ives was pointing, it appeared he was over in Dartmouth Park Hill, supervising the evacuation of the building site next door to Whittington Hospital.

Edwards turned about. Zimin was still waving his arms in the air, but it looked as if the other Russians were about to win the day and make him see reason. Edwards could not have been more mistaken. Suddenly, Zimin pushed one of his companions aside and set off down the path. Sprinting after him, Edwards overtook the Russian and tried to lead him back to the main gates. Within seconds, he found himself surrounded by the entire entourage, all of whom, it seemed, objected to the way he was handling things. Had he been confronted with a crowd of football hooligans, Edwards would have known exactly what to do, but he was completely out of his depth in this situation and, inch by inch, he was forced to give ground.

Donaldson drove past the entrance to Waterlow Park, dropped into third gear and turned into Bisham Gardens. There was still no sign of Lloyd and the others, but Norris had learned over the radio that they intended to leave the A1 at Archway junction and cut through the side streets to Whittington Hospital. Reaching the bottom of Bisham Gardens, Donaldson turned left into Swain's Lane and went on down the hill. As they approached the cemetery, he saw two Zil limousines and a police car parked outside the gates. The cars were empty, Zimin and his entourage conspicuous only by their absence.

"I don't like the look of that," said Attwood.

"Neither do I."

Donaldson slammed on the brakes and skidded to a halt outside the entrance. Leaving the key in the ignition, he scrambled out of the van and raced after Norris and Attwood. Nobody had to tell him what was at stake and he ran as he'd never run in his life before, driving himself on like an Olympic athlete hungry for a Gold Medal.

Attwood heard him coming and pointed to the fork in the track ahead. Overtaking him and Norris, Donaldson veered to the left and, moments later, spotted two uniformed police officers surrounded by a group of angry Soviet officials. They were just twenty yards from the memorial and he raced towards them shouting at the top of his voice.

Magrane had a terrible premonition that the operation was going to misfire. He couldn't see anything from where he was lying, but the building site was deathly quiet and had been so for well over half an hour. It could be that the workmen were having a tea break, but if so, it was an exceedingly long one. A lightning strike? Well, that was a possibility, but now that he thought about it, there had been no sudden cessation of work. The concrete-mixing machines had stopped one by one so that it was some time before he was aware that anything was out of the ordinary.

He stared through the loophole at the bust of Karl Marx. The wind was blowing in the opposite direction, but he thought he could hear voices coming from somewhere beyond the bend in the track. It had to be Zimin, it just had to be him. He had assumed the Russian would come alone, but obviously he was accompanied by a crowd of officials from the Soviet Embassy. Hesitating no longer, Magrane brought the rifle up into his shoulder and pushed the safety catch forward. A figure appeared in view, and then another and another until there was a whole milling throng.

To his surprise, the Russians stopped a few yards from the memorial and began to move off the path into the shrubbery, shepherded there by two police constables. He couldn't understand how Lloyd had discovered the identity of the manufacturer, but that was entirely irrelevant now because he could see the dumpy, unmistakable figure of Comrade Vladislav Nikolaevich Zimin amongst the crowd of Russian embassy officials. His finger curled round the trigger and took up the slack and then suddenly it wasn't Zimin who was in his sights but Donaldson.

Robert was waving his arms and shouting to him. A warning? Hell, there was no need for Robert to tell him the operation was a busted flush when he could see that for himself. Still baffled, he saw Donaldson turn about and in that same instant, noticed two men running towards him. Suddenly, everything clicked into place and he realized that Robert was in serious trouble, realized too that there was nothing he could do now except put down covering fire, and, squeezing the trigger, he pumped off four rounds in quick succession. Thereafter, he kept up a steady but more deliberate rate of fire.

Donaldson had taken cover in a small depression on the other side of the track from the memorial. Raising his head and looking about, he saw the bullets were falling to his right and rear. At first he couldn't think what Magrane was aiming at, until it slowly dawned on him that Andrew was merely concerned about keeping Attwood and Norris pinned down. In a curious way, it was almost as if Andrew were inviting him to come and join him on the roof.

He wondered when Lloyd was going to make a move. Ryan couldn't have been all that far behind them when they arrived in Highgate and he must have deployed the Special Patrol Unit in and around the building site by now. Perhaps he and Lloyd were waiting for somebody to fetch a public address system from the local police station? It didn't seem very likely; knowing how thorough Lloyd was, Donaldson thought he would have radioed ahead and made arrangements to have one immediately available. Whatever else was in doubt, one thing was certain: it would take a lot of time and patience to persuade Andrew to give himself up.

And then it occurred to him that this was probably the very last thing Lloyd wanted. Should he just let events take their course? . . . No, that had never been his style. Jumping to his feet, he ran towards the building site. The wooden fence was about seven feet high. Timing his approach, Donaldson launched himself at it, planting his left foot against the boards to give himself the extra lift he needed to get both hands on top of the fence. Finding a hold, he levered himself up and over the fence.

Once inside the compound, he moved to the fire escape and made his way up to the roof where he saw Magrane lying in the far corner.

In a surprisingly cheerful voice, Magrane said, "Better late than never, Robert."

"You could say that," Donaldson panted.

Magrane clucked his tongue. "You're not in very good shape, are you, Robert? I hope to God you haven't left the car too far away. Still, I daresay we can afford to wait until you've had time to catch your breath."

"It's time to call it a day, Andrew."

"What?"

"Lloyd has got this place surrounded."

Magrane digested the news in silence, his face gradually

clouding in anger. "I always knew that bastard would get me in the end," he said. "Maybe I'll get lucky and take him with me."

"For God's sake, don't be stupid."

"Stupid?" Magrane's voice rose an octave. "Why is it stupid to kill Lloyd?"

"Beause . . ." Donaldson floundered, wondering what he could say to Magrane that would persuade him it was futile to offer any resistance.

"Because what, Robert?"

"Bloody hell. Listen, Andrew, Lloyd is prepared to offer you safe-conduct providing you agree to leave the country."

"Bullshit."

It was bullshit, but Donaldson was stuck with the story now and had to go with it. "Do you think I would lie to you, Andrew?"

"No."

"Then trust me."

"I trust you, Robert, but not Lloyd. He wants to bury me."

"Be sensible, he can't afford to have any witnesses. If Lloyd attempted to kill you, he'd have to put me away too. Right?"

"Yes."

Magrane sounded doubtful but he sensed that Andrew wanted to believe him. "All right then," Donaldson said, "just you watch this."

Donaldson stood up and looked around him. The hospital was next door and he could see Quinn peering down on him from one of the wards on the top floor. The rifle wasn't in view, but he knew the sergeant had been issued with a Lee Enfield Mark IV that had been modified to take a 7.62mm round.

"Nobody is going to shoot at us," he roared, "you have my word on that."

His voice echoed across the building site and he was certain that it had carried to the marksmen of the Special Patrol Unit on the second floor of the adjoining flat. Magrane hesitated and then smiled in a way which seemed to say, "What the hell, let's give it a whirl." Donaldson watched him slowly get to his feet and sighed with relief. It was over. Magrane was coming towards him, holding the FN rifle at the point of balance in his right hand. One, two, three, four, five paces; he was halfway there now. With an encouraging smile on his face, Donaldson beckoned him to come on.

The gesture seemed to puzzle Magrane, as did a faint swishing sound above their heads. A frown creased his forehead and, jerking his head to the right, he saw the marksmen on the adjoining roof. Reacting instinctively, he brought the rifle up into his shoulder. The safety catch was already in the forward position and, traversing from right to left, he began to empty the magazine. Somewhere between the fifth and sixth round, Quinn took aim and fired. At a range of a hundred feet, he could hardly miss, and Magrane appeared to leap up into the air like a skater attempting a double axel, except that he landed on both feet and then went over on to his back and lay still.

The bullet had hit him behind the left shoulder and exited through his chest, but he was still alive when Donaldson bent over him.

His lips moved and then with a tremendous effort, he whispered, "What am I doing here?"

It sounded like an accusation.

22 . . .

It was a very small, very private affair. Donaldson thought it was just as well Virginia Magrane had decided she didn't want her husband to be buried with full military honors, because the Ministry of Defence would have declined to provide a bugler and a firing party. Queen's Regulations were quite specific about who was and who was not entitled to have one, and Andrew most definitely wasn't. Tamblin had advised him not to attend the funeral and Vaughan had said that if he felt obliged to go, he was on no account to wear a uniform. He had chosen to ignore the advice and disobey the order because he couldn't forget that Andrew had given fourteen years to the Army and that for the greater part of his service he had been a damn good soldier.

He glanced at Virginia Magrane, who was standing between her parents, and marvelled at her composure. Of course she'd had time to recover from the initial shock of his death because almost a fortnight had gone by since Magrane had been killed, but he had an idea that Virginia hadn't found it necessary to look too far for a comforting shoulder to cry on. The boyfriend was there in the background, a somewhat unprepossessing man with a droopy moustache. From what the verger at St. Paul's had said, Donaldson gathered that he had made all the arrangements for the funeral, and that had to be the final insult. He couldn't understand why she had decided to have Andrew buried in South Harrow. He wondered if it had something to do with the fact that she was Catholic, but that didn't make a lot of sense. There were several Church of England cemeteries much nearer to home than the one in Eastcote Lane. It seemed that, even in death, Andrew was still surrounded in mystery.

The priest closed his prayer book and, drawing nearer to Virginia, murmured a few appropriate words of sympathy. The boyfriend eyed the threatening sky, unfurled his umbrella and held it above her head. The rain, which so far had held off during the short service at the graveside, began to fall again and, grateful for an excuse to leave, they slowly drifted towards the gates on the main road, Virginia sandwiched between the priest and the boyfriend, her parents following a few paces behind.

Donaldson waited until they were out of sight and then with a swift salute, he also turned away from the grave and set off down the path. There was a small building just inside the gates and, as he approached it, a familiar figure left the porch and came to meet him.

"Linda." He stopped in his tracks. "This is a surprise. I didn't see you in church."

"I arrived too late for the service." She smiled wryly and fell in step beside him. "I came by train and I didn't allow enough time. Anyway, when I did find the cemetery, I suddenly got cold feet and decided I had no right to be here."

"I know the feeling." He pointed to the Ford Cortina parked outside the gates. "Can I give you a lift back to town?"

"Well, that's very kind of you, Robert. Are you sure it's not out of your way?"

Linda was distant and cool, but that was hardly surprising. Whether it was deliberate policy or not, he had been denied the opportunity of seeing her again before returning to Wilton. He had telephoned to explain his abrupt departure, but although Linda had said she quite understood, it was obvious that she was hurt when he told her he didn't know when he would be up in London again. Vaughan had seen to it that he had been given enough work to keep two men busy for a fortnight, but of course he couldn't prove it was intentional and she had thought he was just making excuses, and it certainly had sounded like that.

"It's no trouble," he said. "I'm staying at my club in London. I'm on embarkation leave."

"What?"

"I've been posted to Fort Bragg as an exchange officer with 82nd U.S. Airborne."

"That's a bit sudden, isn't it?"

Linda was no longer cool and distant. In fact, her expression showed that she was sorry to hear that he was leaving the country.

"It is, but that's the Army for you." He opened the near door so that she could get into the car. "The officer who was holding the appointment got himself promoted and they decided I should fill the vacancy." Linda ducked her head under the sill and scrambled into the Cortina. Donaldson closed the door, waited until the oncoming bus had overtaken them, and then, moving round the car, got in beside her. "I'm told it's a plum job."

"You deserve it, Robert."

"You think so?" He shook his head. "I didn't get the post on merit. I have a hunch that Lloyd pulled a few strings and the Army Board thought it might be a good idea if I left the country for a while."

"Now you know that's not true. I'm not a military expert, but it's obvious to me that you're a very competent officer."

"Oh, I'm competent all right," he said bitterly. "I set Andrew up."

"Nonsense. You did the best you could for him. It's not your fault that Magrane went haywire."

"I made him come to me, Linda. Things might have been different if it had been the other way round."

"I don't see how."

Donaldson lit two cigarettes and gave one to Linda. For some moments he sat there, listening to the rain drumming on the roof of the car, uncertain whether to confide in her or not. Finally, he decided he had to tell somebody what was on his mind and he knew she was the only person who would listen to him.

"I heard a swishing sound a few seconds before Magrane opened fire. Usually when a bullet passes over your head it makes a distant crack and then moments later, depending on the range, you hear the rifle shot. A bullet from a pistol makes much less noise because it has a much lower muzzle velocity."

"But you'd still hear the shot, Robert."

"Not if the gunman were using a silencer. Lloyd was on the second floor of the adjoining block of flats. His chances of hitting Magrane were about zero, but I don't believe that was his intention anyway. He wanted to draw Andrew's attention to the other marksmen because he knew how Magrane would react. Don't you see, Lloyd was counting on him to open fire."

He did not add that he believed Magrane would still be alive today if he hadn't escaped from Bethnal Green Police Station and if he hadn't been so goddamned curious when he was made Assistant Operations Officer. Lloyd could never have let Magrane get into court. He knew too much about the SAS, about Northern Ireland and Oman—and about Lloyd.

Linda stared through the windshield, deep in thought. "You can't prove that, can you?" she asked presently.

"No."

"Then my advice to you is to forget the whole thing. It's an interesting theory but that's all it is." She opened her handbag and looked inside to make sure she hadn't left her purse behind at the booking office in South Kensington. "Come on," she said briskly, "you look as if you could do with a drink and I still owe you one from Keebleloch. Where's the nearest pub?"

"The Tithe Farm is just down the road."

"Local knowledge?" She turned to him with a quizzical smile.

"I was born not far from here."

"Really? I didn't know that."

"There's a lot you don't know about me," said Donaldson.

"That sounds like a challenge," she said cheerfully, "one I can't possibly ignore."

It was what he wanted to hear and he knew what he was going to do. Tomorrow he would walk into the Military Secretary's Branch at Stanmore and tell them what they could do with their posting, and then, while the iron was still hot, he would hand in his resignation.